THE ROMANCE REWIND

THE ROMANCE REWIND

Sarah Everett

G. P. PUTNAM'S SONS

G. P. PUTNAM'S SONS
An imprint of Penguin Random House LLC
1745 Broadway, New York, NY 10019
penguinrandomhouse.com

Design by Rebecca Aidlin
Text set in Adobe Garamond Pro

Library of Congress Cataloging-in-Publication Data is available.

First published in the United States of America by G. P. Putnam's Sons, 2026

Manufactured in the United States of America
LSCC

ISBN 9798217002986

1st Printing

The authorized representative in the EU for product safety and compliance is Penguin Random House Ireland, Morrison Chambers, 32 Nassau Street, Dublin D02 YH68, Ireland, https://eu-contact.penguin.ie.

To Fey,
for Christmas, New Year's, and Easter

One

I can always tell when Jason has a secret. He starts to do everything at double speed—speaking, eating, driving. It's like he physically can't wait for the part where he gets to unleash his surprise on the world.

Tonight, Jason starts rambling from the moment he picks me up at my house, all the way down the interstate and into the city, and he doesn't stop even when he's taking his first bite of spanakopita. That's how I know our dinner at Apollo's is going to be special. That—and the fact that today is exactly one year since our very first date. It's the only anniversary I like to think about this time of year.

So far only I've given Jason his gift. My adorable hand-drawn "Our Relationship Is a Toddler" card sits next to his plate, as he's halfway through a monologue about the weather. Seriously. If his nervousness wasn't so darn cute, it would be infuriating.

"And that, of course, doesn't predict that we will have a warm fall either," he says, chewing as fast as he's talking, "but what the El Niño effect does do—"

"Babe," I say, unable to take any more, "you're going to choke on your food and not get to tell me what's going on."

I'm expecting my comment to draw one of his to-die-for dimples out of hiding, to coax his broad shoulders into relaxing, but Jason coughs a little instead. "How do you know . . . I mean, who said there's something going on?"

"Oh please," I say, rolling my eyes.

Jason Riddick is known for many things in our town, but being nervous is not one of them. His composure under pressure, pinpoint accuracy, and just-this-side-of-tolerable confidence make him the best captain the Sterlingwood High soccer team has ever seen.

I lean forward so my elbows are on the table. "You're about as obvious as a zit on photo day. Just tell me already."

Jason makes a face. He thinks people only use similes to show off a high SAT score.

I let him gather his thoughts while I covertly check that my lipstick is still flawless with my phone. I always wear at least one thing that accurately captures my mood, one thing that reveals what I'm feeling to whoever is paying attention, and tonight's confident red lip is my open secret.

"Here you go."

The waiter refills our waters, and I give him a smile and a "Thank you."

Tonight, my best friends, Amber and Monique, have a bet going on whether Jason is going to give me a promise ring, pull out tickets for some romantic weekend trip he's planned for this fall, or ask me to senior prom eight months early. Personally, I'm leaning toward the promise ring. I know promise rings are a million years old and dumb for a thousand reasons, but in old-money families like Jason's, they're still very much a thing. His great-grandfather gave his great-grandmother a promise ring, because that's What Was

Done back in the day. But then his grandfather did the same, and so did Jason's father. Now, it's pretty much tradition.

The thing about me and Jason is that we're just the right amount of in love.

In high school, there are always those couples who are radioactive together. Couples whose screaming matches are resolved only with equally gross public displays of affection. But Jason and I are solid, emotionally healthy, mature. If we were doing couple superlatives in this year's yearbook, we would win Most Likely to Still Be Together in Twenty Years. The two of us just make sense.

"Zadie," Jason says, and he's tugging on the collar of his polo shirt like he's uncomfortable. Maybe his dinner is too hot. "I really—I thought maybe we'd talk on the ride home? Just for privacy?"

"The ride home?" I'm incredulous. "If you think I'm waiting that long, you're insane."

"But the thing is—"

"Jason," I whine, because he's still not getting to the point, and my fingers are zinging with an energy that feels electric.

I'm picturing it already, the way the restaurant—which isn't super full now that Maine's vacation season has ended—will break into applause when Jason gets on one knee with his open ring box.

"Whoa, whoa, whoa," Jason'll say, grinning from ear to ear. "We're not getting engaged. We're only eighteen."

Our rapt audience, having abandoned their meals, will whoop and holler when I whisper my teary yes. *Yes, I will promise you my heart until we're old enough to promise our whole lives.*

"Okay, just hear me out," Jason begins in real life. "I know the timing seems off." My brain snags on the word timing, and I think maybe this is a promposal after all? Not the most exciting prospect, but still. "I'm only doing it now because I think waiting too much longer is unfair."

I nod, trying to look like I'm taking in every word he's saying. Really, my phone is now in my lap under the table, stealthily positioned so I can fire off the first of many all-caps group texts. Jason goes back to rambling again.

Something about "the best thing for us" and "You'll understand in time."

It bursts out of me. "Jason, just spit it out!"

And finally, finally, he does.

"I think we should break up."

My mouth is wide open, ready to squeal out an enthusiastic *Yes, oh my God! I thought you'd never ask!*

But those words don't leave my lips.

"You . . . think we should . . . break up?" I repeat, like the words have no recognizable meaning in English.

Jason swallows, takes a drink from his glass of water.

"Is this a joke?" I ask. My eyes sweep around the restaurant's dining room, desperately landing on patron after patron. If just one of them laughs, smiles, blinks, I'll know it's a joke. One of Jason's terrible pranks that he thinks are funny but are really just annoying and poorly thought-out, though I've never told him this.

But nobody is looking at us. Jason gives me a sad shake of his head. "No," he says.

"Is there someone else?"

"No, Zadie. I just don't think this is working anymore."

"Of course it's working. We've been dating one year. Today is one year," I say, as if one year is a guarantee of something. Forever, maybe.

And despite the shock, the pure astonishment I feel, I'm still myself enough to be embarrassed by my shrill desperation.

"I know," he says, quiet, apologetic. "And you can call me an asshole for doing it today, but I just couldn't stand to pretend anymore."

Of all the upsetting, surprising, traumatic things Jason has said in the last five minutes, it is this—this last sentence—that undoes me. *I just couldn't stand to pretend anymore.*

"Pretend?" I repeat.

I feel like I've drifted out of my body. Like I'm standing at the far end of the restaurant's dining room, watching some unsuspecting girl—with perfectly styled hair, her bold red lip for memorable occasions, and a body-hugging dress—get broken up with by her boyfriend. (*Poor girl,* I think. *How embarrassing for her.*) Her voice is loud, growing in volume and pitch each second, unrecognizable to me.

She sounds angry. Heartbroken. Blindsided.

But what do those things actually feel like?

I have to pull myself back into her place to know.

Blindsided is the soft cushion of the chair under my butt and thighs. Angry is the wood of the table beneath my elbows. Heartbreak is the thick padding of carpet under the wobbly stiletto heels I wore for this special occasion. It is the cold emanating from the sweaty jug of ice water by my hand.

I feel all these things, and I feel none of them.

"You've been pretending?"

"I mean, no, of course not," Jason fumbles. He looks smaller, not like the near six feet of boy who routinely blocks balls with his head. His wide shoulders and calves of steel. My Jason is so solid, and this boy is not. "That's not what I mean."

"What *do* you mean?" And then, to my horror—to his probably too—my voice cracks.

My voice cracks, and suddenly my throat is closing up, and the room gets very, very blurry. I am no longer tables away watching this happen. I am beside myself, pleading with everything inside me to *please God don't cry, please not now*. But the hiccup leaps out of me and then an avalanche follows.

I am crying and sniffing and wanting to die from sheer embarrassment, which makes me cry harder, which makes me want to die even more.

I see Jason steal an embarrassed glance around him as he gets up from his chair and hurries over, putting his hand on my back. He speaks quietly and comfortingly to me. And maybe it's that self-conscious look around the room he does or the fact that he doesn't seem to be saying any actual words of comfort, just sort of mumbling and *there-there*-ing, but something snaps in me.

I shrug off his arm and catapult away from the table. I race out of the restaurant, past the lobby, and into the cool night air. It's that idyllic window between summer and fall, where it's lobster season still but the influx of vacationers has dispersed. I should be having the best night, but I'm sobbing as I frantically pull up a rideshare app on my phone.

"Come on, come on," I sniffle, willing the app to move faster and pacing the sidewalk until Jason comes out of the restaurant.

"Zadie," he says, reaching for me.

I fling his arm off with a strength I didn't know I had. I'm suddenly furious. How could he do this publicly? How could he not spare me the indignity of making me cry where everyone can see? "Don't touch me."

"Please, babe. Don't do this. Let's just . . . Let me take you home."

If my voice was something you could hold in your hands, it would be shattered porcelain. Broken and all sharp edges. "I'm not going anywhere with you."

Jason frowns, hands on his hips. "What are you going to do, walk?"

"Does it matter to you what I do?" I spit.

He sighs. "I thought we would be mature about this."

"Did you?" I say, and I'm both ashamed of the mocking tone in my voice and unable to help it. "Why did you think we would be mature about this, when you had never discussed it with me?"

I speak louder as I walk away from him. "Maybe in future when you make decisions that affect us both, you'll remember to check with me."

"Zad," Jason says tiredly. "I'm sorry, okay? I didn't see it going like this either. I thought we'd be forever."

It's like taking my heart to a shredder.

"Why can't we be?" I'm practically pleading. "We're so good together. We're the best together. I just don't get it."

"Please let me take you home. I'll explain on the drive," Jason says, pushing his fist into his left eye.

Is he crying? Can he be . . . is it possible that he's really as upset about this as I am?

The fact is that I don't want him to explain on the drive home; I want him to take it back. To say it was all a mistake, a slip of the

7   *   *   *

tongue, a misunderstanding on my part. Maybe he was black-mailed by someone into breaking up with me. A million wild scenarios run through my head, and I'm willing to accept any of them so long as it undoes everything that just happened.

It's that hope that makes me not book the rideshare.

It's that hope that makes me hug my purse to my chest as I sink into the passenger seat of his SUV.

Jason starts the car.

"So?" I say after a few seconds when the air conditioner has just been whistling in its tone-deaf way. *Please take it all back*, I plead inwardly.

Jason breathes out through his nose. "It's so hard to explain."

He's really doing this. He's really breaking up with me during the first month of what was supposed to be the ideal senior year.

"Oh my God."

Bile rises in my throat. I think I'm going to be sick. I open my purse and start rummaging around for a cough drop or random Tums, anything to calm the upheaval in my stomach. I check under the last book Dad and I buddy-read for our Father-Daughter Book Club, bookmarked and on its third reread.

We're stopped at a red light when Jason scrubs a hand over his face.

The light turns green, and he lifts his foot from the pedal, and we start to roll forward. "Okay, so it's like this . . ." he says, at the very same moment I whisper his name and then puke the dinner I barely touched into my purse.

"Jesus, Zadie!" Jason shouts, horrified. "Not in my c—"

But before he can finish his sentence—before he can freak out about his car's leather interior or give me an explanation for why he would break up with me after one incredible romance-filled year—before he can say anything at all, there is the smashing of metal. A burst of light. Three panicked car horns. And the loudest explosion I've ever heard.

Two

When I wake up in Sterlingwood General, in a room that smells of hospital, the first thing I feel is grateful. The difference between living and dying is so tiny, the space between heartbeats, but somehow I'm here.

"Oh my God, she's awake!" someone—I'm pretty sure it's Amber—shouts. "You're awake!"

"My head," I groan, as Amber hurries over and kisses me repeatedly on the cheek.

"How are you, honey?" My mother hovers over me too. I can hear the relief in her voice, though she's wearing a prominent frown. "I thought the doctor said she didn't have a concussion. Why does she have a headache?"

"It might just be the stress," Monique offers. Missing every social cue, Mo starts to explain that headaches can have many causes, from dehydration to anxiety. "Since they said she passed out on the way to the hospital, it was likely the shock—"

"That's very interesting, Monica," Mom says, cutting her off. "Do me a favor and get the doctor?" It's an order, but Mom makes it sound kind. She is never not delegating—Sterlingwood's mayor first, everything else second.

Mo hurriedly does as she is told. Being low-key afraid of my mother means she'll answer to anything, even the name "Maureen," which was what Mom called her when Mo first moved to town at the start of high school.

"You have to be more careful," Mom says, squeezing my hand.

I give her a weak smile, because I know exactly what her tenderness means: *I was scared. I'm glad you're okay. Please don't ever do this to me again.*

Mom and I have a way of communicating without words. In our silences, we say the important things. Promise not to hurt or embarrass each other.

The woman Mo returns with seconds later is in colorful floral scrubs with lavender bottoms and a white shirt with purple flowers.

"Welcome back, Zadie!" the nurse says, all cheer. Under the fluorescent lights of the hospital room, everything feels too bright.

There's a stinging pain in the back of my neck and an ache going around the crown of my head.

"I think I'm having a migraine," I tell the nurse, and she nods, scribbles something on a chart, then begins to take my vitals, asking me a bunch of questions.

"What's happening?" Mom asks. I've heard her assistants joke that my mother wants regular progress reports on progress reports.

Before the nurse can answer, a short, ancient-looking man enters with a stethoscope around his neck. "How's the girl doing?" he says. If I wasn't feeling so gross, I'd blanch at being called *the girl,* but what it reminds me is that there is also *the boy.*

"*Jason!*" I say, shooting upright and wincing, all while the nurse is taking my blood pressure. "Is he okay?"

"Well, I don't know if *okay* is the word," Monique mumbles, eliciting the fastest smack from Amber.

"What do you mean? What does that mean?" I scan the room, desperately searching for information on somebody's face.

"He's not awake," the doctor says, pushing round, owl-like glasses up his nose. He comes forward, tips my chin up, and shines a penlight in my eyes.

"He's sleeping?" I ask.

"He's in a coma, honey," the nurse says, each word gentle, but it feels like a punch.

"A coma?"

Air is pushing against my windpipe, making it hard to breathe.

"We have every hope that he'll make a full recovery," she hurries to add, "but he took a harder hit than you. An especially bad one to the head."

Amber sniffs loudly.

When my dad died last summer, thirteen months ago to be exact, I discovered that the worst kind of pain feels like nothing—blank, flat, dry—until it feels like everything.

But Jason isn't dead, and this pain is different, a sharp, twisting feeling in my chest.

"Can I see him?" I ask.

Mom pats my hand in my lap. "Maybe just focus on getting better," she says.

"I want to see him," I say, ferocious suddenly.

I want to confirm it—that the Jason I know, who is always on the move, always doing *something*, is really hurt enough to be unconscious.

The nurse readjusts my arm cuff and instructs me to lie back down. She tells me she has to restart the measurement.

"Is he going to be okay?" I manage to squeak out.

Both the doctor and nurse seem reluctant to make any promises. "We're doing everything in our power to get him better," the nurse says, as the doctor begins inspecting my neck, rambling about whiplash. Mo interrupts to ask him a question, but I hardly hear a word anybody says.

The nurse discharges me an hour later. "You're free to go and check on your boyfriend," she says, giving me a final squeeze on the arm.

I have just enough presence of mind to think *ex-boyfriend*, a heaviness sticking to the pit of my stomach.

Amber offers to give me a ride home after we check on Jason, leaving my mother free to follow the nurse out of the room and pepper her with questions. Monique pouts about having to leave because her grandparents don't like her to stay out this late. Together, Ambs and I take the elevator to level three.

"If something had happened to you, I would have gone to jail for what I would do to the driver who caused the crash," Amber tells me. I manage a weak smile and decide not to point out that she is a generous five two and has not a violent bone in her body.

"What would you do? Overfeed him to death?" I tease, even though I still feel awful.

My body aches with dull, unspecific waves of pain. Like when you have the flu and can't really say what is hurting. And then there's my heart, still smarting from Jason's words.

"Well, there's a reason they call it death by chocolate," Amber says. She gets more serious suddenly, squeezing my hand in her small one. "I hope you get that you're, like, crucial to us. Nobody else knows Mo is terrified of grasshoppers or remembers my fifteen stupid allergies." She lowers her voice. "Or knows that my parents are basically just roommates, and I never, ever want to be like them."

Amber's sweet words form a lump in my throat, but I say, "Maybe I plan to blackmail you all."

She ignores me. "Who else keeps a list of everyone's birthday in our grade?"

"It's called data."

"Data that somehow always makes it into the morning announcements."

I don't bring up the point Jason made a couple of weeks ago—that more people hate getting called out on their birthday than appreciate when someone remembers. That, for being only vice president of Sterlingwood High, I take on too much.

I change the subject. "So who was the driver? What even happened?" I ask Amber as we approach the ICU.

"There was a four-car pileup. Apparently, some cargo truck driver was following too close." She rolls her eyes. "He's totally fine, of course. But they're saying Jason braked out of nowhere."

Was it because of my puking?

I tell Amber what I can remember about the accident itself, leaving out everything beforehand. No one I know saw me falling apart. If I never acknowledge it, my humiliating public meltdown might as well not have happened.

One of my earliest memories is of being at the Yellow Mart in Sterlingwood before my parents' divorce. I'm five, and right before I die of complete boredom, listening to my parents argue over cereal brands, Dad steals me away for the most fun game of hide-and-seek-and-chase. One of the funk songs Dad likes is playing loud on the store's speakers. We're grinning so hard that our faces feel like rubber, and everything is wonderful until I hear an earth-shattering crash. A gigantic pyramid of baked beans has crumbled right at Dad's feet. We are both laughing as we get to work rebuilding the tower. Mishaps like this seem to follow Dad, but today when I look up from the mess, for the first time ever, I am aware of them. The woman who grabs her son's arm and marches off, like he might catch something contagious just from being near us. The elderly man who curses under his breath and mutters about "people these days."

Other shoppers around us meander, stealing glances at our chaos. For a second, I see the two of us from their perspective: loud and Black and *messy*.

Maybe Dad notices me freeze up, because he sends me to Mom while he gets a staff member and finishes cleaning up. I find Mom in the freezer aisle, where a woman in a mustard yellow sweater is hugging her, congratulating my mother on being elected to city council. The woman's eyes are admiring, pleasant, calm. My mother is beautiful, admirable, with her slicked-back bun, subtle brown lipstick, and impeccable posture.

I never tell Mom about the tower crash, but the next time we go to the store, I stay with her.

Softer eyes and kinder smiles and fewer whispers. Every time.

And it becomes my unspoken motto.

That memory passes, an inconvenient ghost flittering through my mind. When I come back to myself, Amber is whispering as we walk, "So what was the surprise? What was he trying to ask you?"

My voice is pitched unnaturally high. "Jay?"

I had everyone believing he was going to practically propose to me. That he was going to promise me forever. My lipstick from this evening is all rubbed off by now, and with it, every trace of certainty I had in anything.

"Did he ask?" Amber's eyes are round as saucers.

I try to think of how to break it to her. *No, he didn't ask. He said it was over.*

The shame feels so heavy.

I suddenly see it in my head, my superlative: Zadie Cartwright, Most Likely to Lose Everything.

How do I tell Amber about the breakup without making it sound like it was me, like it was a *Zadie* problem? After all, I don't know for sure that it was.

I open my mouth right as Amber squeals.

"Oh my God, he *did*, didn't he?" She grabs for my hand. "Where's the ring?"

"In . . . his car." The lie tumbles out without me thinking. I am a storyteller, my father's daughter.

Amber's face twists in horror. "No! You lost it in the wreck?"

The muscles of my neck feel bunched, sore, and tight. "It's crazy, right?" I say, half-hearted.

"That sucks so much," she says, starting to tear up like she's the one who has lost something precious. "I'm so sorry, Zadie. You have to tell the police."

I nod, knowing full well that I will do no such thing.

I'm only too relieved to step forward and speak to the unit clerk when we reach the ICU. "Can we see Jason Riddick?"

Amber taps my shoulder. "Um, is it okay if I don't . . ." She looks as white as a sheet of paper. Mo's thing is surgery and diagnoses and obscure medical facts. Amber can hardly look at a scratch. "I just . . . If there's blood . . ."

"Oh."

I don't want to see Jason by myself because I don't know how I'll cope if he's swollen or unrecognizable.

I almost say we should forget the whole thing and just go home, but despite being the sweetest human, Amber has zero discretion. Everyone will know by tomorrow morning if I couldn't hack seeing Jason sick. Besides, I'm suddenly overwhelmed by this need to protect Jason if he does look bad. I should get to see him first. I should make sure what people hear about him is flattering and honest and fair.

"I'll be right back." I leave Amber and follow the nurse down the hall.

My heartbeat quickens as she opens his door. The beeps of a dozen machines should sound like hope, but they make the hairs on my arms stand up. I slowly shuffle forward.

A huge breath escapes my lungs when I see him. Minus a wide bandage around his head, some bruises and cuts on his face, and an elevated leg in a cast, he still looks mostly like himself. Like the strong and handsome Jason I know. He looks like he's sleeping.

"How is he?" I ask the nurse, suddenly on the verge of tears. I don't know if it's relief or exhaustion or both.

"He's stable. That's the most important thing. Feel free to talk to him. We have every reason to believe he can hear."

The thought makes a chill run over my skin, like stones skipping on water. "Really? He can hear us?"

"Oh, yeah," she assures me. "Now, you have a job to do: Tell him all the reasons he should hurry back. Tell him you're waiting for him, and it's rude to keep a lady waiting."

For the first time in what feels like forever, a small smile tugs at my lips.

The nurse pats my shoulder. "Let me give you two some privacy."

When she shuts the door, I stand staring at Jason.

I'm not sure what to do. It's bad enough he's fighting for his life, but now I don't even know if he would want me to be here.

Still, I force myself over to the side of Jason's bed and take his hand.

It feels stiff and big and unfamiliar. I squeeze.

"You're going to get better, okay?" I tell him, more demand than request. "You're going to play this season and go to college and do everything you've ever wanted."

Even as I say this, I'm staring at his broken leg and wondering if my words are possible. What if he never wakes up again? What if he never gets to do any of the things he always talked about— playing for his dream school, making the national team, playing for an international club?

A new feeling stretches over me: guilt.

If we hadn't been fighting, he might not have been so distracted. If I hadn't thrown up. If I'd handled the breakup better.

I hoist myself up into his bed and slowly tuck myself into his side, careful not to dislodge or break anything. "I'm so sorry, Jay," I tell him, holding his hand again.

"And listen," I whisper, "I forgive you for the . . . what you said before the crash . . ." I can't even say the words out loud, like speaking them might make them real. "We'll talk about it when you're awake."

I kiss him, a long, heartfelt kiss on his jaw, where he's already developing a five o'clock shadow.

Hopefully, by the time Jason wakes up he'll have changed his mind about the breakup. But there's a thought percolating in my mind, like a slow-kindling fire. It's what the nurse said about Jason possibly hearing everything we're saying.

You have a job to do, the nurse said, and maybe she's right. Maybe this is on me.

Maybe I can fix everything that went wrong with us so by the time he comes out of this coma, it makes absolutely no sense for us not to be together.

All I have to do is figure out why he felt he had to end things.

All I have to do is read an unconscious boy's mind.

Three

I don't remember falling asleep, but I must drift off for a few minutes.

I'm still lying on Jason's bed when, without warning, his door swings open and what seems like all of Sterlingwood comes bustling in. First, the Riddicks: Jay's mom, Cara, and dad, Rhett. His uncle Tommy and little cousin, Joey. Then, the soccer team, complete with coach and assistant coach. There's fourteen players, and they're all dressed in their soccer uniforms.

Great.

I realize that some kind nurse must have let me sleep, as I climb down off the bed, adjusting my dress. I must look awful with my smudged-off makeup and no-longer-controlled edges. Both coaches squeeze my shoulders, and all of Jay's friends hug me and tell me how sorry they are, how glad they are that I'm okay.

None of his friends say anything about Jason having broken my heart. Honestly, none of them even look like they have a clue, and I start to wonder if it's possible Jason told no one what he was planning to do. My first thought would have been to get his friends to tell me what he told them.

"Zadie, he's coming on back to you. Just give him time," Coach Kyle says, and something about his ferociously tender confidence makes my stomach twist.

I give him a sheepish smile. "Thanks."

"Fellas, thank you for wearing your uniforms and coming out so late and on such short notice." Coach Kyle addresses the team like they're in a mid-game huddle and not an intensive care unit. "I thought it would only be appropriate to bring Jason some of our team spirit, because he needs it right now more than ever."

A few people yell "Hell yeah" and echo his words. I quietly slip out of the room and head to the family waiting area, feeling the pinch of guilt under my skin. I know that technically I'm not doing anything wrong in letting everyone think I'm still Jason's girlfriend. Jason and I were broken up for maybe ten minutes. That can't be worth announcing. Plus, if I have my way, we're probably not even staying broken up.

Still, maybe I should try to tell *someone*. I find Amber in the waiting room.

"Ambs, I have to tell you something," I say, after I've apologized for abandoning her and falling asleep in Jay's room. She's flipping through a magazine next to a vending-machine feast of chips, pretzels, and candy.

"Don't even worry," Amber says, grinning for the first time since I woke up. "I already sent the word out and everybody's going to look for the ring . . ."

I think I've misheard her.

"Wait, what?" I frown.

"The ring. Sterlingwood is on it."

Sterlingwood is like an entire human body. It functions as a unit, thinks as one group. If she says the town is on it, then the *town* is on it.

Dread creeps over me as she continues to explain.

"I told everyone Jason gave you a promise ring but it got lost in the wreck," she says. "I put it out on social."

"Amber!" I'm horrified. "Why would you do that? Are you *crazy*?"

"You'll find it faster this way. Maybe even before Jason wakes up—"

I bury my face in my hands, every cell in my body buzzing with horror. Now what am I supposed to do?

Either I play along and hope Jason follows my lead when he wakes up—if he wakes up—or I have to tell the truth and out myself as both a liar and the girl who wasn't worthy of Jason Riddick.

I'm pretty sure that I can only live with one option.

"You don't understand," I tell Amber desperately. She looks at me with furrowed brows, a bit startled.

"What don't I understand?"

"The ring isn't—" Before I can finish, Amber's phone trills with Dolly Parton singing "I Will Always Love You." It's way too loud for a hospital waiting room, and she quickly answers it before one of the nurses can complain.

"Hello?" she whispers into the phone, and then she motions at me. "It's Talon."

Amber's latest boyfriend, Talon, is what we respectfully refer to as a stoner. Dirty Converse, weed, and skateboards are Talon's whole life. Despite not being her usual type, at three months in, he is easily Amber's longest relationship yet. For such a big romantic, Ambs is terrible at relationships. She's great at getting into them, frequently obsessing over someone for weeks before finally asking them out (or getting them to ask her out). There'll be the first two weeks of grand gestures and epic declarations and "I think he's the one" before it all just . . . peters out. Surprisingly, Amber and Talon still appear to like each other right now, as she delves into a long, whispered conversation with him, repeating the whole story about the accident and the ring. Amber's run-through is detailed, dramatic, and almost gleeful in the moments she forgets to be somber. My head spins suddenly, and I drop into the nearest seat to regain my balance.

"Well *apparently* someone else our age was in the accident, but I still haven't heard if it was anyone we know." Amber's voice is stressing me out, so despite not feeling great, I push up and walk through the halls until I find a restroom far enough away to feel safe.

As I feared, I look like the cargo truck personally ran me over multiple times.

I tie my microbraids into a bun on the top of my head and clean up my smeared makeup. But I'm woozy, the way you are when you haven't eaten in a while, and it trickles all the way down into my body until I feel like a shell of myself. Maybe I just need some sugar.

I splash cold water on my face to wake up.

Amber's call with Talon has reminded me of exactly why I don't want her to be the first person to hear about me and Jason. She'll be sweet about it, comforting, but I know a part of her will just be dying to share it with someone. The news will be everywhere by the end of the night, and being the talk of the town because Jason broke up with me is the last thing I want.

God, I can picture it already. Everyone's sympathy—faux kind smiles and condescending hand squeezes—or worse, diverted gazes and whispers, their quiet confirmation that I was never good enough for him.

Zadie Cartwright, Most Likely to Think She Was Better Than She Is.

I call Monique. I won't get Amber's softness from Mo, the empathy and determination to be on my side *no matter what*. It's the reason I'm far more likely to confide in Amber when I just need a sympathetic ear. That, and I've known Ambs way longer. Both my friends held me and cried with me when my dad died. Still, with Mo, I know I'll get bluntness and possibly a talk about right versus wrong, aka why I need to fess up and tell the truth. But maybe Mo will understand why I lied about the ring after everything that has happened.

Mo's phone rings and rings, but she doesn't answer. Chances are, she is already safely tucked in bed, as per her grandparents' wishes. Mo and her siblings spent years in foster care before being adopted by their grandparents four years ago when she moved to Sterlingwood. Mo is half-Jamaican and has all types of feelings about being saved by her white grandparents, but the fact that they all love each other is indisputable.

I decide to leave her a voice memo.

"Mo, it's me. I need you to promise not to judge me for what I'm about to tell you."

I've heard that confession is good for the soul, so I swallow my nerves and spill my guts in the note. About how Jason broke up with me, about how sad and confused I feel, about wanting to know why, and the lie I fed Amber about the ring. I'm just getting to the end when someone beats insistently on the door of the restroom.

"One second!" I say, squirting soap into the hand without a phone.

Knock knock knock.

"I said, one second!"

But when the pounding continues, I quickly end Mo's message.

"I have to go, Mo. Some psycho won't let me even wash my hands. Love you, bye."

Knock, knock, knock.

"Oh my God, can I finish?" When I open the door, I'm shocked to see Marcus Riddick. Marcus with his lazy grin and his messy, shoulder-length dirty blond hair. He's wearing a soccer shirt, but he's paired it with jeans. It occurs to me that he was the only player on the Sterlingwood Silvers who didn't show up to Jason's room earlier.

"M&Ms or Skittles?" Marcus says, apropos of nothing, smiling broadly at me. I tug at my sleeve when what I really want is to shut the door in his face. A long time ago, Marcus decided our "thing" was playing an everlasting game of This or That. I did not agree to any such thing, so I completely ignore his question.

"Did you get the time wrong?" I ask, and it comes out more snide than curious. His cousin is in a coma, and he can't even be bothered to show up to see him on time.

My real concern is that I thought I was far enough from the ICU that none of Jason's teammates or family would be around, but I don't know how long Marcus has been standing out here. If there's any justice in the world, Marcus cannot be the first person to know about me and Jason.

That sleepy smile stretches across his face now. "Something like that," he says, voice gritty like he just woke up from a nap.

25 * * *

"Did you . . . How long have you been waiting?" I ask him, trying not to show my panic.

He yawns. "Just got here. You done?" he asks, but he's already pushing in past me, completely oblivious to the concept of waiting his turn.

"Oh, don't worry about it, Marcus. I was just leaving, anyway." Mom would call my sarcasm unbecoming, but in this case I would say it's justified.

Marcus is holding on to his belt like he wants to start undoing it, and since that's a show I have no intention of seeing, I hurry out of the restroom, slamming the door shut behind me.

Then I look at my phone and see that my voice recording has disappeared. "Please tell me it sent," I whisper, checking Mo's and my message thread.

There's nothing.

"Oh my *God*."

I must have accidentally deleted it when I was talking to Marcus. I check that I didn't mistakenly send it to anyone else, and it doesn't look like I did.

The entire thing has vanished, lost in the ether, when I'd just summoned enough courage to tell Mo.

I don't feel brave enough to record it all again right now.

Defeated, I walk back to the visitors' room in the ICU, where Amber is still waiting. The snacks have mostly been devoured, various wrappers and half-empty packets discarded on the table, and she's now surrounded by a bunch of soccer bros, Jason's friends and teammates. It's like they're expecting Jay to suddenly jolt awake, expecting that they can just camp out here for a few hours and then they'll get their captain back—ready to play, his capable, steady self. I hope they're right.

"Make space for the missus!" Tyler Manning orders, tugging at his faux-hawk. He likes to think he's the de facto leader when Jason isn't around, mainly because he's the goalie and wears the No. 1 jersey. He also bribed his way into being the most unserious student body president of all time, but that is neither here nor there.

The guys all make a big show of hugging me again and asking how I'm doing and moving up on the couch for me. Being Jason's girlfriend is like an exclusive VIP pass, one I didn't even know I wanted, one that allows me to fit in anywhere and everywhere I go. I sit down between Amber and Holden Ash, who is asking if his yearbook quote can have profanity.

"Only if you don't want to be included," I tell him.

Being head of the yearbook committee is tiny in the grand scheme of things—it's definitely not student vice president or valedictorian, which I'm also on track for—but somehow it feels like the most consequential role I'll have all year. I'm in charge of capturing some of the final moments of our high school careers, of preserving memories that reflect the best of us and how we want to be remembered for the rest of our lives. People think yearbooks are supposed to mirror the people in them, but I see it differently. When someone's kid or grandkid pulls out the yearbook in forty years, you'll want them to see you as you want to be seen, not as you actually are. It matters how you present yourself—and in the yearbook you're frozen in time. I want us to look classy and timeless.

Holden is still asking me questions when someone hollers, "Yo, Plan B!"

Everyone turns around to watch Marcus's arrival, his grin wide.

"It's Discount Riddick, mothereffers!" another person yells. It's no wonder Marcus is so insufferable. If I got this kind of reception every time I entered a room, I too would have an unquenchable ego. Jason is the only person I know who, despite being treated like a king, still knows to keep himself in check.

"How's it going?" Marcus says, coming around and exchanging back pats and fist bumps with everyone. When he reaches me, he holds out his fist to me, like he expects me to pound it. I keep eating my Twizzler and just roll my eyes. He seems to enjoy this, if his smile is any indication. And he would enjoy it, because Marcus Riddick is the worst. He's like the anti-Jason, which is probably where the irony comes in that they are cousins. Uncensored (as in, if I didn't have the rest of the yearbook committee to think about and Other Repercussions), I'd give him Most Likely to Be Doing Something Annoying at Any Given Time, because it fits seamlessly.

Josh Faraday says, "You didn't make it for the group thing, Plan B! Coach is *pissed*."

Marcus laughs. "Coach is always pissed. Well, off to perform my familial duties," he says, saluting us as he heads toward Jason's room.

"Yeah, go wake Sleeping Beauty!" Holden tells Marcus, but the joke falls flat. With how uncertain everything is, it feels cruel rather than funny. As Jason's girlfriend, I should scold his best friend, but I don't. Amber's sharp "*Holden!*" and the resounding silence is the only backlash he gets, though, because Marcus's smile does not falter even a little before he disappears into Jason's room.

Josh lets out a giant yawn, and Tyler snickers. "Past your bedtime, Faraday?"

"It's, like, tomorrow morning already," Josh says defensively, and doesn't bother to stifle a second, longer yawn.

Amber turns to me. "Oh, Zad, weren't you trying to tell me something before?"

I blink at her. It's absurd how unfazed Ambs is about the notion of creating a spectacle. Because that's exactly what this would cause.

"I was?"

I've suddenly realized just how grateful I am that my message to Mo never sent. In this moment, I decide: I'm not going to tell anyone what happened between me and Jason earlier tonight.

I shouldn't have to, when the breakup is never going to last.

"Oh, I was just going to ask if, um, you knew what happened to Jay's car?"

Amber beams, because of course she does.

This breakup is not a big deal, I tell myself.

It's not relevant, and it hardly counts, and I shouldn't have to face the fallout of us not being *us* on my own.

29 * * *

Four

Mom insists I spend the weekend resting, which I take as permission to not think about anything stressful and simply cozy up in bed and read. A few months before Dad died, I researched a list of books everybody needs to read in their lifetimes, and it became the official reading list for the Cartwright Father-Daughter Book Club of Best Books to Read Before You Die.

For more than one reason, I wish we'd picked a different name.

All the way to August, Dad and I spent hours on the phone discussing George Orwell, bell hooks, Emily Brontë, and Dad's favorite, Zadie Smith. Dad took it as a personal challenge to argue any point that was opposite to mine, to "make me think." He was immovable in his opinions and completely obnoxious when he managed to win me over to his side. He used to say that, at its core, every story was about love.

I think that was true about his story too. One great big adventure that he incorporated me into whenever I visited him in Portland after the divorce. He'd take me to all the museums and galleries and bookstores he loved, cherished coffee shops he liked to attempt to write in. We'd act like tourists and overdose on lobster, go to concerts of Dad's favorite musicians that he only sometimes had tickets to. Meet up with his eccentric artist friends and whichever woman he happened to be dating at the time.

We were still doing our book club, smack in the middle of *To*

Kill a Mockingbird, when his heart stopped, but when I got to the end in September, I flipped to the beginning and immediately started again.

Today on my Mom-imposed "me time," I reach for my twenty-fifth book once again, but I can never do it. I can't read another book on our list without Dad. I go for a walk because my muscles are itching for a run, despite where I'm sore from the crash. I wear a T-shirt with one of Dad's favorite bands on it, always funk music. I didn't inherit his musical taste, but I saved his T-shirts, his old music records, as many of his books as I could stand to keep. As I walk, I try to think of only happy things. So *not* the book list I will never finish, *not* the stress of making plans for the future, *not* the heartache of losing the boy I love.

But it's pretty much a lost cause.

It turns out, you can't outrun your life.

*   *   *

Part of me wishes I could go on "recovering" into the new week, but by Monday, even I've exceeded the amount of moping I can tolerate, so I'm back to school. It turns out there's only so much BookTok recommendations can do to fix a broken heart. If I was brave enough, I'd wear my heartache on the outside. I'd walk around in a flowing all-black lace getup like some grieving Victorian widow, but I realize people get committed for that kind of thing.

So I settle for two black stud earrings, the open secrets no one will notice.

As I enter English class, Mr. Tan hands me the essay I turned in a week early last Monday, with a circled red 98. Before I can ask where I lost two marks, he says, "You hanging in there, Zadie?"

Mr. Tan is in his mid-forties, a perpetual wearer of beige cardigans, and one of Dad's old friends. He discovered Dad was M. L. Cartwright, the author of *Moon Over Hanover*, during a parent-teacher conference, and Dad was never able to shake him again. Mr. Tan has been giving me sad eyes for a month, since the one-year mark of Dad's death, reminding me at every turn that there are resources available if I need them. For the briefest second, I don't know why, I think he's talking about Dad, and I almost blurt out that I'm not really *hanging in there*. That some days I miss him so much my bones ache.

But then I remember what he's really asking: the accident, Jason, Jason's coma.

I just manage to blurt out an "It's tough, but" before I'm flanked by a bunch of people I've gone to school with since kindergarten.

"Oh my God!" Penelope Miller says, throwing her arms around me.

Penny and I aren't friends exactly. With me hopefully going to Princeton and Penny heading to UMaine, there's no way we'll keep in touch once we graduate. Still, she hugs me fiercely now. The kind of hug you give a person you never thought you'd see again.

"Wow, thanks!" My voice is muffled by her shoulder. "I love your haircut."

"Ugh, thanks," Penny says. "Caleb hasn't even noticed."

Before I'm fully out of Penny's embrace, somebody else hugs me, and then another person, and then another. "How are you?"

"Oh, you know—"

"I'm so sorry about the accident."

"I'm so sorry about Jason."

"We've been praying for him."

"We've been praying for *you*."

"You should sue that driver!"

"I heard you had a concussion."

"I heard you broke your neck."

Their voices blur into a swirl of rumors and well-wishes, the kind of recognition you earn when you're affiliated with Jason Riddick. Small towns have their stars, and as the soccer captain, Sterlingwood's answer to a quarterback, Jason is one.

Before Jay and I started dating, I was popular but in a nerdy, friends-with-everybody sort of way. Dating Jason means that the whole school knows exactly who I am. Sometimes I think they know more about me than I do.

Being Jason's girlfriend made running for VP such a breeze that I occasionally wish I'd thought to challenge Tyler for president instead of running for a smaller role so I could focus on college applications. Lord knows student council would be going more smoothly.

"Okay, everyone, back up," Mo says with her trademark intensity, pushing people out of the way like she is my bodyguard. She's been super protective since the accident. Mo might have just moved to Sterlingwood in freshman year, but sometimes it feels like she's always been here.

Right then, Cristin Lee says something that catches my attention. "God, that sucks about the ring. We went out looking for it last night."

"You did?" I croak, stopping before Mo can herd me away. Amber truly opened up a can of worms.

"A bunch of us went out to where the accident happened," Cristin says, all animated, her blond curls bobbing in agreement with everything she says.

"We didn't find anything?" Jazz King is Cristin's best friend, and she has the unique talent of making every sentence sound like a question. "We were so sad? Like, it was super disappointing?"

On the one hand, it feels nice that so many people are willing to sacrifice this kind of time and energy for me and Jason. On the other hand, I feel like the worst person in the world for lying.

"We're doing our own search party tonight. There's a sign-up online," someone else chimes in.

"Guys, seriously, you don't have to do all this—" I'm saying, half hoping the ground opens and swallows me, when Mr. Tan claps his hands to get our attention.

"Okay, friends, time to talk some Wordsworth."

My heart is weighed down by guilt as I slink into my usual chair next to Mo.

"Mo, people are like hardcore looking for the ring." I grip her arm. "This is insane."

She shrugs at me like, *hey, to each their own*. She's too focused on her laptop screen, working on her app. Mo is convinced that making a health app, combined with her killer GPA, is her ticket into any premed program she chooses.

"Yo, Mr. Tan," Holden says, falling into a seat in the back of the classroom, where he'll proceed to sleep for the next period. "Tell us again why you became an English teacher. I'm really struggling to pick between majors on my college apps."

A bunch of kids snicker, but Mr. Tan's entire face lights up. Soon our English teacher is three-metaphors-deep into his biweekly speech about how he started college as a—you won't believe it—math major but slowly felt the call of the written word. It's a sure-fire way to derail any lesson with Mr. Tan and today—maybe because it's Monday, maybe because Jason's in the hospital, unconscious, instead of across the hall in Ms. Gardner's class where he should be—it's exactly what we need.

The embarrassing truth is that I really am struggling to pick a path. Last night I Googled "best college major," because I'm that desperate. It was thirteen-year-old me who decided on New Jersey. I've told exactly one person the full story, which is that I researched the overall best Ivy League college using three different methods, and it was just Princeton that came out on top. Since then, it's been my "dream school," and one of the key things everybody knows about Zadie Cartwright is that she knows where she's going. What they don't know is that I have no idea what I'm going to do when I get there.

So I should definitely be taking in some of Mr. Tan's wisdom right now, but my mind won't let go of Jason. I miss being able to text him random thoughts, miss the cute little GIFs he'd send to let me know he was thinking of me. It occurs to me that whatever the reason a person is gone—whether it's a shocking, out-of-the-blue breakup, a random crazy coma, or even death—missing someone you love will always feel achy and empty and sad. It's just that sometimes the feeling is temporary, and sometimes it's forever.

For the rest of the day, my brain is so fuzzy I can hardly think. Time moves like a toddler having the hiccups, jerky and inconsistent, and I'm having trouble staying present.

During my second-to-last period, I'm discreetly scrolling through the string of *I love yous* and *good night beautifuls* and *hey I'm heres* between me and Jason when my head starts to really hurt. It's kept doing that on and off since the accident.

My eyes are suddenly stinging at the bright fluorescent classroom lights, so I ask Ms. Gonzalez for a hall pass and head to the infirmary. When I get there, I hear laughter coming from the room. I push open the door and turn to my left as Nurse Diamond's still-smiling face goes from relaxed to alarmed. She's sitting at her desk, the two bunk beds for sick kids behind me.

"Oh, Zadie! How are you, honey?"

"Good," I say on impulse. "I mean, I'm having a kind of headache?"

"In what way?"

I tell her about it, the way sound is starting to distort and everything is too bright.

"Hmm," she says. "Sounds like the start of a migraine. All our beds are taken, but . . ."

"I was just leaving," a familiar male voice says, before the owner emerges from behind me where the beds are.

Marcus Riddick. He is wearing a collared gray button-down over a black cotton shirt and black jeans. In last year's yearbook, Marcus put "Heath Ledger circa 1999" as his "style inspo." It was too specific a reference to not look up, and while I can confirm that, with his dirty blond hair that hangs down to his shoulders, Marcus *does* look exactly like that, his inspiration is too ancient to be as cool as Marcus thinks it is.

"Hold on, Marcus," Nurse Diamond says. "Let me just check if I have any more ice packs."

As the nurse disappears into a back room, I notice that Marcus is giving me one of his easygoing smiles. His hair is slightly ruffled. He's clearly spent the whole period in here.

My eyes give him a quick sweep, looking for any ailments. Predictably, there are none. I mean, he's noncommittally holding ice to his left elbow, but that's Marcus in a nutshell: noncommittal, indifferent, unbothered.

"Good nap?" I ask. In the background, a kid groans like they're in pain.

Marcus's smile gets wider. "Not bad. Though those pillows could stand to be a little softer. I go wild for duck feathers. What's your preference?" he asks with a completely straight face. "Firm? Medium?"

"Marcus, get f—"

"Okay, here we are," Nurse Diamond says, returning with a blue ice pack. When Marcus takes it, I stop myself from pointing out that he is putting ice on the wrong arm. Typical that he can't be bothered to get his story straight.

"Thanks for everything, Melissa," Marcus says.

I manage not to roll my eyes when he leaves.

"Zadie, let me get you Advil for your head," Nurse Diamond says, only too happy to attend to me now that her star patient is gone.

I've had a couple of migraines before, and they were so awful I thought I might be dying.

"How's Jason?" Nurse Diamond asks as she shakes two pills into a small plastic cup. "Marcus was telling me they saw some improvements in his scans."

"Was he?"

Last I checked, Marcus hasn't been back to see his cousin since Friday when the whole soccer team was mandated to be there. I've been there every day since, and I haven't seen him once.

As I head over to the vacant bed, I tell her about the small hopeful changes with Jason. It's the bed Marcus must have just been in. I find myself wondering what he was *really* doing here. Probably his favorite pastime of getting out of class or hiding from some girl whose heart he broke.

After taking the two pills, I fall asleep.

When I wake up what feels like five minutes later, the room is shadowed and dark, which makes no sense. I groan and turn over, confused and bleary-eyed.

"Good nap?" a voice says.

"Oh my God!" I shriek, shooting up, only to slam my head on the top bunk. "Ouch."

"Careful. There's a bed there."

It's freaking Marcus again.

I narrow my eyes at him. Look around at the empty infirmary. "What time is it?"

"I'm guessing like five p.m. The infirmary closes at four, but when Melissa tried to wake you, you apparently begged her to let you keep sleeping."

"I absolutely did not," I say, on the simple basis that begging doesn't sound like me. Plus, I only shut my eyes for a few seconds.

"So Nurse Diamond just left?" I ask.

"She had to pick up her kids, so I offered to keep an eye on you."

"Oh my God," I say, standing more carefully, smoothing down my skirt. "I don't need you to babysit me."

"Well, when you have a head injury and come in complaining of a migraine, you do. Are the doctors sure you don't have a concussion?" There's a hint of worry in his voice.

"Yeah, they think I—wait, what do you care?"

Marcus blinks at me. "I don't." The split second of hurt I feel is made the tiniest bit better by the nearly imperceptible wince Marcus gives at his own words.

"Whatever. Don't ever watch me sleep again. It's creepy."

"Oh, you wish I was watching you, but alas." He holds up a thick fantasy novel. He's dressed for practice, so I get the feeling that's where he's supposed to be. Marcus Riddick as an avid reader is so inconsistent with all the things most people know about him, which is why he seems to do it only when nobody else is around.

"I hope it has plenty of pictures," I say, as I head for the door.

Marcus laughs, a deep rumble from his chest. "Good one. Very original."

Fat headphones now over his ears, he starts to lock up the infirmary. I look over at him with the express purpose of marveling at Nurse Diamond's bad judgment, leaving a senior who thinks class schedules are a suggestion in charge. But he's already looking my way, so I quickly glance away.

I actually liked Marcus a lot when we first met. It was July last year, a month before Dad died, that Penny threw a big start-of-summer party. Marcus had just moved to town, and I had no idea who he was at the time, but somehow, we spent a whole night talking on the back steps of Penny's house. We talked books and our families and expectations and college. It was also when Marcus first started trying to make This or That happen. I thought he seemed sweet and funny and genuine. And it goes without saying that he was not bad on the eyes. But then his true colors came out. We were barely two weeks into September, barely two weeks into the school year, when I found out what he really thought about me.

I head to my locker, pulling out my backpack and books. The school is deserted. But as I exit the building, Marcus is a mere second behind, both of us deliberately not walking together the whole way to student parking.

The ground makes the occasional crunchy noise under my boots as the first few brown and yellow leaves speckle the lot.

I pick up my pace and have almost reached my car when Marcus calls my name. "Zadie!"

I sigh and turn around. "What, Marcus?"

He closes the distance between us. "Forgot to mention: I hear congratulations are in order."

I frown. "Congratulations?"

Now that he's stopped in front of me, I can see that his eyes are dancing. They are unsettling for how different they are from Jason's. I've always thought there was one variety of brown eyes. Jason has beautiful, familiar dark brown eyes. Warm, steadfast eyes. Marcus's are a lighter brown with flecks of yellow.

At the look of confusion on my face, he gestures to his ring finger. "It's so romantic when teenagers take a marriage vow when they can barely vote or see an R-rated movie."

God. The promise ring.

"Oh, um . . ."

He's clearly needling me, but the lack of expression on his face makes me doubt myself.

I stand straighter, feign smugness. "Yeah, well, we're in *love*."

Marcus smirks, like I've just told him a good knock-knock joke. "So I'm told."

He starts to move in the opposite direction, pulling his head-phones back over his ears.

"By the way," he pauses, speaking too loudly because of his music. "How surprised do you think Jay will be to find himself engaged to the girl he broke up with by the time he wakes up?"

I can't move, can't breathe, can't speak.

"Yeah." Marcus grins. "That's what I thought."

And then he crosses the parking lot and is gone.

Five

So much for my hope that Marcus didn't overhear my voice note to Mo.

The only thought more infuriating than realizing I might have to talk to Marcus Riddick again is accepting that I might have to *bargain* with Marcus Riddick.

Since our run-in on Monday, I've been scoping out who knows what about Jason and me, and as far as I can tell, only Marcus knows about the breakup. And for some reason, he's kept it to himself. I'll need to shake the truth out of him and beg him not to breathe a word to anyone.

My soul and dignity in exchange for his silence.

How is deadbeat Marcus my biggest problem? I whisper to myself as I ring the doorbell of Jason's house. I smooth down my dark blue dress, fix my hair while I wait.

After Jason's family held a service at the Lutheran church this afternoon, they're now hosting a reception for friends and loved ones in their house.

The good news is, I'm pretty sure Marcus will be here today.

The bad news is, I'm pretty sure Marcus will be here today.

"I have a surprise for you, Zadie!" Jason's mother singsongs when she opens the front door of their house for me.

"Don't try to guess," Mrs. R tells me, which, of course, makes me desperate to guess.

My obvious hope is that it's Jason, that he's out of his coma, but since I saw him earlier this morning, I know that can't be it. And Mrs. R is excited now, but no way her reaction would be this muted if her son was awake.

"I promise, I won't," I say as I move into the house. The Riddick house is something you would find in *Architectural Digest*. Not those expensive houses with vintage furniture that pretend to be homey, but the rich-and-proud-to-be-rich houses. Everything is sleek and modern and neutrals-colored.

The only time Mom has ever been here, she oohed and aahed over everything, polite to a fault until we got into the car. Then she told me it looked like a "McMansion."

"It just doesn't have a very attainable, lived-in feeling," she said. *Attainable* is one of Mom's words. It means to be *of the people*, to be thought of as normal, down-to-earth, trustworthy, all things that my mother is always aspiring toward as a politician. Other words for attainable: *approachable, relatable,* and *electable*.

I wouldn't describe our house as lived-in either, but that's not something I'd ever tell Mom.

"Oh my God, don't look now, babe, but this absolute stunner just walked in," Amber loud-whispers to her boyfriend, Talon, as I enter the living room.

"Where? Where?" Talon swivels around, pretending to look. Then he nuzzles into his girlfriend's neck. "Only stunner I see is you, babe."

"Wow. I don't know whether to feel rejected or objectified," I deadpan.

"Maybe both?" Amber suggests, taking my hand and pulling me

into their group. "Why are your nails giving *Night of the Living Dead*, and why do I love it?"

"Thanks," I say. My nails are painted black with silvery glitter dust today.

The open secrets started when Dad died. So many times since that day in August, I've wanted to not do my makeup and not put in my contacts and just dress like a slob because what does anything matter when my father is gone? But I never had the courage to do any of that. I've remained tidy, affable Zadie Cartwright, with her carefully chosen clothes and cute hair and flawless makeup. Instead, I started to choose one thing each day that would reflect how I truly felt. Something subtle.

At least the nails aren't clashing with my church outfit.

The Riddick house is big enough for the twenty-five or so of us who just left the service and are having lunch at their house. Of course, the meal is catered, people in uniforms slipping between and around us while classical piano music floats through the house speakers. The somber, formal tone reminds me of Dad's wake. I remember feeling like I was drowning in a sea of faceless bodies that day, all of them dressed in black. Nobody knew what to say or do. It felt utterly hopeless too; nothing I did could bring Dad back.

Today, though, there is an unspoken undercurrent of hope, like we are just simply biding our time, going through the motions until Jason wakes up.

Mrs. R is settling down next to her husband, who is showing Coach Kyle and his wife ancient photo albums of Jason as a kid. Jason's parents have shown them to me multiple times over the past year. Jason playing soccer. Jason winning the golden boot, the mini-league version of MVP. Jason meeting his idol, Cristiano Ronaldo.

I'm only the slightest bit grateful that their spiel is directed at someone else today. "Where's Mo?" I ask. It's weird that she's been gone for this long.

"Somewhere around here," Amber says, voice strangely high-pitched. Behind her, Talon points at Amber then makes exaggerated throat-slashing gestures at me.

"You cut . . . kill . . . killed her?" I say, trying to do my best with his clues.

"Are you miming behind my back again?" Amber asks, turning on Talon. "It's really not in your skill set, babe. And Zad, I love you, but if I had to choose between having you and a walrus on my charades team, I'd pick the walrus."

"They don't even have hands," I point out with a laugh.

"Exactly," Amber says.

"Epic," Talon remarks, and based on his laughter, I take it he found Amber's comment funny.

"Fine. Mo and I had a baby argument," Ambs admits. "And she stomped off."

"An argument? About what?" I ask, alarmed. My friends and I never fight. I call our trio a friend-ocracy because whenever two of us disagree, the third casts a tie-breaking vote. Amber and I have been pretty much inseparable since the day in kindergarten when she gave Brady Westhaven a valentine that he rejected. Rightfully annoyed, Amber picked it up from where it had been discarded on the floor and gave it to me instead. Amber being as famously glamorous and tender-hearted (even then) as she was, I intrinsically understood the value of what she was offering me, and we've been a pair ever since. Then, years later, after showing Monique around the school when she first moved here, I invited Mo to sit with me and Amber at lunch. I was overjoyed to finally have another Black person in my class.

Amber and Mo could not be more different. Ambs with her expensive everything and heart made of actual mush, and Mo with her backpack full of pins depicting great scientists, plus the marker-tattoo she wore on her wrist for all of junior year that read WWAFD (What Would Alexander Fleming Do?). Then there's the app Mo is trying to launch before winter break (she's looking for investors and everything). But Ambs and Mo quickly discovered that they both have an affinity for true crime podcasts and almost always agree on who the killer is, which is no small feat. I can't stand true crime, but somehow the three of us make it work.

"I don't remember," Amber says now, clearly lying. "Honestly, it was so stupid."

I don't like any of it: the fact that my friends are fighting at all, and the fact that it's not over something minute enough for me to just tie-break away. "If it was stupid, why hasn't she come back?"

"Maybe she got caught up in another conversation?" Talon offers.

"I'm going to check that she's okay," I say.

Amber sighs. "Sure. Fine."

"Epic," Talon says, and I try not to flinch. Talon uses that word like most people use "awesome" or "big" or "happy" or "sure." Basically, most things in his mind are epic.

My search for Monique takes me throughout the entire downstairs level of the house, which is roughly the size of my whole home. I traipse through the family room and the piano room, and then open the door that leads into the garage. There, I come upon . . . Marcus Riddick.

There are three expensive cars in the massive garage space, but all I see is him.

He's slumped over in a chair, legs outstretched, head thrown back. For one second, I worry he's not breathing and my heart flips in my chest, but a big noisy inhale quickly cures me of that concern.

"Unbelievable," I mutter to myself. Marcus gets his legendary status from the time he allegedly crashed so hard after a game that he made it all the way to Cranwell before he realized he'd been sleeping in the back of the wrong team's bus, and no one laughed harder than Marcus.

Before I can take this opportunity to confront him, to tell him that I've been looking for him for days, my phone vibrates with a text from Mo.

SOS is all her text says, and I'm already moving back the way I came. I slam the door shut as I leave, the image of Marcus jerking awake in alarm bringing a smile to my face.

On driveway, a second text says before I can send one asking where she is.

On my way, I write back.

* * *

Mo generally doesn't send SOS texts; she answers them, always ready to fix a problem. Maybe it's a side effect of being the oldest of four kids who were left to raise themselves. Or maybe it's just the personality you need to want to cure the world's most pressing diseases in your lifetime.

I button up my cardigan because outside is getting more Maine-y by the day. I know it's controversial, but I love that we get actual seasons, that the air gets sweater-weather cool in fall and the kind of cold that forms icicles in your nostrils in winter.

I find Mo sitting on the driveway, looking miserable. She's not even working on her app, which she is *always* doing. I plop down next to her and rest my head against hers. "What happened?"

She echoes Amber's words. "It was stupid." We are both silent for a while, then Mo says, "Do you know Ambs thinks she's found her soulmate?"

I groan. Because three months is in no way enough time to know someone is your soulmate. Plus, Talon is in his second senior year. I like him, but I might be fighting with Amber too if she told me he was her one true love.

For all the guys Ambs has dated, it's never felt like we actually had to share her with anyone until Talon.

"If I hear him say the word *epic* one more time, I'm going to throw something," Mo says.

We burst into laughter, but then she continues, "We're *eighteen*. We're supposed to be living our best lives, making memories before college. It's never going to be like this again, where we all live in the same town and know all the same people and see each other every day. Everything's going to change. I feel like I'm the only one who realizes that, and it sucks."

Mo has always liked it best when it's just the three of us—no boyfriends, no stragglers—and I wonder if she is already anticipating facing UMaine alone next year. Ambs and I have known for years that we wanted to leave for school—her for culinary school in New York and me for the best school I got into. If it's New Jersey I go to, New York is pretty close, but it's not like Amber and I are going to the same place without Mo; still, it must be hard to be the person getting left behind.

"I know. I don't think I'm ready for how much things are going to change."

"And then don't even get me started on the concept of soulmates," Mo rants. "It's so obnoxious. Like, why is everybody trying to couple up when we have our whole lives ahead of us?"

Her words remind me of Marcus's sarcasm the other day. *It's so romantic when teenagers take a marriage vow when they can barely vote or see an R-rated movie.*

"You think me and Jay are obnoxious?" I ask, terrified to know the answer. First, because Mo is not necessarily Jason's biggest fan. Second, because it feels like her verdict matters.

Monique tilts her head as she thinks. "Well, not really."

A week ago, that answer would have thrilled me. It would have been proof that Jason and I are the exact right balance of in love. That we're Not Like Other Couples. But now her response startles me. She *doesn't* think Jay and I are soulmates, or she doesn't think we're obnoxious?

"You guys are tolerable," she clarifies. "Most of the time. I mean, you don't always have to be together, which is nice."

"Right, but you think we're soulmates?" I ask, feeling around for some sort of assurance. *No, Jay would never voluntarily break up with you. You guys are so perfect. Couple goals.*

She bites her lip. "I don't know if soulmates exist."

"They do," I insist. "Not everyone finds theirs, but when you do, it's forever."

I know I sound as love-crazed as Amber, but what is a breakup, or fight, or coma, or a hundred little bumps in the road in the face of forever? And Jason and I *can* still have forever.

She sighs. "I don't know, Zadie. I think I'm just hangry."

"Well, wait until you see how much food Jason's parents got. It's like they want to feed the whole state."

Mo snort-laughs. "They better be giving the leftovers to the food bank."

We walk back inside arm in arm, her mood significantly lifted, but my mind is whirling with questions and doubts.

We've just found Amber and Talon at the dining table when Mrs. R stands, eyes bright. "There you are, Zadie! I think I've held you in suspense long enough, and I'm so glad I get to do this in front of everyone."

Immediately my heart starts to beat like a bongo drum in my chest. *Oh shit.* I never got to talk to Marcus. Maybe he told his aunt that me and Jason broke up. Maybe she's about to embarrass me in front of everyone.

"Come over here," she says.

I take faltering steps around the table and to the front of the dining room where she's standing. I hope my smile is solid, that my eyes are bright, that I look as calm as a cloudless day. Inside, though, I'm barely keeping it together.

And then she reaches into her pocket and holds out something. "The police found the ring!" she squeals.

Instant applause fills the room as I just stare at her.

Finally, I manage to croak, "The . . . ring?"

Mrs. R nods and opens her palm to show me a gold ring with a small aquamarine stone.

"Oh my God," I say, because there is a ring. In her hand.

"How . . . I mean, where . . . when did they find it?"

"This morning. They found it under the driver's seat," she says. "May I?"

Too stunned to do anything else, I nod, and she puts the ring in my hand. Mrs. R hugs me as a chorus of *awww*s fills the room.

I swear she can feel my heart hammering in my chest. She can feel my muscles twitching. My feet are ready to run me out of this room to hide under any piece of furniture where I can take cover.

It has to be a coincidence. Someone rode in Jason's car, dropped their ring in there. Right?

I slide the ring on quietly, reverently, as everybody watches. And then they cheer again.

Okay, but . . . I think. Maybe Jason bought the ring before he decided to break up with me.

My smile stays firmly in place as everybody applauds; Mrs. R's eyes are getting teary, and Jason's father is rubbing her back. The only person who looks even the slightest bit displeased is entering from the far side of the room. I flash back to days ago, to his grin when he told me he knew Jason broke up with me.

And I can't help it; I'm a little bit smug.

Sure, none of this makes sense.

Sure, any minute now, my delicately woven web of lies is going to strangle me. But for one wonderful moment I am winning, and he is not.

I smile as I twist the ring I've never seen before around my finger. It's slightly big.

"It was in his car the whole time?" I ask.

"The whole time," Jason's father says. "Imagine that."

* * *

The conversation bustles the whole of lunchtime, and I eat as much as I can. But my stomach feels wobbly, my chest tight with unease.

Was Jason deciding *between* giving me a ring and dumping me? That makes no sense.

My head has started throbbing and my brain feels like it's going to combust from what has just happened, so at the earliest opportunity, I push my chair away from the table.

"Bathroom," I mumble to anyone who's listening, which is probably no one at all. In the guest bathroom, I carefully reapply my lipstick when all I want is to duck out, swipe off all my makeup, and cozy up with a book. But I can't.

I put a note in my phone to call my doctor about the headaches I've been getting since the accident and straighten up. For now, I need answers.

I take my shoes off at the stairs while Jason's mom is asking the catering staff to bring out dessert, and I tiptoe up.

I sneak past the second-floor bathroom and the laundry room. I've been to Jason's room plenty of times, and I know that his is the third door on the right.

There must be some logical explanation for everything that has happened over the last week. Starting with the breakup, ending with the ring. I just have to find it.

Once I'm inside Jason's room, I'm hit with it.

That musky old-man cologne. I've never loved it, but Jason picked his signature smell before we got together. Apparently, fancy signature scents are a rich-people thing. I breathe it in and I miss him. I realize I haven't smelled that exact scent in the week he's been in hospital. I miss the solid feel of Jason beside me. I miss that untouchable warmth he has that feels like comfort, like home. Jason always made me feel safe.

I touch his quilt, his pillow. And then I drop down on my knees and start looking, rummaging inside his bed frame and inside the shoebox under his bed. Both contain things I hope his mother never finds, because—

I shriek as the door of Jason's room opens and closes. Marcus hurries in and claps his hand over my mouth before I can shriek even louder. He smells clean in a different way to Jason's room. Woodsy and fresh.

I bite Marcus's hand before I can do something humiliating like sniff him, and he lets go.

"What are you doing?" he asks.

"What are *you*?" I say, enraged to be caught on all fours searching through Jason's unmentionables.

"I wouldn't look in there if I were you," Marcus says.

"Thanks for the warning. On time as always," I say with an eye roll, as I shove the box deeper under Jason's bed. I'm surprised that Marcus knows what's in there.

Marcus and Jason have always had a complicated relationship, just like their fathers. Jason's father, Rhett, is the older brother, the businessman, the former soccer pro. Marcus's father, Tommy, wanted to build a life without their father's money, which made things significantly harder for him, but he opened a car repair shop when he moved back to Sterlingwood last year. He has had to raise Marcus and Joey alone since his wife left soon after Joey was born. Sometimes they get along great, but most of the time Marcus and

Jason want to kill each other. I used to think it all came down to competition—being in the same sport, jockeying for positions and team captain and game time and all those things, but Marcus doesn't seem to actually care about having any of that. Maybe it's just the principle of the thing; no one wants to feel like they are a dimmer version of the sun.

Marcus is watching me, considering, his eyes narrowed. "So. Was it planted by you or planted by someone else? How did you do it?"

"How did I do *what*?"

"The ring," he says. "How did you get it in the car?"

I'm practically beaming. "I didn't," I say. "Clearly, Jason meant to give it to me all along and only broke up with me to . . . to . . . throw me off. And obviously it worked."

I pull myself up into a standing position, trying to hide my wince as a wave of nausea rushes over me.

"That doesn't make sense," Marcus says.

"Consider the fact," I hiss, taking a step closer to him, "that you don't know everything, Marcus."

"I didn't say I do."

"Jason loves me." I am so supremely full of confidence that I feel light as air. I take off the ring, hold it in my palm. The truth is that it feels strange on me. Too big, yes, but wrong in a multitude of ways. I don't normally wear rings, and it's a *promise* ring, and the whole thing feels weirder than I thought it would. So old-fashioned and slightly child bride–ish. "It all makes sense now."

"Except that it doesn't," Marcus says, eyeing the ring. "He could have surprised you without dumping you."

The word *dumping* makes me flinch.

"Let me see it," Marcus says.

"See what?" I ask, even though I know what he wants is in my palm. I take a step closer to him, stopping because he's blocking the door.

"The ring."

"Have you ever heard of the word *please?*" I taunt. But I'm standing too close, and I'm the one who pays for it. I am aware of him. His gaze, the warmth radiating off him, the head's difference between us. He must feel it too, this restless vibration. The feeling that we're *both* standing too close.

Suddenly, I'm thrown back to last July, to loud music and a summer dress, my then-favorite lipstick and warm, thick evening air. He swallows as he looks down at me, and I can't tear my eyes from the way his throat bobs.

In just that one moment of distraction, Marcus snatches the ring from my palm. I am furious. I swipe for it, but he raises it over my head, holding it up against the light.

"It doesn't look fake," he says.

"Marcus, give it *back!*" I say as he easily moves it out to the side, away from me again. I lunge right. He holds it out left. I spin out to the left. He holds it up over his head. All out of options, I jump as high as I possibly can, knocking into his chest. He is so caught off guard that the movement sends us tumbling backward.

Marcus hits the ground with a loud *oomph*, and I fall onto him.

And then the world fades.

Six

Someone grumbles. It sounds like my bed. My bed is grumbling.

No, not my bed. My couch, maybe. But it's harder than that. A park bench? There's a board underneath me that is moaning as I shift on it, trying to get more comfortable. It is solid and warm but in a way that is familiar and nice and feels—

"Oh my God!" I shout, as I jerk up and away from Marcus Riddick. Marcus is my bed, my human park bench. "What the hell are you doing, you jackass human?"

Holding me to his chest is what he was doing, but before he can try to make up some explanation, I've catapulted several feet from him.

Marcus sits up, slowly and stiffly. "What am *I* doing?" he asks, creaking like old furniture. "You're the one who slammed into me."

Instead of pointing out that none of it was intentional, I scramble even farther away from him and push up from the ground to a standing position. I'm mad that I just had to tackle him to the ground to get something that rightfully belongs to me, and even madder that the DO NOT TACKLE MARCUS RIDDICK alarm bells did not go off in my head before I jumped him. And now I'll never be able to wipe the memory of the feel of his body from my mind.

Speaking of my mind, what the hell *was* that?

It's almost like I fell, blanked for a second, and then woke up basically cuddling with him. But it's not like I hit my head or anything. It was more like a sneeze. A consciousness-losing split-second sneeze. Maybe I fell asleep for a microsecond. But I'm not about to admit that to Marcus.

"Where is the ring?" I demand, even as a flurry of muffled laughter sounds not too far from us. "The next time you take something of mine without my permission—"

"I didn't *take* it. I just wanted to see it."

Not moving from the ground, Marcus holds out his palm. "You're . . . really going to wear it?" he asks, voice soft.

I take it from his hand, careful for our fingers not to brush. "I am." I make sure to sound more certain than I feel as I put the small circle back on my ring finger.

"I'm going back downstairs. Please wait five minutes before following me," I tell him.

"Five minutes?" Marcus protests. "Am I supposed to have food poisoning?"

"Not my problem. Have chickenpox, for all I care," I say, moving toward the door of Jason's room and then . . . I freeze. "Marcus?"

Because right as I'm standing there, the door of Jason's room starts to wobble. No, not wobble—*disintegrate*. One time, at a sleepover at Amber's house, I got so wasted I felt like the ground was moving. Maybe someone spiked Mrs. R's punch. I wouldn't put it past the soccer team, but as I whirl around to look at Marcus, he is staring open-mouthed at Jason's closet door to my right.

"What . . . the fuck," he half whispers, half growls.

I follow his gaze to the closet, and it is disappearing before my very eyes, the walls crumbling, dissolving into nothing.

"Marcus, what's happening?" I whisper, so afraid I can hardly move.

"I don't know, but . . . you're seeing this too, right?" Marcus asks.

The answer is obvious, but I ask it back. "Are you?"

"Yeah," he says. I'm instantly certain that this is more serious than spiked punch, because now a bright light is stinging my forehead. *Sunlight.* It's so radiant, I have to hood my eyes with my hand to look up at the sky.

The sky. Which has replaced the ceiling in Jason's room.

The sky that is the fading dusty orange of sunset, but with the almost-brightness of dawn.

"This is not okay," I say, unable to think of better words, more eloquent phrasing.

I reach for the closest wall for something to lean against, but it's gone instantly too, melts away into more nothing. I spin, looking around for Jason's bed, but it's gone. His dresser: gone. The huge TV he got for his birthday: disappeared. When it was just here seconds ago.

This is absolutely not okay.

I feel delirious, like I just spent hours staring at the sun and then stepped into a dark room, when the opposite is true. I was in a dimly lit room and I'm now under the sky. I start to feel lightheaded, all the blood gushing through my veins, pumping from my heart, faster, faster. I could run a marathon. I could—

I think I'm about to have a panic attack.

"Oh my God."

Maybe I'm being punished for all the lies I've told the past few days.

It's like the universe is doing an actual scenery change, remaking the background of everything around us until the carpet we were just lying on has turned to gravel.

"Are we dead?" My voice sounds high-pitched and vulnerable even to me.

Marcus doesn't answer me, but his expression is wild, stunned. Under any other circumstances, it would be funny, seeing Marcus "doesn't give a shit" Riddick look like he's seen a ghost.

"Marcus?" I whisper.

"It's okay," he says instantly, as if feeling the urge to comfort me. Frankly, it is patronizing.

"Oh my God, we're dead."

"We're not dead," Marcus insists. "We're, um . . ."

"Losing our minds?" I half shriek, because that's not the least bit reassuring either. Maybe . . . maybe I'm high. I whirl on him. "Did you drug me?"

"Jesus, Cartwright, don't even joke about that," he says, and he seems legitimately disgusted.

"Then we're dead," I say, the only rational explanation I can see to all this. It's devastating: the work I've put into having a good life, and I barely got to live it.

But Marcus shakes his head. "Think about it: a universe where we died and ended up in the same place?"

"Not possible," I say quickly, just like he knew I would. I look around as if checking for signs that say PURGATORY THIS WAY or PROCEED TO SOUL PATROL. Slowly, the spotty background starts to come back into focus, and instead of simply seeing all the things that are gone, I see the things that replace them.

The parking lot is half-full, bordered by trees with dull-looking leaves. Though the bite in the air makes me think of autumn, the flower beds are crowded with still-alive bluish-purple flowers, violets and daisies and poppies. In the distance you can see the highway and the lake. It feels familiar, but it takes a second to figure out why. I look around until I start to recognize the path, the trees, the sign outside Dot's Arcade. The lobster shack beside it. Okay, so maybe we're really not dead. We wouldn't still be in Maine if we were, right? And definitely not in Sterlingwood.

Maybe I'm hallucinating. I blink once, twice, hard, but nothing changes.

"Hey!" Marcus yells suddenly. He's calling out to a group of middle-school-aged kids crossing the parking lot, walking toward Dot's Arcade. He starts to hurry after them.

Suddenly this seems like a great idea—maybe someone knows something about what happened to us, why we're here. I follow Marcus's lead, only more politely. "Excuse me! Hi!"

Seconds later, I'm cupping my hands over my mouth and yelling too. "Hey! What's your problem?"

Marcus has gone quiet and stopped walking; he's clearly thinking something derisive if his smirk is anything to go by.

"What?" I demand.

"Nothing," he says. The kids completely ignore us as they go into Dot's; they don't even glance our way. There are five of them, young and fresh-faced. They remind me of me and my friends when we were in middle school, happy and carefree, laughing as they disappear through the aqua-colored doors.

We're on our own again.

The migraine I had at lunch is gone, but my head doesn't feel fully clear.

"Maybe I have a concussion," I muse out loud. "I fell on you and got a concussion." I was sure I didn't hit my head just now, but maybe I did.

"You don't have a concussion. I broke your fall," Marcus says helpfully. "It's more likely *I* have a concussion. Fuck, do *I* have a concussion?"

I roll my eyes. "You're literally fine, Marcus."

"No. I think I have a concussion."

I turn away from him and speak compassionately to myself. "It's okay, Zadie, you're hallucinating. This is all a bad . . . episode. A bad dream."

"A dream!" Marcus snaps his fingers like I've just said something brilliant. "We're dreaming."

"You think so?" I ask, embarrassingly hopeful.

My brain latches on to that hypothesis but when I pinch myself, I feel a very sharp, very real pain on my forearm. *"Ouch!"*

"That doesn't work," Marcus says belatedly. "Pinching yourself? That's a myth."

"How do *you* know?" I say, rubbing my arm.

"You've never been in a dream before?"

I look at him like he's batshit, because I think he actually might be.

"So, if I'm dreaming . . ." I begin, trying to voice out the different scenarios.

"Who says *I'm* not the one dreaming?" Marcus asks, as if now is the time to argue. "The dreamer is the main character, usually the only one who's aware that they're in a dream. So you know what that means."

I frown. "No, I don't actually."

"Well, since we're having this riveting discussion, we have to both be in a dream. I'm pretty sure it's *our* dream. We're co-dreaming."

I make a face, mostly because there is an unfortunate logic to his theory.

"Okay, hypothetically, one of us is dreaming. Or both of us are," I add reluctantly. "Maybe when we fell, we like *both* got a concussion. It knocked us out, and now we're in a weird dream?"

"Sounds possible," he says, but his voice doesn't have the urgency I would expect. It doesn't contain the sheer panic mine does.

"Marcus, we were just at lunch. And now we're not. Jason's parents are probably going crazy looking for us."

"Nah, because time works differently in dreams. They probably haven't even noticed we're gone."

"For someone who knows nothing, you sure know a lot about everything," I deadpan. "Where are you going?"

Marcus is walking in the direction of the arcade. "What do you want to do? Just stand here all day?"

I scan around us, unsure of what to do. It is still blindingly bright. We are very clearly outside the arcade strip on the northeast end of town. "We should try to get back to Jason's, shouldn't we?"

"*That's* what you want to do? You find yourself in a dream where you can do literally anything in the world—"

"How do you know we can do anything in the world?"

"—and your first impulse is to go to Jason's?" Marcus asks, disgusted.

"Okay, so what's your brilliant plan?" I ask, folding my arms over my chest.

Marcus points toward the arcade. "I'm going in. Mind-blowing, right?"

"Oh, yes," I say, all sarcasm. "Dream big!"

But as he gets farther away from me, I start to panic. I don't want to be left out here all alone. What if something happens?

Marcus is taking the steps up into the arcade when a car suddenly pulls up behind us. It's loud and big, a black SUV like . . .

"Jason!" I yelp his name, so full of a million feelings that I'm not sure I can even tease them apart. On the one hand, it's Jason. He's climbing out of his car, looking like himself. Tall and strong and handsome as ever. He's running over to the passenger's side of the car. *Running.* As in, his leg isn't broken.

"Holy shit, this is a dream," I whisper.

I'm in a dream.

But I'm just so incredibly happy to see him that I don't even care. Even if he was limping or looked totally different, if he wasn't dressed in a polo shirt, his hair sleeked back like he wears it when he's trying to make a good impression. I don't care what it is or why he's here or *how* he's here. Or how any of us are here.

I rush him. Like a bull charging, I hurry around to the SUV passenger's side and throw myself on him. And find my body . . . on the ground. Hugging air. Hugging nothing.

I'm so stunned, so confused I can't process it.

I look to the stairs of the arcade where Marcus is standing, smirking at me.

"Jason!" I say again. I'm so pathetic, I know, grabbing for his pant leg to stop him turning away, but my hand goes right through his body. And not only does he appear not to hear or see or feel me, but he's opening the car door for someone. He's here *with* someone.

Who?

I just have the presence of mind to realize that he's wearing the dark blue polo he wore on our first date when she steps out.

"Holy shit," Marcus and Jason say at the same time.

Jason is grinning from ear to ear.

Marcus looks horrified.

I can only stare as—the girl, Jason's date—*I* step out of his car.

Seven

The girl who looks like me is younger, with her hair in a bun the way I wore it all last year.

"Stop," she says, giggling. She's wearing a light blue dress I got from a vintage store in Portland when I was visiting my dad. It's the dress I wore on my first date with Jason a year ago. Our first date to the arcade. Our first date ever.

She *is* me.

"Stop what? Telling you how incredible you look?" Jason asks, just like he did that night. "Don't ask me to do impossible things, Zadie." I watch as Jason puts a hand on her—my—lower back and leads her into the arcade. They disappear inside, chatting and laughing.

It takes a full five seconds for the shock to wear off. Five seconds in which Marcus has somehow made his way over to me. When he holds out his hand, I realize I'm still on the ground. I let him pull me up, surprised for a half second by how small my hand feels encased in his.

"Well, that was awkward," Marcus says with a smirk.

I say nothing as I start toward the arcade again. In a couple of quick strides, Marcus is caught up to me.

"What are we doing? You up for a game of Sliders?" he asks.

"No," I say. "We have to follow them. That was us! That was me and Jason on our first date."

"And you don't think we should just leave them be?" Marcus asks as he holds open the bright blue door for me.

"Leave them *be*?" I repeat, hoping he can hear how preposterous that sounds.

I scan the moderately busy arcade, a dimly lit room full of jittery strangers and chirpy machines in mid-game mode. I follow the music to where I remember playing Dance Dance Revolution with Jason. We are doing just that now—we, as in Jason and the other me. Laughing at Jason's two left feet as I kick his butt in the first dance-off.

"Argh!" Jason says, his cheeks flushed from either the dancing or embarrassment. "That was just a warm-up. Best of three?"

"Best of *five*," the other me says, and Jason and I shake hands. "May the best dancer win." Conveniently, I hadn't mentioned that I had an advantage over Jason: I danced most of my life, until ninth grade when I heard that track and field was looked upon more favorably on college apps.

I remember all this, being so nervous for this date that my palms were sweaty the whole time. By the time I got home and called Amber and Mo to tell them, much of the night had receded into fuzzy detail.

Beside me, Marcus shifts uncomfortably as we watch Jason and Zadie flirt, making excuses to touch each other and bump hips and hold hands. Marcus is leaning against an old pinball machine but somehow, incredibly, he's not going through it. And yet when he reaches out to touch Other Me and Jason, his hand passes right through them. Because, well, dream logic. If this really is a dream.

"Wait, so *how* do you get your hips to do that shimmy thing?" Jason asks Zadie.

"It's really happening," Marcus grumbles. "I'm going to have to watch my cousin try to get laid all night. This must be what actual hell feels like."

"*Shhh*," I hiss, because he's ruining it. The night is going so well, and they are totally vibing, Jason and the other Zadie. "Isn't Jason just, like, electric?"

"Yeah, you know what? This isn't going to work for me," Marcus says. "It's been really . . . really fucking weird. But all the best to you."

"Where are you going?"

I watch him get all the way to the door of Dot's Arcade, lift the handle . . . and then he appears next to me again, like magic.

"What the *fuck*," he growls.

I'm incredulous. "Did you just . . ." I begin, but he's already walking determinedly back to the door. He's reaching for it. Nothing is going to stop him this time. Nothing *can* stop him this time except . . . the same thing happens again.

Holy shit.

He's beside me again.

"I don't think you can leave me," I say, not unsmugly, despite the plethora of questions I have myself. It's almost as if Marcus and I are tethered by some invisible force.

Marcus curses repeatedly under his breath, clearly displeased about the latest turn of events, as we go back to watching Zadie and Jason.

"I feel like I'm watching a movie," I say out loud.

Zadie and Jason are characters I vaguely recognize. This Zadie looks confident and sure of herself, not at all like how I feel on the inside. She doesn't look worried about if her hair is out of place or if her breath will be okay by the time Jason kisses her good night.

All the other reasons Jason is the model boyfriend aside, he had a way of bringing out *this* Zadie, and I think it's a little bit miraculous the way certain people and things make you a certain person in their presence. I miss the way I was with him, the way we were together. So sure of our place in the world, so *right*.

"Jay," I say, reaching for his hand on his machine. "Can you hear me?" I say quietly. "It's me. It's Zadie."

Jason just keeps playing, saying something to the Other Zadie and laughing with his head thrown back. He looks happy, lively. So, nothing like the Jason I saw earlier today.

"Jason, can you hear me?" I say, slightly more forceful. I try to grip his arm, but my fingers slip through him instead of wrapping around his bicep. *"Jason!"*

"He might be a one-Zadie type of guy," Marcus says with a half-hearted smirk.

I sigh and go back to quietly watching, mentally running through solutions to this impossible problem: how to get someone to notice you when you're not in the same reality or dimension.

Jason doesn't seem to have felt a thing, not a chill or a shudder, nothing that alerts him to my presence.

In front of us, Jason and Zadie are sharing popcorn and Jason leans in to wipe some salt off the top of Other Zadie's lip.

"Thanks," she whispers as their eyes lock. His gaze lingers on her mouth, and she self-consciously licks her lips. I remember this exact moment, but being able to zoom out on it, to see both of us, is so different. Not only do I not hear or feel Zadie's thundering heartbeat, but from this angle, I can see how much Jason likes her.

"Marcus," I say in a whisper. "He totally wants to kiss her."

Obviously, I know how this story ends. Jason waits until they're outside, going home for the night, before he leans in. He'll walk her to her door, kiss her again. Then he'll go home. She'll go inside her house and scream because there's no one to hear her. As she changes into her pajamas, she calls her friends and tells them it was amazing. Everything was perfect. *Jason* is perfect.

"Yeah," Marcus says flatly. "Seems like it."

As they finish up the last game, Jason's hand rests on Zadie's lower back and my heart flitters. Marcus trails behind as we follow them out of the arcade.

"I've been thinking about this for a while," Jason says when they reach his car.

"You've been thinking about me?" Other Zadie takes a brave step closer to him. Jason touches her cheek.

"Of course I've been thinking about you," he says. "And I'd really like to kiss you now, if that's okay with you. But I don't want to push my luck . . ."

Zadie leans up and presses her mouth to his. It catches him by surprise, but then he kisses her back, holding her face in his hands.

I don't even notice Marcus has tried to leave again until he re-appears beside me.

"Just don't watch," I tell him, feeling a little guilty that he's so uncomfortable. "I'll tell you when they're done."

I'm playing with the ring Jason's mother gave me as I watch them. "He's so respectful." I know if someone zoomed in on me—the real Zadie or dream Zadie or whatever I am—they'd see me starry-eyed, practically swooning at the couple in front of me. I feel butterflies in my stomach at the phantom touch of Jason's lips on mine.

"Sure," Marcus says. He pushes his hands into his pockets, looks down at the ground.

Other Zadie is whispering to Jason, "I like the way you kiss."

In fact, she likes it so much that she puts her full weight on Jason. He holds her by the waist to steady her.

"Slow down," he says against her mouth. Suddenly, I'm embarrassed to be standing there next to Marcus, watching this with him. It's obvious the other Zadie got so lost in the moment that she forgot herself. If she could, she'd wrap her legs around Jason's waist and kiss him silly. On a first kiss.

Zadie Cartwright shouldn't be that kind of girl.

It's true, though, that I've always liked how Jason kisses. Controlled and sweet. His breath is always fresh. Never too much tongue or teeth or pressure. He knows exactly what I like, and in return, I've always wanted to give him more.

"Let's just . . . take it slow." There's a look of hesitation on Jason's face, but it's gone a second later.

"What's happening?" I ask Marcus, as a clear sheath starts to fall between us and them. It's like someone stretched out a droplet of rain. Marcus and I look at each other, but even he is beginning to blur, to fade. His legs are gone, his voice echoey.

It's happening again. We're leaving the dream.

"Hold on," he says, reaching out his arm, but I'm losing him to the pulling feeling, the tornado-like vacuum, the blur of colors and light and sound.

He's gone.

They're gone.

I'm gone.

Eight

I jerk upright, breathing hard, sputtering in the way a dying fish would on dry land, and immediately I try to situate myself.

My body is drenched in sweat, but the room around me is painted black even as a sliver of moonlight slips in from a crack in the curtains. There's a dresser across the room, a table I recognize, bookshelf overflowing. I'm in my room. In my house.

I feel around in the dark till my hand finds the nightstand beside my bed. My glasses. My phone.

It's 7:44 in the morning.

"What the hell," I whisper to myself. That was . . . the most bizarre dream I've ever had in my life. The service and lunch. The ring. Fighting with Marcus and waking up at my first date with Jason. I must have imagined it all.

But my phone says it's Sunday.

The service for Jason was supposed to be on Saturday.

I lift my hand, and the stone Mrs. R gave me gleams in the dark. Yesterday was real.

Yesterday was real, and yet I have zero memory of how I got home, or of anything that happened after Marcus and I had that weird episode.

I wonder if this whole thing is because of the car accident. Maybe I really did have some sort of concussion, and now my memory is getting patchy. Or maybe I'm not getting enough sleep. Ever since the crash, my sleep has been a little inconsistent.

"Please don't let me be losing my mind," I say, pleading with some nameless, shapeless entity.

I Google "side effects of head injury" and come upon a horrifying list of things that might explain why I'm suddenly getting headaches, why I found myself in a memory from the past, why I don't remember how Saturday ended at all.

I head out of my room to find my mother. Maybe she'll insist on taking me to the hospital when I tell her what's been happening.

"Mom?"

Downstairs, Mom is pacing the dining room floor, her cell phone in hand. Her hair is in a bonnet, she's still in her pajamas, and the person on the other side of the line is speaking in an urgent tone.

". . . obviously launch the offensive, but we don't want to be caught on our back foot," Mom's chief of staff is saying, and she's nodding even though he can't see her.

When Mom first ran for mayor, I worried that she'd fall on her face, embarrass us. After all, Sterlingwood has never elected a person of color for mayor. Like, ever.

If Sterlingwood is like a body, all its organs and tissues coordinated and genetically the same, then people like us and Mo's family are moles. Small, superficial but glaring differences, to be monitored at best, and feared at worst. My parents were both from bigger cities, Dad from Boston and Mom from Portland. They met in Portland when my father accidentally sideswiped Mom's car, one of his famous mishaps. Already, Mom had a plan to settle into small-town life, then work her way up in politics.

Mom went into office when crime was up, when the town was in debt, when simple things like garbage collection and library fees were huge points of contention. But if there was one thing my mother knew, it was how to clean up a mess. I should have known not to doubt her.

"Can I talk to you for a second?" I ask.

Mom frowns her disapproval at me. "Not now, Zadie."

She takes the phone off speaker and I feel small as I decide to wait my turn.

Just the way she takes care of so much else in this town, my mother took charge and organized Dad's funeral, delegating every-thing so I didn't have very much to do. She handled the drudgery of letting people know. She handled the flowers, the obituary, the eulogy, all the work that gets heaped on you for simply loving someone who's died. Dad wasn't her husband anymore, but he was still my father, still her ex.

While I wait, I make breakfast. Mom rarely gets to eat in the mornings because she's always rushing out, but if I'm quick and strategic, I can get her to have something on the run. Since she's not in a hurry today, I take my time making scrambled eggs, toast, and black coffee, even though coffee without sugar tastes like I imagine engine oil would. I present it all to her while she's still on the phone, and she squeezes my arm in thanks. She also takes that moment to lift my hand up and inspect the ring on my finger, and I can tell she's pleased. We've never talked about the promise ring, but I know Mom approves of Jason. As far as sweet, wholesome boyfriends go, it doesn't get much better than him.

From her one-sided conversation, I manage to glean that the drama is about a new attack ad coming from Sterlingwood's right-wing party, Mom's toughest competition, if you can call them that. They were the runner-up to her in the last election, with just twentysomething percent of the vote. Throughout this latest election cycle, they have released a few weak anti–Mayor Wendy ads, twisting her words or using unflattering photos, but none of it has worked. My mother always looks, acts, sounds immaculate. Mom's reelection campaign is basically a technicality at this point, and she's pretty much guaranteed a new three-year term. But for the first time that I remember, she seems worried.

Mom guzzles the coffee then picks at the rest of her food while she continues on the phone. Right then, she glances at me. "Honesty matters to me. You know that."

Her look and the word *honesty* jolt me, and I start to wonder if maybe I'm misunderstanding this whole thing. What if someone found out I lied and told Mom or is trying to use it against her or something? My heart dips, and despite myself, I speak again. "Is everything okay?"

Mom covers her microphone. "Zadie, I am having a conversation. Please be patient."

Okay, so not about me, then.

I feel like a little kid who has been chastised—stung, then ashamed.

The last thing I want is to stress Mom out, to make her deal with crap that isn't important, or to have her think I'm one more mess she has to tackle. I'm going to deal with this myself, I decide, as I jump in the shower and start to get ready for the day. All that's really happened is that I've had a couple of headaches and relived one of my favorite Jason memories. Talk about blowing things out of proportion when I should be thinking of it like a gift, being able to see me and Jason like we were. Young and in love and at the start of forever, instead of at the end of it.

Last night reminded me that we had the best first date ever . . . except for the kiss.

Maybe Jay didn't like the fact that Zadie kissed *him*. I've never known Jason to be that uptight, but something was off. And even though Jason's not here for me to ask, I want to know what it was.

So I do the next best thing.

*　*　*

I corner Amber and Mo the next day after school. Technically, I'm just driving us to Amber's house, but it's as long a drive as there is in Sterlingwood, and short of dropping and rolling out of my car, they're stuck with me. I turn down the K-pop girl band Mo has just introduced us to.

"Noooo," she cries, bereft. "We were just getting to my solo."

"Oh, trust me," I say. "We know."

Amber giggles, and I clear my throat.

"Hey, when you kiss a guy, let's call him Bromeo, and he tells you to slow down, what does that mean?" I ask. "Some girl from yearbook was asking earlier."

I get away with "asking for a friend" because, between dating Jason and track and yearbook and tutoring, a surprising number of people have randomly confided in me the past year. It's like that weird thing that Mr. Tan calls a parasocial relationship. People feel like they know you, even when they don't, and it makes them trust you, even if they shouldn't.

"Was this girl trying to do *more* than kiss Bromeo?" Amber asks, as we pull into her driveway. Ambs lives right by the lake in a massive sprawling mansion that only two orthopedic surgeons can afford. We're supposed to spend the afternoon working on college apps, but I can't think of anything less appealing.

"No," I say, then quickly try to make my answer less definite. "I mean, she didn't *say* she was."

I turn off the ignition and grab my bag from the back seat.

I haven't told Amber and Mo about what happened at Jason's house or about the dream. There's really no need to. But what's weird is *they* remember me coming back down the stairs on Saturday afternoon. They remember us hanging out after, going to the movies later that night. There is a version of reality that continued *with me in it*, even if I have no recollection of it.

"Maybe Bromeo was saving his first kiss for his wedding day, like on all those tongue-wrestling-virgin videos online," Amber suggests.

Mo makes a face as she follows us into the house. "Tongue-wrestling?"

"Oh, it's a whole thing," Amber says. "It's this trend where people save their first kiss for their wedding, and it's horrific. It looks like their mouths are fighting. And I'm not even being mean to virgins. Nobody's first kiss is good. It's a scientifically proven fact."

"I guess we're just tossing out the word *science* these days." Mo sighs, plopping down on the sofa in the living room and already pulling out her laptop and a million brochures for premed programs. She would fight someone on the sanctity of science.

Amber pokes her tongue out in response to Mo's comment.

"I don't think it was Bromeo's first kiss. Just *their* first kiss," I say.

"But did Bromeo kiss her back?" Amber asks, truly getting into this.

"Yes," I say.

"Maybe yes, or definitely yes?"

"Definitely yes."

"Then maybe he didn't want to be in a relationship. Not everybody is built to be in a relationship," Mo says. "Maybe he just wanted to hook up."

I frown because that doesn't seem right either. I'll admit that, at first, it was a little odd that after going to the same schools all our lives and barely acknowledging each other's presence, the most popular guy in Sterlingwood would suddenly start paying attention to me. Mo was immediately suspicious, and even Amber, whose middle name is Supportive, took a moment to warm to the idea. But from the moment we started talking one day in study hall last fall, Jason could not have been more straightforward about his intentions. From following me on socials to constantly texting, Jason never hid the fact that he was interested in me. He definitely wanted more than just a hookup.

Amber heads to the kitchen where she's trying out a recipe I found for the internet's Best Mini-Sandwich. More than happy to put off thinking about apps for just a little longer, I follow her.

"I don't think that's it," I say loudly so Mo and Amber can both still hear. I pull out plates as Amber starts to cut up vegetables.

"You know, some guys can be old-fashioned about making the first move," Amber says. "Even feminists."

"You think so?" I ask. "But Jay . . . I mean, *they* would just say so, wouldn't they? If they wanted to make the first move?"

"Not always," Ambs says. "That's why you never want to be too forward in a new relationship."

It doesn't surprise me that Amber has strict rules, being the romantic she is, but I am kind of stunned that this is one of them.

"Really? What even is being too forward?" I ask, frustrated.

As we cook, Amber lists her no-nos. "Calling him your boyfriend before he calls you his girlfriend."

Shit. "I did that with Jason," I blurt out before I can stop myself.

When Amber looks surprised, I feel compelled to explain. "I happened to be introducing him to someone—I don't remember who—and I couldn't just be like this is Jason, who is of no affiliation to me."

Amber laughs, but then she waves a hand. "Well, you know you two don't count. You're an anomaly. But for the rest of us mere mortals, you *definitely* don't want to initiate the 'what are we' talk."

My face starts feeling hot because I did that too.

"And not to be old-fashioned or anything, but you might as well kiss him goodbye if you say 'I love you' first," Amber says.

What is this, a firing squad? I fan my collar as Mo wanders into the kitchen. "A girl can't say 'I love you' first? That's some medieval bullshit," she says.

Amber pops a baby carrot in her mouth and shrugs. "I don't make the rules."

Later, we settle in Amber's living room and get to work. Ambs seems to have no problem filling out her application to the Culinary Institute of America—we very maturely love to say she's joining the CIA—but it's like I'm tackling a wild boar with every word of my Princeton essay.

I have known my whole life that I wanted to go to Princeton

University. From the moment I understood the concept of college, at least.

That's it.

That's what I have after the first hour. And it's clearly a lie.

I feel a little better when Mo presses her fingers to her temples like she's communing with the dead and says, "Oh my God, it's coming to me! I have a name for my app!"

She is obviously accomplishing just as much on *her* admission application as I am. In between wanting to gouge my eyes out because of how lame my essay sounds, I can't stop thinking about the weird dream and the Jason kiss and the fact that I have no explanation for either.

"What's the name?" I ask, happy for the distraction.

"Zebra."

Amber makes a face. "Zebra?"

Mo nods excitedly. "It's spot-on for a diagnostic-tool-slash-health-anxiety app."

I'm embarrassed to admit that, despite her explaining it more than once, I still don't quite get what Mo's app is supposed to be. To be fair, she's spent months not talking about it because she's superstitious; she's just starting to share bit by bit.

"Pitch it to me again," I say, sitting up straighter. "Pretend I'm one of your investors."

Mo takes a big breath like she's waited her whole life for this. "Okay, so you know how when you tell the internet your medical symptoms, all you ever get is, like, Say Your Goodbyes, You're Dying of a Terminal Illness?"

Amber and I both nod. "I got that I had meningitis the other day," Ambs says.

"It probably also told you that you had the flu or allergies or whatever, but what you *focus* on is the fatal illness because, like, duh. Health anxiety.

"So, my app is going to emphasize the other less serious things it could be, and tell you why you're probably fine, and also give you a meditation. Like, *Hey, bestie, I know you think you have meningitis, but it's probably just a head cold. Make an appointment with your doctor and let's do this breathing exercise.*"

"Wait, that sounds amazing," I say, because it does. I could have used Mo's app yesterday in the aftermath of my dream. "Why's it called Zebra though?"

"Because there's this thing in medicine that they teach new doctors: When a patient comes in complaining of something, imagine their symptoms as pounding hooves but think *horses* not zebras. It's just a saying that reminds you that the most likely explanation is usually the simplest and most common one. It's probably *not* the rare brain-eating amoeba, but a normal headache, you know?"

"I guess the name makes sense when you explain it like that," Amber says, and I nudge her, because could she sound any less enthused?

"It's brilliant," I say, and Mo beams.

"So, anyway, that's how I intend to get rich and famous," she quips.

"It's about time Stephen King learned to share!" I say. Dad loved that a writer was the most important thing to come out of Maine; he had a million terrible Stephen King jokes, but today my friends just give me blank looks. I let the pinch of sadness pass and change the subject.

"I can be the Zen voice-over reading the meditation on your app," I offer.

"And I'll just ride your coattails and bring you snacks," Amber says, but she sounds half-hearted about it.

I try to focus again: *Zebras, not horses.*

It's the analogy I need right in this moment. My weird dream was likely just that—a weird dream. Nothing to worry about. And Jason's expression was probably a small involuntary twitch of his facial muscles. It's the easiest explanation.

But a tiny fleck of uncertainty remains.

What if I'm wrong?

Nine

Jason's friends are on the soccer field after school the next day, warming up before practice, and I am, ostensibly, taking pictures for the yearbook.

"I have a question for you guys," I say.

"For the last time, Zadie," Holden says, "no, I will not break up with Bennett to date you."

I roll my eyes but fight a smile. "That's not the question."

"Oh, fine. Yes, I will," he says, putting an arm around my shoulder.

"Aww," Josh says. "I thought you were going to ask why I wasn't wearing any underwear and if it's because my mom didn't do my laundry."

"Not my question either." I love being around Jason's friends, being accepted by them. Before dating Jason, the soccer jocks intimidated me. Now I know they're mostly secret softies.

"I really think we'd get away with it if you posed as me to write my Spanish test next week," another of the boys says. "And all my tests."

"So *anyway*," I say, speaking over all of them. I play with my black heart necklace, today's open secret. "Do guys like it when girls make the first move?"

"Yes," Holden says unilaterally. "Is your friend Amber coming? I heard she brought cupcakes today."

I ignore his question. "Yes? That's it? That's the official answer?"

"Yes," Holden says, stretching his calves.

"Go on," I implore. Softies or not, boys are the worst to have a serious conversation with. "Explain."

But just then Coach Kyle appears, and practice starts. I sigh in frustration, then go into official yearbook photographer mode, walking around and taking pictures. I am packing up the school's digital camera at the end of the day when Holden runs up to me. "So the consensus is yeah."

"Huh?"

"On girls making the first move. Everyone said yes except Tyler, who said no, and Josh, who said, 'Depends.' And Marcus, who said, 'It's hot as hell.'"

"Marcus?" I've been trying not to pay him any attention the last couple of days, given that I feel like I'm walking around with a giant neon sign that screams I HAVE BEEN DREAMING ABOUT MARCUS RIDDICK.

As if summoned by the mention of his name, Marcus looks over at exactly that moment. He's laughing at something someone is saying, and his smile fades. His T-shirt is tight across his broad chest, hair pulled out of his face, and I inhale as if I'm the one breathing hard from playing. Our eyes are like fingers, light and lingering, brushing a second too long on a handshake. I should roll my eyes or something, but I don't. "That's . . . good to know" is my lame response, as I finally tear my gaze away.

Holden's methodology is the furthest thing from scientific, but I don't think it's wrong either. Jason might not have liked something about our first kiss, but I highly doubt it was me liking it too much.

Then because I have nothing else to lose, and because it's easier than checking if Marcus is still looking over here, I tell the truth. "I just remembered Jason asked for us to take it slow on our first date. He seemed, like, hesitant. I wish I could ask him what that was about."

Holden gives me a suspicious look. "You don't know?"

I shake my head. "No."

"Your dad had just died, right? I'm pretty sure he wanted to make sure you weren't rushing into anything."

It's weird because Jason and I never really talked about my father's death. It came up here and there, of course, but it was never something we sat around and specifically discussed. To be honest, I doubted Jason—or anyone—wanted the boring, undignified details of how I was crying myself to sleep or trying to remember the last thing I'd ever said to my dad or thinking about random lines from random books Dad and I had spent hours dissecting over the phone. But hearing Holden's take, hearing that Jason *was* taking it into consideration even when it didn't seem like he was, feels like the sudden clearing of an overcast sky. It makes total sense. Why didn't I ask Holden sooner?

"You really think so?" I say, close to tearing up.

I feel completely stupid for ever thinking Jason might be old-fashioned or anything but thoughtful.

It's just the coma, I tell myself. It's missing him and not being able to hear his reassuring voice.

But what it shows me is that reading an unconscious boy's mind might not be as impossible as it sounds. If I ask the right questions, I can absolutely figure out what Jason was thinking.

* * *

"I love that you visit every day," Jason's mother tells me, holding my hand with the ring when I stop by the hospital later that week. It's part of my daily routine—wake up an hour earlier than normal, go for a run, go to the hospital, then go to school.

"He would do the same thing for me," I say, because I do *think* he would. Before we broke up, anyway.

I have taken up conversing with Jason as if he is awake. I almost feel like if I just keep talking, at some point he's going to be forced to give in and speak back. So I make all sorts of bargains with him in my head. I fill him in on trivial school news and silly student council drama in exchange for the answer to whether he still loves me. I read him the scores of his favorite soccer teams in the hopes that he'll tell me when the thought of breaking up first crossed his mind. I even play some of the country music he likes, and that one is for the ultimate truth: why he broke my heart.

The thing I'll never admit to Mrs. R or to anyone is that most of the time I feel like I'm playing pretend. I don't know that Jason can hear me. I feel like I'm shouting across the Grand Canyon, across consciousness, across waking and sleeping, and all I hear is the echo of my own voice.

"That's the beautiful thing about finding your life partner so young," Mrs. R is saying. "Everything is so simple."

The words *life partner* make me choke on my saliva. An image of two mules being chained together for eternity suddenly flits through my brain. I mean, sure, a promise ring is a commitment, but life is, like, so many more decades. It's college and marriage and kids and houses and retirement. Things I can't even begin to think about when I'm in high school. We talk about forever all the time, but I have no idea if I want all *those* things with Jason. Or if he wants them with me. The realization that he probably didn't at the very end doesn't even sting, because what does either of us know about the future? But I have to act like I deserve the ring she gave me. I have to act like I deserve Jason.

"So simple," I tell Mrs. R, though the truth is that nothing feels simple at all.

When I get home that afternoon, I go for a shorter stress run, sweating out all the questions and frustration and uncertainty. After, I'm legitimately researching mind-reading when someone knocks. Three precisely spaced raps are my only warning before my door swings open and Mom walks in. "You decent?"

"Yep!" I say, eyes immediately jerking over the pile of laundry I haven't put away yet on my computer chair. I also haven't vacuumed in almost a week or finished my homework. My immediate thought is to reach for the "near-death experience" excuse, but thankfully I don't need to. Mom doesn't mention any of the things we can both see I haven't done.

It's evening but she's still dressed in her work suit, hair styled, makeup on. "I have a proposition for you," she says, sitting on the edge of my bed. "What do you say we get dinner together, just the two of us?"

I immediately sit up straighter. "Right now?"

The last time Mom and I went out to dinner was my birthday, and Mom's assistant, A.J., joined us so they could "work out some things" while we ate. I felt like a third wheel, unnecessary, on a night that was supposed to be mine. Mom's schedule is insane since she's campaigning for reelection in addition to her regular duties, so the idea of having her full attention for even a couple of hours sounds like a dream. Maybe I actually will tell her I've been feeling off. Or maybe I can tell her something bigger, like about how I've gotten in further with the Jason lie than I ever meant to. Maybe she'll be able to help me figure some way out, or tell me that it's not as big a deal as I think it is, and we'll just laugh about the whole thing.

The thought makes me feel something I haven't felt since the accident: hopeful.

"Not tonight," she says quickly, "but let's aim for as soon as you send your last college application in."

I force a smile. "That sounds great."

"We can do an early fall lobster dinner since we finally have our town back," Mom says sassily. She's referring to the fact that Sterlingwood—like most coastal towns in New England, really— is overrun by visitors from May to August. As mayor, she actually loves this increase in tourism, but people who live here have been known to use words like *insects*, *deluge*, and *vermin*. Real Sterling- wooders know, though, that you just have to wait out the summer, that the lobster will still be there after everyone has gone home. Peak season is not four months long, as many people think, but all the way up to December most years.

"We'll make a thing of it," Mom promises. "But anyway, I have something for you."

My stomach is as tight as a clenched fist. "You do?"

She hands me a piece of paper with a name and email address

scribbled in her slanty handwriting. "This is the contact information of my friend who went to Princeton. You should write him and find out about his experience, let it whet your appetite. Actually, his daughter started at NYU last year. She might have tips on the process in general.

"She might even make a good case for New York," Mom says with a wink.

I feel hot and itchy, like I might be breaking out in hives. I know Mom is trying to help, but lately the sheer act of talking about college fills me with dread. Talking to one of Mom's friends about it or having someone suggest more options will only make that worse.

"Oh, um, thanks."

"You should write tonight."

I take a risk and try being honest. "I actually think I need, like, a weeklong break from thinking about college. I'm pretty overwhelmed with school and Jason and stuff."

"I understand," Mom says, and I can tell she's trying very hard to be sympathetic. To not tell me what she thinks I should do, the way she might order a staffer to do something. "It is October, though, Zadie."

"I know," I say in a small voice.

"I don't need to tell you how important early decision is," she says. "Not to mention that this is one of the biggest choices you'll ever make in your life."

I shrink in my skin. "That's why I'm taking my time."

"Take all the time you need, sweetheart," she says, squeezing my shoulder. "But don't waste it."

Before they divorced, Mom used to call Dad out for wasting

time. He was forever late, for one thing. Then, when he wasn't try-ing to write that elusive second book, he always had big ideas, new products that he was working on or investing in at any given time. For years, I heard my parents fighting about bad investments, bad deals, but nothing seemed to piss Mom off as much as the time that Dad wasn't using to get a real job or go back to school or "show Zadie what responsibility looks like." And then, one morn-ing when I was thirteen, Dad's things were laid out in small stacks all over the living room. I cried as he stuffed his old Mazda full of his belongings. Pages and pages of abandoned manuscripts, copies of *Moon Over Hanover*, books Dad loved, books to cure writer's block. The Turbo-JuiSIR, a toothbrush that doubled as speakers, a failed prototype for an e-reader. A lamp with a broken shade. The WORLD'S GREATEST DAD mug with no handle. So much of the clut-ter we lived with belonged to him, and now he was gone. Every-thing that remained in his stead had to be faultless.

I take a breath. "I just . . . how do you decide the rest of your life? I want to make the best choice."

She runs her hand over my head. "And you will. You know the right thing to do."

Except that I don't.

I groan in frustration after Mom leaves, because this feels like a calculus problem I can't solve. And suddenly there are no formulas that work, no helpful equations or examples, just this one huge dilemma that feels impossible to figure out.

"What's the right thing to do, Dad?" I whisper. I know he'd say something about love—do something you love, probably—but I don't know what I love. And besides, Dad spent his life trying to write a second book, trying to replicate this dream he achieved in his twenties, trying to do what he loved, and he ended up dying alone. After the breakup, he moved to Portland, had to make a whole new set of friends, worked temp jobs to never make ends meet, and became the one-time writer who couldn't write.

There's nothing worse than loving the wrong thing.

Ten

On Friday night, Amber and I huddle in front of a crackling orangish bonfire by the lake, its warmth swallowing most of the October chill.

An electric buzz is in the air as our senior class gathers under the stars. More of us are slightly farther down the beach, kids playing volleyball and Frisbee, and a few people have even ventured into the inky black water. There's music playing on someone's portable speakers and a cooler full of beer that is bound to taste like soap.

Amber jiggles her keys, uncharacteristically impatient as we people-watch while we wait for Mo. "Have you noticed she is never on time these days?"

"She eats and sleeps Zebra," I say, feeling the need to defend Mo.

"It just feels kind of rude," Amber insists. "Like, I have things I'm excited about too."

"Like?" I prod.

Amber grins. "Well, for starters, I'm pretty sure I'm in love." *And here it is*, I think, heart sinking. The soulmates confession Mo warned me about. "With Pablo Navarro."

"The exchange student?"

"What? No, the poet! I'm reading his book."

I giggle. "Do you mean Pablo *Neruda*?" You don't ace Mr. Tan's English class without knowing a bunch of famous dead poets.

"Yes, him! My bad. Either way, Pablo fully gets love," Ambs

gushes, like they're on a first-name basis. She tells me about the way he writes about passion, like it's a visceral thing. A living, breathing thing. "And that's how it should feel."

Right then, Talon, who has been playing Frisbee, looks over and waves. Amber and I wave back.

"Are you sure you've felt it?" I ask, but Ambs never gets the chance to answer because Mo suddenly appears. The first words out of Monique's mouth are "I hope you're not drinking, Zadie. Not with . . . all the headaches you've been getting." She's panting slightly, like maybe she just jogged the whole way here.

"Wow, hello to you too," I say, positively bewildered.

I notice then that she's wearing a visitor sticker on her hoodie, the kind they give me at Sterlingwood General every time I visit Jay. Mo yanks it off and crumples it in her hand.

"Why were you at the hospital? Is everything okay?" I ask.

Mo flops down on my left side and gives a dismissive wave. "My sister did . . . something to her ankle. She's fine. Anyway, I'm sorry I'm late. Also, I would have texted you, but my phone died."

"It's okay, Doctor Doolittle. I already decided I'm going to be DD tonight," I say, but I don't think I'm imagining that there's a weird tension between the three of us.

Amber is being unusually quiet. When she finally speaks, it's to say, "You know, Zadie is actually capable of making her own decisions."

A beat of silence. "Yeah," Mo says, "and I'm reminding her to make a good one."

"It's f—" I start to say, but Amber speaks over me. "Where do you get off telling people what decisions are good and bad for them?"

She is not wrong—Mo is being just the tiniest bit self-righteous and overprotective—but the bitterness in Amber's voice catches me off guard. She rolls out an imaginary banner with her hands. "Breaking news: Mo is the only one with a brain around here. The rest of us are just idiots. Right, Mo?"

"Um, is that what I said?"

"It sounded a lot like what you said to me. *I'm Monique, the absolute authority on everything.*"

"Wait. Are you serious right now?" Mo gasps, and suddenly they're yelling at each other. I feel like I've missed something.

"Guys! Guys!" I grab both their arms. "Holy shit. What's happening?"

Amber blows out her bangs. "She's so condescending."

"Very useful information. Mo?" I turn to her.

Mo glares at Amber and makes like she's going to speak but ultimately shuts her mouth.

"So no one is going to tell me what this is about?"

There is a very long pause, and just when I think they won't answer, Amber blurts out, "She doesn't like Talon."

"Talon?" I'm completely confused. "This is about Talon?"

"Well, it has to be, since she keeps dropping hints about me making bad decisions."

Oh, Mo. I shoot her a look, because we were doing so well trying not to be judgmental.

But Mo won't look at me. "I said nothing about Talon."

"You didn't have to say anything. The way you treat him speaks volumes," Amber says. "You know, you're not as subtle as you think you are."

"Oh, honey, I was going to say the same about you," Mo says.

And they're back at it, every jab from each of them escalating the situation.

It's like the worst game of tennis, listening to their back and forth. "You guys are giving me a headache. Did you forget we don't fight?" I ask, unable to hide my sadness. "We're Teflon."

Neither of them moves for a second, and then Amber loses her fighting posture. "Fine. I'm sorry," she says.

There is a very long pause, in which I am terrified that Mo is not going to back down.

"I am . . ." Mo looks like she's gritting her teeth, fighting to speak. "Sorry. Also."

"Progress!" I say, raising my arms in celebration. "You know what? I can be DD *and* bartender. I'll get your drinks." I snatch Amber's keys from her lap and walk off before another fight erupts.

I'm digging around in the cooler when I hear a voice behind me. "Zadie Cartwright. Vesuvius or Fuji?"

I twist around to see a grinning Marcus, then turn back to face the cooler. "What am I supposed to be choosing between?"

"Your favorite volcano, of course," Marcus says, like this is completely normal discussion material.

I sigh. "When are you going to let this go? We're not playing a game."

"We could be," he says, raising his eyebrows playfully.

When I don't respond, he says, "I have something to ask you."

I put my hands on my hips. "What now?"

"Hold on," he says. He takes several steps closer until he's looking right down at me, his chin millimeters away from my forehead.

"What are you . . ."

When he leans forward, his woodsy scent wafts over to me, even under the smell of the bonfire. The closer he gets, the more light-headed I feel. A hand touches my cheek. His hand.

"Ash," he whispers, gently flicking something off my face with his thumb before he steps back.

My heart is a thunderstorm in my chest, even as I regain the feeling in my legs. "Oh," I say. I am warm all over. Embarrassed at my overreaction. It's just Marcus Riddick, for God's sake.

"Thanks," I mumble.

Marcus starts talking again, but I can't hear any distinct words. I'm still feeling dizzy from being that close.

"Because if I did somehow hurt your feelings . . ."

A second later, I hear what he's saying. He's actually acknowledging that we hate each other, that he upset me.

"You didn't," I blurt out before he can finish his sentence. He wants me to admit that he hurt me so he can, what, laugh in my face? Feel vindicated by my confirmation than I've been stewing for a solid year over a few comments he made? There's no way I am going to give even the appearance of caring about anything Marcus Riddick has to say. "Some people just don't jibe, and that's what it is."

"Some people just don't jibe," Marcus repeats quietly, like he's running the thought through his mind for inconsistencies. "Okay."

I'm annoyed by his audacity to look both confused and hurt. He was the one who literally announced to everyone that he didn't see what Jason could see in me.

Asshole.

"I have another question," he says, but before I can react, a pixie-like brunette girl rushes Marcus, throwing her arms around him from behind.

"Marcus!" she says.

"Kari!" he says, sounding friendly, if not quite pleased to have her plaster her front to his back. But she doesn't seem to notice.

"Shhh. I'm not supposed to be here," she says, using Marcus as a human wall and periodically peering around him to see what's happening on the other side. She waves at me, then ducks behind him again. I think the joke is that she's a junior at a seniors-only event.

"My question," Marcus says, ignoring her shenanigans, "is whether you would tell someone you know if you had a really weird dream about them."

My brain spins at his question. He's not saying . . . He can't be suggesting what I think he's suggesting.

I look closely at him, trying to grasp the meaning of his words, but his eyes are unreadable.

"Like a sex dream?" Kari, who is clearly very drunk, sticks her head out to join our conversation.

Marcus kind of jumps at her voice, like he'd forgotten she was there. It's a performance, the way he immediately plasters on one of his cheeky grins. "I mean, there's always the potential."

Um, so not the same dream then. "I wouldn't tell them any-thing. In fact, the only person I would tell about the weird things that go on in your mind is your therapist."

Marcus laughs, but there's something odd about it.

I collect two cans and start to leave but Marcus stops me again. "So you don't think joint dreams are a thing?"

"Joint dreams?" I echo.

He looks at me like he's genuinely asking. "When two people have the same dream or are *in* the same dream. Together."

I almost drop the beers in my hand.

"N-n-nope," I say. "Co-dreaming? Doesn't sound like a thing."

I don't know why I say it exactly. Maybe because it doesn't sound like it *should* be a thing. Maybe because Kari is with us and there are a million people around, and it sounds really freaking weird that Marcus and I would have the same dream.

I want to end this discussion, but Marcus won't let it go.

"You don't think sometimes there's, like, something that happens between two people? Like thinking the same thought? Mind overlapping?" The crazy thing is, he sounds completely earnest.

"What if we don't just have to be stuck in our own minds all the time," he's saying, spiraling, "but we can like hop between . . . I don't fucking know, Cartwright. I just . . ."

"Marcus, you silly goose," Kari says, whispering like she's telling a secret. "We're all alone in the universe."

I point at her. "Yep. What Kari said. We're all alone in the universe," I say, and then I turn and practically sprint back to my friends.

Naturally, they are talking about—what else?—Marcus.

"What I heard is that Coach Kyle wants him to play Jason's position," Amber whispers to me, Mo, and Talon, who has since joined our group. "But Marcus is being, like, the biggest slacker. Turning up late to practices or not showing up at all. Playing like crap. It's like he *wants* to stay on the bench."

"Big surprise there," I mutter to myself, looking over my shoulder to find him still laughing with Kari. When he glances up, our eyes clash and I quickly swivel back to my friends. From then on, I feel Marcus's gaze on and off, and it's stressing me out. I don't know what the hell the conversation we had was about. Was Marcus really hinting at having had the same dream I did? That's impossible. Sure, something bizarre happened in between the lunch at Jason's house and me waking up in my bed hours later, but it's because I have a head injury. That's why my memory is fuzzy.

* * *

Hours later, when I'm lying in bed, trying to fall asleep, my head calls my bluff.

Before I know it, I'm heaving over a bucket, throwing up everything I've eaten today. I'd think it was a hangover if I had even a lick to drink, but I listened to Mo. Every sound is grating to me just like it was when I went to Nurse Diamond last week at school. The buzz of electricity humming through the walls, my clock *ticktock*ing, all of it makes my brain feel like it's under siege, being scaled by very loud, very bright enemy forces.

Between bouts of nausea, I groan and cover my eyes with my pillow, wanting only peace and relief. I call for Mom, but she must be fast asleep or not home yet, dealing with some overnight crisis, because she doesn't respond.

I can't even cry about this everything-everywhere pain because the crying itself would make things worse. Even the skin over my eyes hurts.

But in a split second, the blackness behind my lids disappears, and the kind of light I've been hiding from all night shines into my room. I pry my eyes apart just in time to see my side table crumble, my door dissolve, my walls vanish.

And then everything begins again.

Eleven

I open my eyes in a stuffy gymnasium where the entire population of Sterlingwood High is screaming a fight song. Next to me, one shouting voice stands out from the rest. *Sterlingwood, Sterlingwood, who are we? Champions, champions, 'cause we win!*

The volume and intensity should make my head want to explode, but they don't. My pain is gone.

I don't understand how. Or why I'm suddenly . . .

A dream.

Holy shit, I'm in another dream. And it's another day I recognize.

The Sterlingwood High Homecoming pep rally. I'm in the stands watching as the entire soccer team bulldozes through the gym in their uniforms, slapping hands with other students, dabbing and dancing and taking dramatic bows like they do at the start of every season.

I have no idea how I got here, because I certainly haven't done anything but upchuck in the last hour in real life.

Right now, though, the person beside me is roaring, and I cover my left ear as I turn to see who has this much team pride.

My eyes nearly bug out of my head. "Marcus?" I shout over the noise to be heard. "What the hell?"

He looks just as stunned to see me, then a little embarrassed.

"You're here," he says. "I thought I was just having a random-ass dream."

Our conversation at the bonfire immediately flies back to me.

"How did . . . I thought we . . . you know what? Never mind." I can't pretend to understand dream logic, so I'm already squeezing through the rows of the stand and heading down the stairs as Principal Collins calls the room to attention.

"All right, all right! Thank you, Sterlingwood Silvers," she says.

"I can't believe it's happening again!" I whisper to Marcus, overjoyed, as we wiggle through the stands. I'm going to get another chance to see Jason.

Not a single person pays any attention to us as we skip down the stairs to the floor of the gymnasium. Just like last time, it doesn't seem like anyone can see us.

"Jason and Zadie are over there somewhere!" I tell Marcus excitedly as we approach the lowest bench. I know exactly when this memory is from.

"Are they," Marcus says, voice flat, but he follows me, anyway.

Jason's height makes him easy to spot in a room full of seated people. And my heart leaps as soon as I see him. His neat brown hair, his easy smile. His presence is as vibrant as the sun. Speaking of owning the entire room, there is no logical reason why the most popular guy on the soccer team should be settling next to chronic overachiever Zadie Cartwright during a mid-October pep rally, but that is exactly what he's doing. Marcus and I stand off to the side, where we have a good view of Jason and Other Zadie. Next to me, Marcus folds his arms across his chest. It occurs to me that this would have been Marcus's first pep rally here, but I don't think he actually attended.

As he sits, Jason casually greets the Other Zadie with a shoulder nudge, and she gives him a subtle smile. He gives her another nudge, more obvious this time, and she shifts away from him, trying to look stern.

"They're keeping things on the DL. Only our friends—my friends and Jason's friends—know we're dating because I wasn't ready to tell everyone," I explain to Marcus. The night before this pep rally, Jason had sent Zadie a text with the words I think it's time for our hard launch 👫

Zadie had written back: Ok don't hate me, but I need a minute.

Jason: Like a 60 second minute or . . . ?

Zadie: Like a week or two minute 😛

Jason: Because of your dad?

Zadie: Because of everything.

And there really were a bunch of things bothering me: Dad had died less than two months before. I still had moments of bursting into tears for tiny things like hearing a song he'd introduced me to or someone quoting a movie he loved or simply because it was early evening, the time that we used to talk on the phone almost every night since I was thirteen. Sometimes, there was no reason. But most of all, I wanted to be sure the relationship was right. Not something I'd regret or feel ashamed of. Not one of those typical high school relationships with the screaming matches and empty promises.

I wanted to make sure we were good together.

"As much as I wanted to be with Jason, I needed to wrap my head around it. I wanted us to figure out what being together meant before we were everywhere." I suddenly notice Marcus is rigid beside me. And that he actually hasn't answered anything I've said in the last couple of minutes. I look over at him, and he is wearing something akin to a scowl, face focused ahead as he watches Zadie and Jason pretend they aren't newly dating.

"Are you okay?" I ask Marcus, tentative.

I can't believe I actually care, but I think . . . I think Marcus is mad at me.

"Is this because of the bonfire?" I say when he doesn't respond. "You're punishing me?"

"I'm not punishing you, Zadie," he says, still staring straight ahead. At exactly that moment, Principal Collins starts reading a long list of announcements, each of them more boring than the last. *Clean up after yourself on the quad. No vaping on school grounds. Actually, no vaping at all, anywhere, unless you want to die.* She tells a string of bad jokes, hands out insanely large bouquets of blue flowers to two teachers going on maternity leave.

"But the dreams aren't a thing, right?" Marcus continues in a whisper, as if he's trying not to interrupt Principal Collins. As if we're even capable of interrupting. "Isn't that what we're pretending?"

"I could have not been pretending," I point out. "What if I just didn't remember the dreams in real life?"

"Co-dreaming," he says, while the pep rally continues in the background.

I frown. "Huh?"

"You said *co-dreaming*. At the bonfire. We only ever mentioned that in the dream."

Shit.

"I'm sorry, okay?" I say, contrite. "Yes, I shouldn't have pretended not to understand what you were talking about. I just . . . I don't know what this whole thing is any more than you do. All I know is it sounds shady as hell to say I've been dreaming about my boyfriend's cousin."

"Ex-boyfriend," Marcus says after a beat. "And, of course, what everyone thought would be your top concern."

"Caring what people think is not a bad thing, Marcus. *Caring* is a normal human emotion," I say, unconcerned about coming off preachy. "People care about other people. They care about their grades. They care about their sport." It's a jab specifically aimed at what Amber told us last night, about Marcus half-assing practices and missing his chance to start a game, to play Jason's position.

"You think I don't c—" He pushes a hand through his hair. "You're right. I'm heartless. So what's happening here?"

I focus on the pep rally again. "It's Kiss Cam Day," I tell Marcus, beaming.

"Kiss Cam Day?" he repeats.

"Remember what I said about Zadie not wanting everyone to know yet about her and Jason?"

"Yes?"

"Well . . ." Right on cue, the catchiest bubblegum pop song bursts from the huge speakers mounted in the corners of the gym. It's "Kiss Me" by Sixpence None the Richer, and immediately, a live video of people in the gym is projected onto the screen. At any given time, the camera seems to target the most awkward pairing of people sitting or standing side by side. Megan Shu and Clark Howie, Braden Young and Hunter G, Vice Principal Moon and Coach Kyle.

And last but not least . . .

I watch through the spaces between my fingers as the camera

pans to Jason and Other Zadie. When the camera lands on them, blowing up their interaction for everyone to see, Zadie looks horrified. She's already shaking her head when Jason laughs, cups her face, and kisses her.

It is decidedly not a kiss between strangers.

"Holy shit," I whisper, feeling like it's happening all over again. I've never been kissed like that in my life. From the vibration of the music to the softness of Jason's lips to the awareness of every passing second and people gaping and the crowd now catcalling and whistling and clapping. It feels like the cameras stay on Jason and Zadie for an eternity. Long enough for the kiss to end, and for her to finally, sheepishly crack a smile. Jason, on the other hand, looks like he always does. Completely unflustered and in control.

I don't know how I manage to tear my gaze away from them for long enough to see Marcus—the Marcus in the dream—enter the gym. He's wearing a backpack that could not look more decorative (read: empty) if it tried, old jeans, and a gray sweatshirt, hood up over his head. He slows as he senses the commotion, finds the screen showing Zadie's and Jason's grinning faces, comes to a complete stop, then turns around and walks back out of the gym.

"Hey, why did you leave?" I'm asking the Marcus beside me, but I never hear what he says because, suddenly, the gym is very, very loud.

Marcus tries to tell me something, maybe in answer to my question, but I just shake my head and point to my ears. "I can't hear you!"

The dream is ending.

It's an undignified ending, like being sucked up by a vacuum, and I'm fighting it, trying to get Marcus and myself to stay in this one perfect memory. But the force pulling us out of the present moment is much, much stronger. Soon, I feel like my legs are disappearing, like bit by bit I am unbecoming.

Reaching for Marcus is a last-ditch effort, but to my surprise, when my hand grazes his, he catches my finger. Holding, holding, *holding*.

And then we are gone.

Twelve

I squint awake to a brand-new morning.

Immediately, I try to fall asleep again. I feel greedy. I want more memories, and I want them now, but it doesn't work. I'm that little kid closing fluttering eyelids at bedtime and hoping it counts as sleep.

I try chamomile tea, a meditation app, even reading the most boring book on Mr. Tan's syllabus, but nothing makes a difference.

"Seriously?" I whisper after one deeply unsuccessful hour. It's frustrating because I have nothing but time today. Nothing but time and college apps and homework. And then it hits me. "Oh God," I groan as soon as I remember.

Today is our very first fundraiser for senior prom. As the vice to his president, I'm co-organizing with Tyler. Could I fake sick?

For the first time in possibly my whole life, I consider not going. Just pulling a total no-show. But not only would that be completely irresponsible, it would also make me feel even more guilty than I already do for all the things I'm lying about.

"Shit," I mutter as I make peace with the fact that not only do I have to go but that I *am* going. Because I'm so late, I won't even have a chance to see Jason this morning. And I didn't see him yesterday either.

"Shit, shit, shit."

I glance at the time and run around my room, trying to pull

together an outfit for the day and do my makeup. I should have chosen my clothes yesterday. I hate that I've been so disorganized lately.

Mom sticks her head into my room while I'm hustling and frowns.

"Where's the fire?"

"Senior fundraiser is today," I say as I put on eyeliner, which for some reason I have only learned to do open-mouthed.

"Oh . . . yes," she says after a moment.

"Will you be there?" I ask.

She's distracted by her phone, murmurs something about if she can fit it into her schedule. This kind of community event would normally warrant the mayor at least showing up. There's no official policy or anything, but Mom likes to stay involved in local events. And in this case, it's her daughter's class fundraiser.

"It's kind of a big deal."

"Mmm," she says.

I try to push back the dam of resentment building inside me at how low on her list of priorities I seem to fall. As she's been getting busier these past few weeks, she's spared me less and less of a thought. Sometimes I get the sense that I'm an imposition, being here constantly. I bet half the reason she can't wait for me to leave for college is to get some space.

The thought makes my chest hurt.

Mom has never really dated since the divorce, and I don't know what kind of things she'll do when I'm gone. I don't know if she will remember to eat meals and make her own coffee and get enough sleep. It's hard to imagine our lives not being intertwined, but at least she's still here, alive.

Mom doesn't notice me fighting tears. She leaves to have a conference call, despite it being the weekend, and I finish getting ready and rush out. I feel a little embarrassed when I turn up at Stanley Lake Park fifteen minutes past our scheduled meeting time and with store-bought ginger molasses cookies. We're doing a joint car wash and bake sale, but thankfully, it's mostly still us seniors here at this point. By some miracle, Tyler is actually doing his job and setting up for the car wash. In my stead, Amber already has people laying out tables of food for the bake sale, checking off the list of baked goods that each person was supposed to bring.

"Thank you so much," I whisper in her ear, tugging at my headband to hide both my rough edges and my mortification. It's black, so at least it fits with my retro Mary Janes and black socks, today's open secret. "I slept in."

Amber grins. "I got you," she whispers.

"Where's Mo?" I ask.

"Late, as per. If I didn't know better, I'd think she was hiding more than that stupid app," Amber says, blowing on her hands to warm them.

The thought has occurred to me, but I quickly dismiss it. Mo is honest to a fault. "She's just out of it," I say, my words forming clouds in the morning chill. Every day the ground accumulates more yellow, pink, brown, and gold leaves. It's like the universe is bargaining with us—more beauty if we tolerate more cold.

If Tyler had any instinct for planning, we would have gotten this fundraiser off the ground first week of school instead of having a car wash when we're halfway to Halloween. But my role is to support him, I remind myself. I take over from Amber, divvying our classmates between the bake sale and the car wash, which Tyler and I agreed beforehand would be one of my duties.

"Nah, I'll take Zeke," Tyler says, after I've claimed his best friend for the bake sale. "Josh too."

"Okay," I say, trying to stay upbeat. After all, I'm the one who's dropped the ball this morning. But then Tyler steals Vance and Austin to work with him when I've already assigned them to bake sale duties.

Hands on hips, I turn to Tyler. "You can't just claim all the guys for the car wash."

"Why not?" Tyler says, popping a Rice Krispies bar in his mouth. "It's not like you're bench-pressing oatmeal raisin cookies over here."

A couple of people snicker, and my cheeks burn.

I pull my jacket tighter over my chest and jut my chin forward.

Our classmates are meandering around, presumably waiting for instructions for where to go, but really, they're probably enjoying the drama. Despite having many reasons to be annoyed by Tyler so far this year, I've tried to respect that *he* is president and keep the antagonism to a minimum. But this is ridiculous.

He wouldn't treat me this way if I had Jason by my side, staring him down. Most likely, Tyler would be asking what he could do for me.

"Last I checked, you weren't bench-pressing cars over there either," I spit back, taking a step toward him to show that I'm not intimidated. There's a flurry of excitement behind Tyler's head, and I notice that at the back of the crowd, Marcus Riddick is arriving.

Great.

Another antagonist to deal with.

Marcus settles next to Holden in the group of kids waiting for direction from me and Tyler. Marcus looks so profoundly sleepy that I bet if someone asked, he wouldn't be able to say where he is.

I return to the situation at hand, straighten my posture. "We're not splitting by gender," I say. "Are we in 1955? The boys run the car wash, and the girls run the bake sale?"

"Well, is it fair if people don't get to decide where they want to work for the day either? That's also discrimination."

I take a deep breath and pray for strength. "Tyler, I'm not about to teach you the definition of discrimination."

"Good," he says.

"As student body president," he begins in his familiar mocking tone. Because it's all a stupid joke to him. "I believe in letting people make their own decisions. I'm not running an automerit system."

I lose the battle and roll my eyes. "You mean an autocracy."

Tyler smirks. "I believe in it so little I don't even know what it is," he says. "People can work wherever they want to, and all my boys happen to want to be with me."

With that, he turns around and leaves, walking across the grass to the parking lot, where cars are starting to pull in for the car wash. About ten of the guys, including most of the soccer team, follow him like imprinting baby ducklings.

"Asshats," I mutter as I watch them go, but the truth is I feel humiliated. Stung and small and powerless.

"You owned him," Amber assures me, even as a few of the girls wander away too, leaving us way outnumbered compared to the car wash. A few stragglers hang out between the parking lot and our canopy of trees, seemingly unwilling to commit just yet. Penny and her group of friends stick with me.

To my surprise, Holden and Marcus shuffle forward.

"Hoo waow ioonn, cooowa," Marcus says, yawning so hard he looks like he's spasming.

Holden looks longingly over at the car wash, sighs, then translates. "He said, put us in, Coach."

Marcus rolls his eyes. "She knows what I said."

"Dude, *no one* knows what you said. Except for me. Because I have ESP."

"You two are making coffee," I say, instead of what I mean to say, which is *thank you*. Thank you for not being like the rest of the other assholian boys who ran behind Tyler. I refer to the sheet on my clipboard. "Do you think you can manage that?"

When both Holden and Marcus look immediately overwhelmed, I turn to Amber. "Ambs, can you help me not regret this?"

"On it," she says. She looks at her phone. "I'm going to text Mo again. Come on, you two."

As she's leading Marcus and Holden away, I can't help but say to Marcus, "I'm surprised you didn't follow Tyler."

"Don't get me wrong. I like sheep," Marcus says, turning to go with Amber. His eyes are dancing, lighter somehow this morning than they were in the gym in our last dream. "But they're also kind of stupid."

My lips twitch as I hold back my smile.

Seeing Marcus takes me back to last night's dream, to that exhilarating Jason kiss, to the floaty feeling of reliving a moment that had already happened. And I find myself wanting to talk to Marcus about it, to make him answer me this time: *Why did you leave?*

We can't exactly talk about it here, so I focus on making sure everybody has their task, and by the time the first of our customers show up, our bake sale is running like a well-oiled machine.

Across the park, the car washers are playing Nelly's "Hot in Herre." It's clear there's absolutely no structure over there, and that they are bound to offend some parents, and that Principal Collins might even punish me and Tyler after all this.

"I'd really like to punch them. I think it would be very cathartic," Mo says, voicing my thoughts when she arrives a whole hour later than our official start time and I tell her what happened. Amber is annoyed with her, but I can't really give Mo a hard time for being late when I was too, so I just put her in front of the cash box.

It feels like the entirety of Sterlingwood comes out to support us, but there's no sign of my mom. I remind myself that she's busy, that she's trying her best.

Across the park, there are more shouts from the car wash crew. I refuse to look over to see whether they are screams of delight or chaos.

I hate everyone, I think as I adjust my headband and focus on doing a good job with my part of this.

To not get worked up and to keep my hands busy, I start to set out a tray of mini tarts and allow myself to revisit last night's dream, savoring every part of it. How in the world do I get back there? I have every intention of becoming a dream expert if that's what it takes to keep seeing these memories. And I *do* intend to keep seeing these memories.

I'm not just enjoying the dreams; they are showing me things. Things I didn't notice when the moment was originally happening.

First, Jason's hesitation at our first kiss. Second, that Marcus really was there on Kiss Cam Day. I can zoom out on the moment and see more than I saw when I lived it the first time.

Somehow, these dreams might be able to show me more about me and Jason than I ever knew. They could show me the good things, the bad things, the moment things went wrong, and they can help me figure out exactly how to fix it.

All I need is the right memory.

Thirteen

I'm triple-checking that the gluten-free goods are being separated from the rest of the baked goods when I hear Amber, Mo, Marcus, and Holden all chatting amiably.

"My nanny taught me to angry-bake," Amber announces after the seventh straight compliment on her lemon bars.

"Angry-bake?" Marcus repeats, chewing vigorously on some fudge. "Is that like a hate-kiss?"

"Marcus, stop eating our merchandise!" I must sound like a broken record at this point, but he just grins. I swear he's doing it to annoy me.

"A love bite, maybe?" Mo offers.

"It's putting everything you feel into whatever you're making. I angry-baked *so* many treats for my parents," Amber says. "I'd just be like, 'You think you're going to work nineteen-hour days and never come to my school plays? Take *this* freaking macaron.'"

Holden roars. "Oh, you really showed them!" I can't get over how helpful he's been, how he's followed Marcus's lead in, like, not being a jerk today. Holden, I've realized, is one of those people who always needs a partner, a second half. His boyfriend, Bennett, is a junior and they can't be together all the time, so Jason and Holden are normally inseparable. But in Jason's absence, Holden seems to have affixed himself to Marcus's side.

Marcus, for his part, always seems to do his own thing. Slipping in and out of groups like he belongs in them but somehow doesn't need them.

"Then I realized you could *love*-bake, and, well, it's what I want to do forever and ever."

"What are *you* doing for college, Marcus?" Mo asks.

"I'll probably stick around here, actually," he says, reaching for a cookie. When our eyes meet, he grins and defiantly eats it, but, really, I'm only listening to what he's saying. "My dad needs an extra pair of hands at his shop and my sister's just a kid, so it helps if I'm here."

"That is so sweet," Amber says.

"An extra pair of hands?" Holden scoffs. "Plan B practically runs that place ever since his dad got sick."

I feel a squeeze of sympathy for Marcus, which is odd since I don't know Tommy Riddick well at all, other than the occasional story from Jason about his uncle.

Everything Holden said, really, is news to me.

I knew that Marcus's dad owned a car shop, but I didn't know Marcus helped out, much less "ran" the place.

"Dude, I'm pretty sure Hailey Chow just got here. Did your ESP tell you that?" Marcus teases Holden. To us, he explains, "Hailey is Bennett's ex."

"Oh shit!" Holden says, immediately ducking to pretend to pick something up from the ground. "Tell me when she walks past."

Marcus laughs. "That's your plan? You want us to tell you when she walks past?"

Everyone is laughing and having fun again, and I wonder if I'm the only one who notices that Marcus successfully diverted the conversation away from his future plans. Right at that moment, though, I notice Jason's mom walking over to our table.

"Zadie! Did you help put this on? You kids have done such a good job. Hi, Marcus!" Mrs. R leans over the table and Marcus kisses her cheek.

"It's so nice of you to come and support us," I say. The *despite Jason not being here* goes without saying.

"Of course," Mrs. R says. "Can I try some of that pie?"

I put a slice of coconut cream pie on a paper plate for her.

"Have you been feeling well, though? Or I suppose it's that you've been busy planning all this?" she says, motioning around us.

I blink at her, unsure of her meaning. Then it hits me.

I've missed seeing Jason twice.

But that can't be what's bothering Mrs. R.

"Yeah, I have," I say.

She takes a bite of her pie. "Mmm," she says. "This is delicious. You did all the baking too then, Zadie?"

It's the most passive-aggressive thing I've ever heard Mrs. R say, and it surprises me. Is it really such a big deal that I missed a couple of mornings with Jason?

"Amber did most of it," I say.

All the weeks I've shown up for Jason seem to be forgotten. Suddenly I'm not his "life partner."

The fundraiser is starting to wind down, so Mrs. R says goodbye and leaves. As we all pack up, I feel uneasy about the interaction with Jason's mother. I'm embarrassed by Tyler's treatment of me too, the way I'm suddenly worth messing with because Jason isn't here.

I go from uneasy and humiliated to angry when two juniors I

know from track come over to ask about how Jason is doing, but instead of asking me, they ask *Marcus.*

"He's making a lot of progress," Marcus says in that annoyingly vague way of his, because, *again,* I'm the one who has seen Jason every day since his accident except two. And now I'm strangely determined to remind everyone here, to remind his mother, that as far as they all know, I'm still the girl Jason loves.

Do you realize what Jason did in last night's dream? I want to yell at them.

He kissed me in front of everyone. And sure, it wasn't my ideal reveal for our relationship, but it was still big.

When I'm carrying some empty containers over to my car, I pull out my phone right there in the park, take a picture of my ring—this glistening symbol of everything we had—and fire off an Instagram post.

Missing my **@JasonRiddick4real**

I think I've let people forget that I'm one full half of Sterling-wood High's power couple. Since this is the first time I've been on socials in a long time, I'm drowning in mentions under #prayersforJasonRiddick. I'm knee-deep in my important work of liking, boosting, and reminding everyone I'm alive when two icy hands slide over my eyes from behind, covering me in darkness and making me squeal.

"Sorry, sorry! You were just such an easy target," Amber says, giggling as she reveals herself.

I slide my phone into my pocket and turn to her. "What's up?"

"I know we were going to hang out, but Talon just got here—he didn't realize the fundraiser started at twelve, as in noon," Amber says.

"He thought it started at *midnight*?" I give Amber a "you've got to be kidding me" look.

She lowers her voice. "It was an honest mistake," she says. "But anyway, I thought maybe the three of us could hang tomorrow and today I could just chill with Talon?"

The hopeful lilt of her voice does nothing to pacify me. "Ambs, we had plans!"

Specifically, we were planning to work on college apps, eat at Tanner's (our favorite diner just off the highway), and basically make a girls' day out of it.

"I know! I'm sorry," she says, then makes a sad puppy face. "Please? Wasn't I so helpful today?"

"You were, but . . ."

"And weren't my baked goods hands down the best of the lot?"

I sigh. "Amber."

She throws her arms around me. "Thank you, thank you, thank you!" she says. She's blowing me a kiss and running toward a blue van at the edge of the park before I can even argue.

"Don't do anything I wouldn't do!" I yell at her back. She waves and keeps running.

"Another one bites the dust," Mo says as we say goodbye to our bake sale crew and finish packing away the last few items. The boys took half the leftovers, and the other half is for Mo's siblings. "So much for *senior year will be all about the girls*!"

"You still have me," I say, because Mo looks particularly despondent.

We're headed toward our cars when the first big wave of nausea sweeps over me.

"Zad!" Mo hurries over to me when I stumble, even though her car is in the opposite direction. "Are you okay?"

I groan as I open my car door. "Yeah, I think I'm just getting another headache. I'll go to bed when I get home . . ."

"Uh, no," Mo says. "I'm driving you. Give me your keys."

I hesitate. "And how will you get home?"

"I'm sure the happy couple can spare a few minutes. I'll get them to give me a ride back to pick up my car. I'm texting them now."

I relent and we enter my car. While Mo turns on the ignition, I lean against the window for the coolness of the glass.

"You really don't need to do this," I say, trying to be brave.

"And *you* seriously need to see a doctor. Maybe we should go to the hospital."

"No!" The fierceness in my voice is a surprise even to me. "I really don't want to."

Mo frowns. "Why?"

"Because . . ." I say.

Because I don't want to see Jason.

The realization sends a shock wave through my body.

I don't want to see Jason.

Maybe Mrs. R isn't crazy after all.

If I go to the hospital, I'll feel compelled to see Jason. And I don't want to see him looking limp and paler each day, like a ghost of himself—not when I can just keep seeing him as he used to be. Healthy and strong and on top of the world.

It makes no sense, but it's the way I feel.

"Because it's not a very big one," I tell Mo. "And I'm pretty sure it's a PMS headache."

Mo is wary but finally says, "Those suck."

"I also didn't sleep too well last night," I say, to really put a nail in it.

"Oh! I was reading this research about how not getting enough sleep, even more than vitamin deficiencies, is like the worst thing for *migraineurs*," she says. "I should really say 'people who suffer from migraines,' but I just like the word *migraineurs*. It sounds like some kind of French delicacy, don't you think? Or like some fancy type of nomad. *Migraineurs*."

"Oh, totally," I say, feigning a laugh. When Mo abruptly ends the conversation, I'm afraid she's seen me grimace and is going to insist on the hospital after all. She's been so overprotective ever since the crash. But she just plays with the air controls in the car, turning down the fan.

Then she says, "I've been thinking lately about how wild it is that no two experiences are the same. Like even migraineurs don't have the same pain. Who knows if we're describing the same things when we talk about headaches? This came up because I was, like, inputting symptoms in Zebra for pneumonia or something, and it just blew my mind that someone might have three of these key symptoms and someone else has seventeen, but it's all the same disease."

"That is kind of wild," I say.

"Then I realized we might not all be having the same experience of *anything*. Like my grandparents' version of falling in love might be different than your experience of falling in love, so is it ultimately the same thing? How can anyone *know* anything? Every-thing is unknowable!"

"That's probably true." Trying to keep up with Mo is making my brain hurt more.

"So then I was thinking more about love and relationships, in general. And I . . . Do you remember what I told you right before you and Jason got together?" Mo asks.

I try to recall what she's talking about, ignoring the pulsing in my temples. "You're not ready to be Aunt Mo-Mo?"

Mo cackles. "Well, that too."

I smile despite myself. "You told me to make sure Jason is good enough for me."

She nods. "Yeah, how did you know he was?" She won't look me in the eye, and something shocking occurs to me. Whatever is keeping Mo preoccupied, making her late and distracted, it's big-ger than an app. Maybe Amber was right this morning; maybe Mo is hiding something for real. "How can we know anything?"

I let myself consider what she's asking. Is she going through something with her family? Is it a guy?

"Like, even now, how do you know Jason is good enough for you?" she continues, and her sudden curiosity about Jason feels as close to confirmation as I'm going to get.

Mo is notoriously tight-lipped about crushes. I think she feels weird about being the only one of us three to never have had a boy-friend.

"Mo, do you want to tell me something?" I wish I could find a more playful way to ask, but when your head feels like a rock concert—and not in a good way—it's kind of hard to be cute.

"I really don't," she says, ducking her head.

I smile. "Don't worry, I see what this is," I say, nudging her with my elbow. I so badly want to ask who the lucky guy is, but I don't want to push. She'd tell me if she wanted me to know.

She shakes her head. "It's not like that. And you haven't answered the question. Why Jason?"

"You know, you're always so hard on him, but he's never done anything to hurt me." Other than break my heart, I don't say. "He's a good guy."

"How do you *know*, though?" Mo asks, passionate. "Someone isn't good just because everyone says or thinks they are."

She's called me out on this before: The truth is that Jason is the king of Sterlingwood High partly because he's white. He's attractive and smart and athletic and all the things a good all-American boy should be. Would a Black guy with all those attributes be considered the same? Absolutely not, and none of it is wasted on me.

I could be just as biased as everyone else.

But it's also more complicated than that because Jason just happens to be, like, the peak of everything good in our town. He volunteers and goes to church with his parents and gets good grades and rarely curses. He likes me. I like him.

My headache is intensifying, but I give a shaky smile. "I'm not going just off what everyone thinks. You know my dad was a big romantic, right? I don't think anyone had as many relationships as he did. I don't need to tell you how they all went," I say, feigning a laugh. "But he did like to say, 'Love is what you do when no one is watching.' When nobody was around us, Jason was still a complete gentleman. And that's how I know."

Mo sighs. Wistfully, I think. My head is hurting so much now that I'm squeezing my fist like it might help.

"You're sure you don't want to go to the hospital?"

"My mom will take me if it gets worse," I promise, trying not to flinch with each road bump Mo flies over. When we get home, of course my mother isn't there. I'm surprised I have the brain space to feel embarrassed about the stark contrast of our cold, quiet place in comparison to the warmth of Mo's always-bustling house.

Mo is waiting with me till she gets a ride, so I pull out glasses of water for us and swallow some Advil covertly.

"Hey, you finally posted the ring on main!" Mo exclaims as she looks through her Instagram.

"Oh, yep. Thought it was about time," I say, but my brave face is starting to wobble. "Do the walls look funny to you?"

"What?" Mo glances over at me like I'm crazy. "The walls are fine."

But around me, the furniture is disappearing, and the ground feels like it's crumbling underneath me. I know immediately what's happening, so I make an excuse to go to the bathroom. Once I shut the door, I sink down onto the floor and try not to die. Seconds later, the walls around me are gone.

Fourteen

I'm on a boat.

Given how ill I've been feeling, its bouncy movement should technically have me regurgitating everything I've eaten. Instead, the pain in my head vanishes as a new world comes into focus around me.

I'm on a spacious motorboat with a distinct front and back section, separated by a large wooden deck space. The front area has standing room as well as two seats for the driver and a passenger, while the back has two parallel rows of leather seats. On the outside, the boat is white and huge.

I've only been on something like it once.

"So what do you think of the *Apostle*?" Jason asks, looping both arms around Zadie's waist as she stands at the helm of the boat.

Other Zadie leans back into him, grinning. "I think I might like your boat better than I like you."

Jason kisses the top of her head. "Wow! The truth comes out." He looks good as always, but it's particularly windy today and a day of tubing and swimming and other hijinks has left him looking uncharacteristically disheveled. I remember finding it endearing and special, like I was one of the few people in the world who knew Jason inside out.

I remember it being an unseasonably warm day for this time of year, and I want to enjoy the romance of this moment, to swing right into the memory, but something is missing. I realize for the first time that these dreams would feel entirely different, lonely, if it was just me reliving past memories.

"Marcus!" I say as soon as I spot him standing a few feet away, staring out at the lake. I can't help my smile.

We're on a boat.

Marcus looks over and winks, and I'm surprised at the lift I feel inside me, a hopeful kick of emotion. That, or my organs are shifting inside me, which seems ominous.

"Zadie Cartwright," Marcus says, both of us ignoring the fact that mere feet from us, Jason and Zadie are talking. Making a Memory. Marcus's hair is pulled back today, and somehow, in an alarming reversal of roles, he looks less tousled than Jason. "Skydiving or paragliding?"

He has to talk loud over the wind.

I sigh, then surprise us both by answering. "What's the difference again?"

Marcus seems more than happy to explain. "Skydiving, I'm pretty sure, is jumping out of a plane voluntarily and falling to your death," he says. "Paragliding, on the other hand, is basically falling to your death while attached to some parachute-like situation."

Leaning in so close his breath is warm against the back of my neck, he adds, "I don't recommend either."

My heart beats just a little faster at his nearness.

"Paragliding," I bumble, "seems more . . . I don't know, serene or something. Like there's more floating and less falling."

Marcus considers this. "More floating, less falling. I can see that."

I try to steer us back (pun intended) to the reason we're here: the Jason and Zadie of it all.

"I have no idea why this memory matters," I tell Marcus, looking around the boat. "It was just a normal day. We had a nice time on the lake."

My mind is racing ahead, already questioning what this dream might reveal.

"Yo, Captain! My Captain!" Holden yells from the back. "What's the rush? Why can't we do one more hour?"

"I told you! My dad already expected us back an hour ago," Jason shouts. I remember that he is not-so-secretly pissed at Holden for smuggling booze onto the boat when that broke Jason's dad's number one rule.

"So what's another hour then? Live a little!"

"My friends are such idiots," Jason fumes, chin on Zadie's shoulder.

"Amber and Mo would have brought lemonade," Zadie teases, a whisper only Jason can hear. "I'm just saying."

"She's joking, but she's also not," I tell Marcus now as we watch them. "I'd asked Jason if Mo and Amber could come and he said there wasn't any room, but there's like eleven of his friends here." I point toward the back of the boat where a full-on party is happening. "Sometimes I think . . . Never mind."

"No," Marcus insists. "Sometimes you think . . ."

"Sometimes I feel like Jay is weird with my friends. There are times when he's normal and chill and it feels like everyone loves everyone. Other times, he only wants to hang with his friends. And if my friends are around, there's this weird, like . . . undertone."

Marcus kneads his thumb against his temple, and I wonder if he's tired of talking about me and Jason. Tired of hearing about our drama. I can't blame him if he is. "I wouldn't worry about it. Jay likes everyone who likes him."

"Everyone likes Jay," I point out. "He's going to be prom king for sure."

"Yeah, but that's all bullshit."

I frown. "Which part?"

"The very concept of prom king, the campaigning, the voting. It's a popularity contest."

I have the same thought I did at the fundraiser; it's something like jealousy at the way Marcus comes and goes in groups, the way he never takes anything, including himself, very seriously.

"There's nothing wrong with popularity." It comes out defensive.

"True. It's just not real, that's all I'm saying," Marcus says, but his eyes are lasers as he looks at me, sharp and focused. Somehow it sounds a lot like *you're* not real. It's as if he's seeing straight inside me, as if he can see all the effort to be liked, to be good, to be *tidy*.

I put both hands on my hips in frustration. "So, everyone who cares how they're perceived is shallow—is that it? Less authentic?"

Marcus sighs, sticks his hands deep into his pockets. "I thought we were talking about Jason."

"We are," I snap. "Why don't you like your own cousin?"

"Of course I . . ." Marcus begins, then changes his mind. "Look. Let's focus on those two."

But Jason and Zadie are just standing at the helm, kissing.

"Doesn't look like we're missing anything," I say, then turn back to Marcus. Suddenly, I want to see him squirm, make him just as uncomfortable as he's made me. "Weren't you and Jason ever best friends?"

He shrugs. "When we were five, maybe." Marcus rubs the back of his neck as he thinks. He seems to be taking my question seriously. "I got a lot of attention when we were kids. I was fast for my age and, honestly, a bit of a show-off. I had the bigger personality."

"You?" I'm incredulous. "I'm not sure I can see it."

"Yes, me," Marcus says, flicking one of my earrings. Today's open secret. Each ear features a small dangling crown—with green, purple, and gold pieces—that Dad got me when he went to Mardi Gras one year. Marcus's action is surprisingly playful and intimate, something you would do to someone you know well. I have no idea why I like it so much.

"Jay . . . didn't love it," he went on. "And one summer he started this thing where whenever our families got together, he would challenge me to a playoff. If I won, he'd sulk through the rest of our vacation. As we got older, he started to win more and more, and to this day that's the only scenario he can live with."

"Is that why you won't try in soccer? So you don't step on his toes?" I ask. "Because if you're trying to maintain some agreement you and Jason have, then both of you are even dumber than I thought."

My sharp words surprise even me, and Marcus narrows his eyes. "Maybe I'm not as good as he is."

"Well, we'll never know, will we?" I shoot back. "Because you're just going to sit on your ass and phone it in. If you don't try, you can't fail, right?"

"There's no agreement," Marcus says with a sigh. "We give each other space, because we disagree on a lot of things."

"Like what?" I ask, half goading Marcus. "What shot to take? Where to sit on the bus? Girls?"

He glances up at my last guess.

"Oh," I say, catching myself. "How could I forget?"

Marcus frowns. "Forget what? What are you talking about?"

I snort. "You know exactly what I'm talking about. I know what you said."

Marcus opens his mouth to say something, but just then the machine-y sound of the boat completely disappears. It's like going from a rock concert to a child's nursery at nap time.

"They're here," I say as the boat is pulling up by the wharf. A middle-aged man comes over and shouts instructions to Jason, helping to get them tied up. Other Zadie packs up, and she and Jason climb out of the boat. At the edge of the lake, rows of multi-colored wildflowers mix in with the wilting grass, but it's the bluish-purple poppies that catch my eye. I know I've seen those before.

"What is it?" Marcus asks, noting my distraction.

"Those flowers. I think they were in the last dream."

Marcus looks confused. "Where in the last dream?"

But I can't remember. It's more like a feeling rather than a picture in my mind, so I shrug and let it go. As Jason's friends disband, Marcus and I stick with Jason and Other Zadie.

They're holding hands and walking down the dock. We're close enough to see them slow, to hear Jason whisper "Hold on," let go of Zadie's hand, and walk the rest of the way down the dock to meet his father.

Other Zadie stays back, pretends to be on her phone while Jason and his father talk in quiet voices, but Marcus and I go close enough to hear. I always wanted to know what they talked about.

"I told you to bring the boat back by four," Mr. R spits. "It's almost six."

Jason is repentant. "Sorry. We lost track of time."

Mr. R says nothing but glances over Jason's shoulder at Other Zadie. "I thought we agreed no girls until offseason."

"Dad," Jason says, sounding both exasperated and strangely pleading. I hold my breath while I wait for Jason's response, a response he knows Zadie will never hear.

Love is what you do when no one is watching.

"It's not serious," he tells Mr. R in a quiet voice. "I swear."

I almost double over from the punch in my gut.

Jason scratches his head, clearly hiding his guilt, as he goes back to Other Zadie.

"Is everything okay?" Other Zadie says, intuiting Mr. R's disapproval.

"Oh yeah," Jason lies. "He's just worried about his boat."

The real me watches dumbly as Jason threads his hand through Other Zadie's again. "What do you feel like for dinner?"

"Didn't you hear? It's always a good night for Tanner's," she says, reciting the diner's catchphrase.

Jason laughs and pulls her into him, squeezing their bodies together for what feels like an infinite amount of time. I know that, in this moment, Other Zadie isn't sure what to think, but she's telling herself nothing significant just happened.

"It's really not a big deal," I tell Marcus now, because I'm trying to convince myself the same thing. I both hate that he's standing here watching this with me and can't think of anything sadder than if I had witnessed that alone. "Sometimes we say what we have to."

Marcus nods. "I get it, but it can't feel good watching . . . that."

"It's truly okay. Can we not talk for a minute?" I say, because my eyes are stinging. Thankfully, Marcus respects my wish. We only stand in silence for twenty, maybe thirty seconds, before a strong magnetic force grabs hold of our bodies. Before my arms turn blurry, then vanish. I'm relieved to feel the force whirling around me and Marcus, a noisy storm we're starting to know well. Relieved to be snatched out of the dream, pulled out of the memory and into real life.

I feel whiplashed when I wake up in my room, as tired as if I'd run a marathon and as sad as if I'd lost something I loved.

* * *

I'm in my bed, alone.

It's early, early morning. Sunday.

In the dark, Jason's words echo. *It's not serious.*

Maybe Jason really meant what he told his dad. Maybe *that* is why Jason broke up with me—I was just passing the time.

The thought won't let me sleep. I sit up, turn on my bedside lamp, and pick up the ring from where I usually set it at night. Once it's on, I twist it around on my finger.

I should hop out of bed, go for my run, go and visit Jason. But I don't have it in me.

I'm wearing the ring still when I log on to social media to see the response to my last picture. And there is a big response. Mo and Amber hype me up in the comments as usual, but this post has the most likes I've ever gotten. Dozens and dozens of comments, each one praising the love between me and Jason. A strange thing happens: the words of people who barely know me make me feel safe and warm. Less alone. Less uncertain.

Of course Jason didn't mean what he said. It *was* serious. I was there. All these people have been there.

What I know is that this ring is on my finger for a reason. Jason and I, together, make something beautiful. Something impeccable. I'm about to close out of Instagram when I see that I have a new message. It's from an account that has no followers and only follows me.

The message contains one line.

That's my ring, Zadie.

Fifteen

Someone knows.

Who is this? I write back immediately.

I get no response.

Please just tell me who this is.

Nothing.

The smart thing to do would be to stop wearing the ring, probably. Stop aggravating whoever it is behind the Instagram account—but people will notice if the ring suddenly disappears from my hand. Besides, I don't want this person to think they've intimidated me. I'm terrified, but they don't have to know that. So I keep it on and try to keep going about my life.

When I arrive at the hospital on Monday to see Jason, Nurse Harlow, the one who told me Jason can hear us, waves at me. "You're back!"

Do the people of this town have some sort of chart, tracking my attendance? It's ridiculous. But it does remind me that I have to do better. I can't miss more days of seeing Jason, so I force myself through twenty minutes of inane rambling at his bedside. I tell him about our friends and how senior year is going and my running times. I read him more soccer scores. I tell him what he's missed in Spanish class, but I am suddenly exhausted.

"I'm mad at you," I tell Jason, letting all my pretenses fall. "I keep finding out new things about you, and I thought they'd help me make sense of everything, but all I feel is doubt."

I touch the ring. "Why did you have this? Who did you mean to give it to?

"And your dad," I say, "I can't believe you told him we weren't serious. Have you been lying to me all this time?"

My eyes suddenly get very blurry. "If we're not us, I don't know what we are. Who else am I supposed to love?"

I hold his pointer finger. "Tell me if you can hear me."

I wait for a squeeze or a tap, but nothing happens. Not even a twitch.

Defeated, I go into his bathroom, pull what I need from the travel bag I take everywhere with me, and redo my makeup. Today's open secret is my nude lip, because I wish I was invisible. In addition, I've been wearing a series of graphic tees all week because I think I'll always feel a little angsty until Jason wakes up.

Then I leave for school.

All day, I keep obsessively checking Instagram, waiting for another message or odd comment, something that confirms to me that someone is out for my blood. In many ways, the possibility that I might be in trouble is worse than if I knew for sure that I was in trouble.

"Diabolical," I say, quietly cursing whoever this person is, as I gather up last period's things. The fact is, it's only been two days, but I am already tired of being messed with. The ring picture has now scored *double* the number of comments I got for the kissing photo that made me and Jay Instagram official last year, post–Kiss

Cam. I know none of this is important in the grand scheme of things, but I find I can't even enjoy the positive attention because this nameless, faceless bully has decided to torment me. And I can't get the support of my friends on all this either.

"Why would they say that's their ring?" I imagine Amber asking, confused, as I blather something about how, funny story, the person is right, and I actually have no idea whose ring I'm wearing. Could be that it's a ring Jason bought, or it's equally likely some random person dropped it in Jay's car when he gave people a ride home after games.

I decide that, regardless of who this is, I'm making the next move. I'm going to figure out who they are before they strike again. I just might need a little help, and I have an inkling of where to get it.

My plan requires me to duck out as soon as school is done, but Amber and Mo are hovering by my locker. "How about 'Love is an open door' for my senior quote?" Amber asks immediately when she sees me, then offers me one of her homemade brownies. "Don't you think it's very me?"

"It *is* very you, but also very *Frozen*," I say, taking a brownie and looking longingly toward the back doors of the school.

Amber sighs as I open my locker and take out my bag. "How about 'All's fair in love and war'?"

"So cliché," Mo says. "And a disturbing sentiment either way."

"You don't think anything goes if there's love involved?"

Mo and I react automatically. "No."

"*You* just haven't been in love yet," Amber says, pointing at Mo. "When you find the right guy, you'll get it."

"Bet you I won't," Mo mutters.

To me, Amber says, "But you. What's your excuse?"

I shrug as I close my locker door. "Love doesn't make everything okay. Like, you couldn't murder people for love," I say.

"But people do," Ambs protests. "Not saying they *should*, but love is that powerful."

I laugh. "I think you might be overidentifying with murderers. Or watching too much *Dateline.* Hey, I have to go. I'm taking pictures of soccer practice for the yearbook."

They accept this excuse, but as I make my way outside, I wonder what Dad the "expert" would say about our conversation on love. Probably something as irrational as Amber, about how love is everything. Love is the only thing worth writing about, worth living for, worth spending money on. All my life, wherever Dad took me—a bookstore or candy store or any type of store—he'd hold out his arms majestically as if he owned the place. "What do you love, Zadiebug?" As long as he could afford it, he would buy anything I picked. The question thrilled me when I was a kid, but it became unbearably stressful the older I got. I so badly wanted to choose right. Choose the *best* thing, so I didn't have any regrets.

Today I sit in the bleachers, finishing my brownie and doing homework until it's getting close to the end of practice. Then it's "go time" for my plan, so I head out to the side of the field with my camera. At this point, most of the team is on the sidelines, cooling off or stretching. Marcus is still on the field, Coach Kyle next to him.

"Plan B stepping in as captain is one thing I never thought I'd see," Holden snorts, coming up beside me.

"What do you mean?" I ask.

"He talked to Coach. Promised to do a complete one-eighty and start taking the game seriously."

My heart skips a beat. "When?"

"Yesterday, maybe?" Holden says. "Who knows?"

I wonder if it's because of the talk in our dream.

And the longer I stick around, the more Holden's words are confirmed. Marcus is playing Jason's usual position on Friday night. Even I, with my minimal understanding of soccer, can see that the coaches are treating Marcus differently than they normally do. Usually, he is on the bench, a substitute for Jay or one of the other forwards, but right now the coaches are watching Marcus like a hawk and nitpicking everything from his footwork to the way he makes contact with the ball.

Marcus looks miserable, and I don't blame him.

He's playing with his shirt off, and my eyes can't help being drawn to his toned abs. Sweat has made his blond hair darker than normal. If someone called Marcus a skinny Thor, they would, technically, not be incorrect. But Jason is definitely more my type. Clean-cut, sweet, disciplined.

"Psst, Marcus!" I say, trying to get his attention as soon as Coach Kyle walks away. "Marcus!"

"Is it dream time?" he asks when he finally comes off the field.

I glance around, horrified. "Would you keep it down?"

Marcus grins, lowers his voice. "I doubt anybody's going to know what that means." His bad mood dissipated as soon as the coaches let up on him.

"You never know," I say, irritated by how paranoid I sound.

He gives me a questioning look, and I take the opportunity to say, "I have to talk to you."

"Zadie Cartwright wants to talk? I *am* dreaming. I don't even have a good This or That prepared."

"Stop it," I insist. He grins as he takes his hair out of the ponytail he plays with and runs his hand through it.

"Am I upsetting you? I really wouldn't dream of doing such a thing."

Oh my God. I turn on my heel as I lament what a shitty plan this was. "Okay, I'm going."

Marcus chuckles and catches up to me. "Fine. I just had to get that out of my system. So?" he says, after we've been walking together a millisecond longer than is comfortable. Last time we were both in this parking lot, he was threatening me, telling me he knew Jason had broken up with me.

"It's not you, is it?" I suddenly feel the need to ask.

"Is what not me?" Marcus looks genuinely confused as he bites into a granola bar.

"The Instagram bully."

Marcus rocket-laughs, a fizzy, unexpectedly delighted sound. Frankly it feels so disrespectful and cruel that I storm ahead and don't stop walking until he catches up to me.

"Hey! Hey!"

"Is everything a joke to you?"

"You know I don't even *use* Instagram, right?" Marcus asks.

The truth is, I don't think Marcus sent me that message. I don't know why, but it doesn't seem like something he would do.

That being the case, I still hate that he's the only one I have to turn to for help.

"Someone's harassing me."

Marcus's face loses its glee. "Explain."

I pull out my phone and show him the message.

"God, what a nightmare." His lips quirk.

"Marcus!"

I reach out to shove him. I'm touching his chest before I realize that Marcus Riddick and I are not the kind of friends—or acquaintances, or dream buddies—who touch each other.

I pull my hand back as if electrocuted, and his laughter fades.

"You're the worst," I say.

We walk in silence for a second.

"So whose ring do you think it is?" he asks.

"Either Jason's or somebody else's. If I knew which, I wouldn't be asking you for help."

"Okay, okay," Marcus says. Then, "Do you even know who Sly and the Family Stone are, or does the shirt just go with the theme of the day?"

I blink at him, because I'm confident I've misheard. "Excuse me?"

As he tears through his second granola bar in as many minutes, he nods at my shirt. Dad's shirt. The words SLY AND THE FAMILY STONE have been pressed on the black fabric in red. "Are you an actual fan, or is it an on-theme thing?"

Never mind that Marcus must have been looking at my shirt to know what it says; the words he's saying are simply not possible.

"On-theme? There's no *theme*." I sound like there's a theme.

"No? I'd have sworn there was, given that you've worn something black every day since the breakup."

I'm frozen. How can Marcus Riddick of all people have figured out my open secrets? I finally say, "Maybe I'm going goth."

"Please. You're clearly upset about the coma and in mourning over the breakup. Probably will be until you know Jay will be okay and that he wants you back." My mouth has fallen open. Marcus grins. "Am I close?"

Furious and flustered, I blurt out, "Stop paying attention to what I do." I realize after I've said it that it's an admission and not the reprimand I meant it to be.

Marcus surprises me by shooting me an annoyed look. "Sure," he says. "I'll get right on that."

We've arrived at his truck now, and he looks at his phone. "Look, I have to be somewhere at five."

"That's in fifteen minutes," I point out. Luckily, you can get most places in Sterlingwood in ten minutes. But if Marcus is too annoyed to help me with the Instagram situation, who else do I have?

I glance around. "I could . . . come with you?" I offer. "To talk?"

"Uh . . . fine?" Marcus says, clearly caught off guard. He opens his door, and I climb into the passenger side of his truck. I try not to notice how many players and spectators might be witnessing me getting into Marcus Riddick's truck. Hopefully they'll just assume we're doing something for his cousin.

As soon as the engine goes on, a man's evenly paced British voice fills the cab, an audiobook. Marcus turns it off right away.

"So?" he says.

The night we met, Marcus told me one of his favorite things to do was listen to audiobooks while he drove, built things, or worked out. I've seen so little evidence of this person I met last July that I've started to feel like he was make-believe.

But I remember everything he said.

"Do you still make birds?"

Marcus gives me a weary look. "I carve birds," he says finally, the slightest hint of a smile on his face. "I'm not, like, the Creator God."

"You promised to show me," I say before I think better of it. The beat of silence that follows feels excruciating.

"I did," Marcus says softly.

I clear my throat. "So, going back to the ring."

"The ring," Marcus echoes, facing the road again. "First possibility is that Jason bought the ring, *owns* the ring, and someone is just harassing you. Second possibility is that he could have bought it *from* someone and they have amnesia." I smile.

"Alternatively, you think the Instagram person is saying they left or lost their ring in Jason's car?" Marcus asks.

"What else could it mean?" I say.

Neither of us has many other ideas, but over the next couple of minutes, Marcus seems to morph back into the easygoing, slightly annoying person I know. Idioms and everything.

"I get that we're a dream team, but what exactly do you want me to do here?" he asks. "Other than kick a soccer ball very accurately at their head for you."

That makes me smile again. "We'd have to know whose head to direct it to," I say.

"Which we don't," he finishes.

I sigh. "I'm trying to keep my eyes and ears open, to use my Spidey sense and all that, but I think I'm in too deep. If I ask people too many questions or act even a little bit off, I'll blow up everything."

"So you want me to . . ."

"Investigate, keep your ear to the ground. Someone has to know some . . . Hey, why are we at Corner Books?"

Marcus is pulling up in front of the only used bookstore in Sterlingwood.

"They're holding something for me."

He raises his eyebrows in question, but I'm already climbing out, following him into the store.

Sixteen

As soon as we enter Corner Books, the smell of paper and dust in the air, I'm hit with a wave of longing so big it overwhelms me. Whenever I think of books, I think of Dad. He read to me constantly when I was a kid. I grew up surrounded, literally, by copies of his books, pages of manuscripts he was trying to finish. And most of the books I've read in the past two years are from our Father-Daughter Book Club. He feels close enough to touch when I'm around books, but then I go back into the real world, and he's so far away again.

"So you're a *reader* reader?" I ask Marcus, speaking over the lump in my throat.

"First, I don't know what that means," Marcus says. "Second, it's not for me."

"Who's it for?"

He doesn't answer because Stan, the eighty-year-old man who owns Corner Books, has spotted us.

"Ah, Marcus Riddick! Back so soon?"

"I can't get enough." Marcus grins as the man goes behind the counter and looks around for something.

"And with a different lady on your arm this time," Stan says with a wink. I feel myself blush down to the tips of my toes. Of course the bookstore is somewhere Marcus brings girls on dates. I should have stayed in the truck.

Marcus is trying to rectify the situation with a "Zadie's my . . ." at the same time that I'm saying, "We're just . . ."

But both our voices fade when Stan pulls out a copy of *Little Women*. It's a leather-bound version, elegant and classic. Clearly very expensive.

I gasp. "Oh my gosh."

"What did I tell ya?" Stan says, talking to Marcus but grinning at me. "Works every time."

But Marcus is opening the book, flipping to the last page. I see his face fall as he lands on it.

"Not it?" Stan asks.

"What are you looking for?" I ask as Marcus shakes his head.

"Every copy of *Little Women* in the state, it seems like," Stan jokes. "Ah well. Not so lucky today, I guess."

"I'll take it anyway," Marcus says, pulling out his phone to pay for the book.

"You don't have to do that," Stan says, waving his hand. "I'll just return it. Say my customer wasn't happy. No harm, no foul."

But Marcus won't hear of it, and somehow he gets Stan to charge him for the book, and we walk out with it.

"You don't like it?" I ask once we enter the truck, and Marcus puts the book in his glove box. I take it out before he closes the compartment.

"It's incredible," I say, running my fingers over the binding. "I would have loved this as a kid."

Marcus nods. "Yeah, she would too, but she's looking for a specific one. It's leather-bound and has gilded pages, and it's been written in by my mom."

I'm confused. "She?"

"My sister. Joey."

I wait for him to explain. "My mom used to have a copy of the book as a kid—she mentioned it in one of her letters, and now Joey wants . . ."

"That exact copy," I finish.

"Something like that. I'm running out of places I can even check for used copies."

I bite my lip, not quite sure if I should say what I want to or not. But I can't help myself. "I thought you weren't in touch with your mom? I thought . . . I mean, Jason said . . ."

As soon as I reveal that I've ever asked Jason about Marcus, I want to kick myself.

"It must have come up," I finish pathetically.

"We're not in touch with my mom, but, um . . . Joey is."

All the joking around I've come to expect from Marcus, the various unreadable expressions, it's all gone, and instead, there's a very clear look on his face that says closed for discussion.

"That's great," I say, because I can't imagine what it's like to have a parent who leaves you intentionally but still finds time to write. Even when my dad moved, I still saw him often, heard from him all the time. Him being gone now is not a choice.

We drive in silence and then Marcus is pulling up next to my car in the school parking lot.

"You said I said something," he says, when he stops the truck.

"What?"

"In the dream, on the boat," Marcus says. "You said you knew what I said. What did I say?"

Ugh, it's the last thing I want to talk about right now.

"It's fine, Marcus. We really don't have to get into it. I've moved past it."

"See, there you are again with one of those *comments*."

I'm surprised by the passion in his voice. "What comments?"

"'How could I forget' and 'I've moved past it' and 'You know what you said,'" Marcus says.

"Yes, well, all those things are true."

"What the hell did I say?" he asks.

I sigh, trying to decide whether it's more humiliating to talk about it or not talk about it. "You said you didn't see what Jason saw in me. I believe your exact words were 'Why would he be interested in her?'"

When you'd met me one time, and I'd stupidly poured my heart out to you, I almost add.

Marcus blinks, and I wait for a denial. But it never comes.

"That was only because . . ."

"Oh my God. So you admit it," I say, vindicated but also weirdly hurt, despite knowing all along that Marcus sucks as a human being. "You think I'm not good enough for Jason."

Marcus turns so he is more fully looking at me in his truck. "Why the fuck would you not be good enough for Jason?"

I cross my arms over my chest, embarrassed by the sudden impulse to cry. "I don't know. You tell me."

"No, seriously," Marcus insists. "Why the fuck would you not be good enough?" And I realize for the first time that he's looking at me as though I have three heads. "You're smart and funny and beautiful as fuck. You're the person everybody in this school wants to be, and you wouldn't have it any other way. When I asked why he was interested in you, I was asking because you're not his usual type."

My mind is still stuck on the words "beautiful as fuck," but with a concerted effort, I say something else.

"You said he was out of my league."

"No," Marcus says. "I said *you* were out of *his* league. Where the hell did you hear all this?"

"Word gets around, Marcus."

"Whose word gets around? Give me a name."

All my intel obviously comes from Amber, but I lie. "I don't have a specific name. It just got back to me."

Marcus looks furious now. "Why would you not come to me with that shit? Why wouldn't you ask me straight out?"

"We barely know each other," I point out.

"Ask me whatever else you want to know," Marcus implores.

But my brain is acting like it's been taken over by a swarm of bees and all I can hear is those words again.

He thinks I'm beautiful.

"Those are all my questions," I say, undoing my seat belt. All my bark and bite are gone. "So, um, keep me posted if you hear or see anything suspicious. Like, with the Instagram bully."

Marcus looks like he's fighting a smile. "That's their name? The Instagram bully?"

"What else am I supposed to call them?"

"I don't know, the Ring Bandit, maybe?"

Despite myself, I laugh. "We are not calling anyone the Ring Bandit." I push open the door of Marcus's truck.

"Fine, I'll ask around. Keep you informed if anyone has a push pin with your face on it."

"Ha ha," I say, sliding out of the truck. On the signboard in front of the school, the details of this week's game are displayed for all to see. "You know, everyone is talking about you."

"Who's everyone?" he asks, with none of the panic I would have at such a statement. "Same person who told you I hate you?"

I roll my eyes. "No, everyone means the *entire* student body," I say. "Rumor has it, you're starting in the match on Friday, and I for one am excited to see it."

Marcus groans and scrubs a palm over his face.

I laugh. "Who knew Marcus Riddick could be shy?"

He doesn't deny this statement.

In fact, all he does is call out right before I shut the passenger door. "Hey, Cartwright?"

"Yes, Riddick?" I can't help my smile.

"If I do some investigating for you, I need you to do something for me," he says, and one of my eyebrows skirts up. What can Marcus Riddick possibly need from me?

"Okay?"

He looks out the window, in the direction of the soccer field the team just had practice on. "Don't come on Friday night. To the game."

That snaps me out of any haze I've been in, and I'm incredulous. "What? Why not?"

"Because it's going to be a bloodbath, and I don't want you to see me at that level of not caring."

I know that he's making reference to when I told him he didn't care about anything, but I don't quite understand *why* he is.

I want to delve into a speech about how not trying is an excuse to not fail, and honestly, it's the saddest type of failure, but Marcus just agreed to do me a favor. And he knows too many of my secrets.

So I just say, voice steady, "Silvers are the defending champions, Marcus."

"I know that," he says, one hand on the wheel.

"Okay, well, you're their interim leader. And Jason loves this team."

"You're telling me a lot about my own team," he says, a small smile on his face. He rubs his chin. "I just think you should spare yourself the hassle this time. There's no way . . . There's just no way . . ." *we win.* I hear his unspoken words, and I want to tell him that it doesn't matter.

I want to climb back into his truck and argue with him, but that seems a little much, so I just nod and shut the door. Head back to my own car.

And now, in addition to who my bully is, I also have questions about Marcus. Why does he so badly want me not to see him play? Maybe he's going to throw the game. I don't really know how you can do that with so many players on the pitch, but I'm sure it happens. Maybe I should contact Coach Kyle or something.

I decide against doing that, and then, for reasons I don't understand, I spend the entire evening searching for used bookstores near and far that carry copies of *Little Women.* I do the same thing over the next couple of nights, and then on Thursday I compile a list and text it to Marcus. I've never texted him before, even though his number is saved in my phone.

He doesn't respond at all until the next day when I send an additional Good luck with the game!!! just before last period. I hope, implied in all the superfluous punctuation is the fact that this game is a really freaking big deal, and even if they don't win, he has to at least *try*, and I'm definitely going to be there and . . . and . . .

All he says is: You promised.

So.

I guess I really am not going to the game. It feels like he's implying that he won't help me figure out my Instagram nemesis's identity if I go to the game. It's very unfair.

The only silver lining is that Amber and Mo decide not to go as well, so I invite them over for a girls' night. (An actual girls' night, meaning no Talon.) It's a mini-intervention designed to ease some of whatever pressure has been causing their squabbling lately. And I decide it's working when I'm washing the mask off my face and listening to my best friends laughing together in my living room as they try to learn a TikTok dance.

My phone vibrates in the pocket of my pajama shorts, and I pull it out. There's no live stream of the match, but I've been keeping up with the score online, holding my breath as the Silvers beat the Buffalos 3–1.

So it's extremely surprising when my text is from none other than Marcus.

> Thanks for the links. I'm going
> to check them out tonight.

I could act like a normal person and wait five minutes to text him back, but *screw it*, I don't.

Me: You're welcome.

Me: I saw you won. Congrats! Seems like you really didn't care.

A few minutes go by before he texts back.

I'm not hiding in the bathroom, watching my phone screen, waiting for his response. But I'm also not *not* doing that.

Marcus: Yep, we did win. Thanks to astronomical levels of not giving a shit.

Translation: I tried really hard actually.

He texts again.

Headed to dreamland anytime soon?

Me: I think so.

His response: Maybe I'll see you there.

Is he flirting with me?

There's something different about texting Marcus now that I know he thinks I'm beautiful. But maybe he says it to girls all the time. Maybe he means beautiful, like, mind-wise. Which is also great.

Eventually, I just write back Maybe you will, and I hope it is true.

Seventeen

But the next dream doesn't come.

Instead, over the next couple of days, I face the single other thing I dread more than continuing my Princeton application: Reading the next book from our list without Dad. Book No. 25. When we decided to do the Cartwright Father-Daughter Book Club, Dad had this big box of books sent to me. On Sunday, I pick a random novel from the box and read the first page. It takes exactly forty seconds before I can't continue. Every word feels like slugging through mud, even though I know in theory I could love this book. If Dad were reading it too, miles away in his little apartment in Portland, I *would* love this book.

I pick up another, and the same thing happens. A third book, and now my head feels thick, like the words are sticking to the inside of my skull.

I've been battling myself for a whole hour before I realize that sticky feeling inside my brain is actually a headache. Maybe it really is time to do something about these things.

"Mom?" I call as I open the door of my room and go to hers. It's empty.

Downstairs too.

I grab a glass of cold water and two pain tablets and shuffle back up the stairs where I realize that, in addition to a bunch of texts from Mo and Amber, I have a message from Mom saying she'll be working late over the next few days.

"Whole house to myself. Woo-hoo," I say flatly, because I'm probably the lone teenager who would give anything for my parents to be home. I'd pick either of them over getting to throw a raging party or not do chores or sleep in till midday.

I go to bed early, but it's a restless sleep. Soon, I'm jerking awake, tripping over the side of the bed to reach my waste basket, and then again in my rush to the bathroom. I throw up everything I've eaten into the toilet bowl, flush, then stay there on the floor of the bathroom. The coolness of the tiles against my right temple is sweet relief.

Okay, so maybe this is more than a headache. It's like every pain I've felt before in my life has condensed into one or two pulse points.

I try to reach for my phone, but I realize I left it in my bedroom.

My head feels like something detonated in there. It is a dull throbbing pain in the front of my head and behind my eyes that refuses to stop, no matter how much I plead with it to.

When I feel a little less nauseous, I rinse my mouth and shuffle back into my room. Just the slit of moonlight bleeding in over my bed feels aggressively bright.

I curl up on my side as I fall back into bed.

I can't really sleep because my head hurts so much, but I'm also not fully conscious.

"Mom?" I croak out again, knowing what her text said but hoping that somehow she's come back early or changed her mind. Some type of maternal sixth sense that brought her home to take care of me. But the only sound is the hammering in my brain.

And when I wake up, I know that hours have passed, but I have no sense of how many. I must be missing school.

There's a pounding sound that gets louder and louder. Except—wait. For the first time, the noise is coming from outside me. The front door.

I groan, wanting the sound to stop.

It's only the hope that maybe it's my mom coming home that gets me up, blanket dragging behind me, shuffling to the front door.

I wince at the sunlight when it opens.

"Hey."

It's Marcus. At my front door. Of my house.

"I was just driving by. It's kind of stupid, actually, but I . . . You okay, Cartwright? You don't look so good."

"It's just a migraine." My voice is a dry whisper, and my mouth feels like cotton wool.

Marcus frowns. "It doesn't look like it's *just* anything." He sounds almost disapproving. And concerned. "Do you . . . do you need anything?"

I feel too gross to speak, so I nod. He reaches forward and gently brushes his thumb over my still-wet cheek.

I start crying for real.

"Hey, it's okay," he says softly. "Just tell me what you need, and I'll do it."

And so what happens is that Marcus Riddick leads me back up the stairs and into my room. My waste basket still smells like the nasty contents of my stomach. In fact, I'm pretty sure it still *contains* the nasty contents of my stomach, but Marcus acts like he doesn't notice.

He disappears for minutes-long stretches, coming back with something new each time.

A cool washcloth for my head. A glass of water from the kitchen. Somehow, he figures out when I took my last pain meds, and he gives me two new tablets. Different than the first ones I took. "I think it's fine," he says, reading something off his phone as he holds them out to me. "Yeah, I'm pretty sure it's fine. It should actually help, taking them together."

Later, he opens my window and a touch of cold air comes in.

The acrid smell recedes.

I feel marginally more human.

Right around the moment the thought of food no longer revolts me, something smells like burnt toast. But it's a bowl of noodles he sets down in my lap after he's helped me sit up. "Something smells burnt," I tell him.

"Don't worry about it," he says.

"You burned *toast?*"

"Don't worry about it," he says again. "It's the fever talking."

"I don't have a fever."

There's a featherlight grin on his face.

He takes my bowl away when I finish eating, and as I'm falling asleep I ask the question I'm afraid of: "You're leaving?"

"Do you want me to?" he asks.

"No."

"Okay," he says. "I'll be right back."

I know the minute I'm feeling better because a few things happen in quick succession. I remember that Marcus is *here*. I remember that he is not bad on the eyes, that he called me beautiful. I remember that he has seen my puke.

So I jump out of bed and race for my dresser. I'm hurriedly filling in my eyebrows when I hear him speak.

"Are you serious right now, Cartwright?" he asks from the door-
way. "You're dying and you're putting on makeup?"

"I'm not *dying*," I say, and my voice comes out hoarse. I clear my
throat. "I'm not dying. I just look hideous."

He sighs and sinks into the desk chair beside my bed while I
hastily finish my brows. I meet his eyes in the mirror as I dab on
some lip balm.

"You look good," he says, almost under his breath, holding my
gaze through the glass.

My face burns. "Please, you know you say that to all the girls,"
I joke.

He breaks our eye contact. "What girls do you think there are?"

"Huh?"

"I don't really pay attention either way, but what do . . .
people . . . think?"

"That you're a hot soccer player and you can have any girl you
want?"

"See, this is what I mean when I say gossip, popularity, all of
that shit doesn't matter. There's no truth to it. I mean, don't get
me wrong. I definitely haven't been celibate since I moved to
Sterlingwood . . ."

I make a face. "Marcus, there's really no need to tell me how
much sex you're having."

He rubs his jaw. "I just mean that there's not, like, a string of
girls."

Why are you telling me this? I want to ask.

Instead, I infer, a little bit breathless, "There's *a* girl?"

He stares at me. "Yeah," he says. "I've been trying to get over someone all year."

For a reason I don't understand, my chest gives one quick, slight ache. No, I *do* understand. It's because it's sweet, so unlike everything that comes to mind when I think of Marcus Riddick. How has he turned out to be so different than who I always thought he was? I wonder what kind of girl gets to be the recipient of Marcus's attention, his affection. I wonder why my lungs sting from something that can't be jealousy but feels a little like it.

"Is she from your old school?"

"Hmm? She's . . . yeah, before."

"Oh," I say. Give him a smile. "She's lucky."

Marcus surprises me by standing then. "I should get going. Before your mom gets home." Somehow it is evening again. I spent nearly twenty-four hours in bed.

"How did you . . . why did you come over? You said you were driving past?"

The strangest thing. Marcus Riddick *blushes.* "We didn't dream all weekend," he says. "Not that we have to dream every day, but then you weren't at school and I . . . I started to wonder if something had happened."

"Well, thank you," I say. "I feel so much better. I always . . . I miss my dad a lot when I don't feel well. He always took care of me when I was sick. I got my appendix taken out a few years ago and it literally felt like a weeklong pizza party. My mom doesn't . . . She's not . . . Well, as you can tell, she's the mayor." It's such a stupid comment, but somehow, I think he might understand.

"Yeah," he says.

He pushes his hand through his hair. "It's not a problem," he says, taking a step back and sounding weirdly formal. "Let me know if you need anything else. And you should really see your doctor."

"I will this week," I say.

He nods, turns around, and shuts the door of my room. A few seconds later, I hear the front door close. When I peek out the window, I see his truck backing out of our driveway.

I exhale and sit on my bed.

Marcus Riddick was just in my house. For hours. Making me noodles and cleaning up my pukey trash can.

What. The. Fuck.

When the world becomes weirdly wobbly, I figure it's just more of the same topsy-turvy nonsense of the last day. But then my dresser disappears, my box of books from Dad.

Everything starts to vanish.

And that's how I know I'm entering another dream.

Eighteen

We resurface in Jason's house.

I can tell, because he's the only person I know who has a cinema room. Also, Other Zadie and Jason are making out in the second row.

"Ah, fuck." Marcus reacts like there's hot sauce in his eyes.

"We're horny teenagers. What do you expect from us?" I say, with no real bite in my voice. It's because Marcus has turned his full attention on me—the real me—and looks like he's trying to see through me. I tuck a falling braid back behind my ear and look at anything but him.

"How are you?" he asks, voice gentle.

"Never better!" I say. Somehow it comes out . . . sarcastic?

I try again. "I'm great!" I say, but it sounds too chirpy, insincere. Finally, I drop the facade. "My migraine's gone. Thank you."

I get a Marcus Riddick smirk for my efforts. "No, thank *you*. Now I know your laundry pile is even bigger than mine."

I frown, even though he's kidding. "That's not normally how it is," I say. "It's because I've been sick so often. I do laundry twice a week—once for sheets, once for clothes."

"Sure, Cartwright."

His grin tells me he's toying with me, but I find myself unable to stop defending myself. It's like a disease.

"No, seriously. I'm so good at laundry, sometimes I go over and do Mo's," I say. "But lately the only times I don't have a headache are when we're dreaming. The pain always ends as soon as a dream starts."

Marcus frowns. "What do you mean *always*? Your headaches are bringing on the memories?"

"Well, I've noticed some . . . I'll tell you later," I say, as in front of us, Holden, Bennett, Amber, and Mo suddenly burst into the cinema room. Jason and Zadie pull apart. Mo and Bennett are carrying backpacks, and Amber and Holden have both come bearing trays of food.

I notice Zadie is wearing her favorite green belted wool coat, a sign that it's cold enough for snow outside, that it's officially winter in Sterlingwood.

"Bro, where's everyone else? I thought you said you were having a party," Holden says, going forward and back-thumping Jason.

Jay sighs. "I had strict orders that we were going to have a Not-Party," he says, shooting Other Me an exaggerated sideways glance.

He and Bennett greet each other as Other Zadie says, "Well, don't make me sound like your mother." She's handing out golden headbands with HAPPY NEW YEAR on them.

"Not my mother. Just the old ball and chain," Jason says.

"Jason!" Zadie cries, as Mo says, "Yeah, that's super gross."

Jason holds up his hands, but he's laughing. "I kid. I kid."

In real time, I feel compelled to tell Marcus. "That's the kind of joke Mr. R would make." As a defense of Jason, it falls flat.

"Oh, I know," Marcus says, and I can't tell what he thinks. Whether he's judging his cousin (and uncle) for being sexist or me for tolerating it.

"He really never talks like this," I say, right as Holden turns to

Mo and nods at her. "How's life on the robotics team? That's where you're from, right?" Then he cracks up at his own joke.

Mo gives Zadie a wordless "Is this for real?" look, and Other Zadie pretends to kick Holden. "We're not taking dickish behavior into the New Year," she announces.

Beside me, Marcus snorts.

I look at him, but he's carefully watching my friends.

Ambs, who has been quiet so far, blows a paper horn. "I actually think New Year's is more romantic than Valentine's Day."

"That's a weird take," Jason says.

"I'm a weird gal," Amber says brightly.

"I like any holiday where there's no school," Bennett says.

"I like any holiday where there's food," Holden says.

"I like any holiday where lists are involved," Other Zadie pitches in, and everyone laughs, the atmosphere getting a little warmer.

"It's New Year's Eve," I tell Marcus, stating the obvious.

"No way," he says, sarcastic.

This is . . . not one of my favorite memories. I'm a little surprised that Marcus and I landed here, that the dream gods would send us to this night rather than, say, the night Jason and I exchanged *I love you*s.

"So what's on the agenda for this Not-Party?" Holden asks.

"Scary movies? We are in a freaking cinema," Mo points out.

Jason, never one to let a compliment on his state-of-the-art home theater system slide, says, "Yeah, everything in here is the best on the market right now. The speakers, the seats. The screen is the big thing, though—here, let me show you the picture quality."

Other than soccer, the only thing Jason will geek out over is technology.

In answer to no one's question, he picks up the remote control and points it at the television, and the screensaver image, a ring of blue poppies, disappears from the giant television screen.

"Did you see that?" I ask Marcus. "It was those flowers again."

"Uh, no," Marcus says.

"Some of these movies aren't even officially out yet, but you can see them in insane quality. Whatever you want to watch," Jason is saying. He flicks through a list, calling out some titles.

"I've seen all those," Amber says. Coming from a similar wealth bracket, she's the least impressed by extravagance.

"Does anyone want to just talk?" Zadie offers, her voice pitched high like she's surprising herself just as much as everyone else.

"God, really?" Jason doesn't just seem uninterested; he seems annoyed. But Bennett is on Zadie's side.

"I'm down."

Amber nods. "Yeah, let's do that!"

Holden groans. "I'm feeling the emptiness of the amounts of booze I am not currently drinking."

"Holden, grow up," Mo says. "Let's take a vote."

By a vote of four to two, sitting and chatting wins. A resigned Jason turns off the television and slumps into a theater seat.

When the six of them eventually lower themselves to the ground, passing snacks between them, Marcus gives me an incredulous look. "Cartwright, tell me we're not here to watch these people *talk*," Marcus says. "On New Year's Eve. In a dream world where we can probably fly."

I focus on Other Zadie and Jason and our friends. "Shhh, I'm listening. Maybe there's something Jason or Zadie says that is significant."

Marcus sighs. "Holden's a dumbass, but he might be right just this once."

"Shhh," I say again.

"The rules of the game," Amber says, "are that you can pick one person to direct a question to, and they have to answer with total honesty. Then, after they answer, they ask someone else a question."

Other Zadie claps. "I love this. Our little truth circle."

That night, I remember feeling like everyone could see straight through my attempts to be light and jokey, the attempts I'd been making for the last week. The last few months, actually. Fall, then Thanksgiving, then Christmas, then the prospect of a new year, the first without my father. But from the perspective of the real me, months older, I realize that nobody else can see what Other Zadie is feeling.

"Jason, you start," Zadie says, squeezing his knee next to hers. She sits up straighter, waiting for the game to begin.

Jason sighs. "Okay, my question is for my moronic midfielder. What happened in the Freeland game?'

"What the hell? That's your question?" Holden laughs. The question is a reference to something that happened on the pitch at some point, a reference that only Holden and Jason understand.

The game devolves from there. A series of inane questions about bad hair choices and embarrassing moments and the whole time I watch, I feel the same way I felt the night it was happening: just the tiniest bit devastated.

The six of them could have really talked, told each other the truth. It's not that they don't tell each other the truth usually, but Zadie has the sense that there are always pieces missing when she and her friends talk. Hidden meanings and half-serious jokes, and then there are the things they just don't tell each other.

"What's Zadie thinking?" Marcus asks me.

I hesitate a second, because a question like that would have changed this night for Other Zadie. It's only Marcus, but I take the opportunity to tell him, anyway.

"She feels lonely," I say. "And she misses her dad. She hates that she wants to talk about it so much because bad things happen all the time and it's been half a year, and shouldn't she be back to normal by now? At the start of junior year, I loved talking to Jason because he made me laugh and he was sweet. He cared about all the things I cared about when my dad was alive: school and movies and friends and homework. In the weeks after Dad died, being with Jason made me feel like myself, the version of me from before. We never actually talked about my dad, which was fine. We started hanging out just a few weeks after his death, and I didn't *want* to talk about it. But as time went on, I'd see things that reminded me of Dad, remember things he said and want to share them with Jason or even just with my friends, but for some reason I always felt like I couldn't."

I don't know at what point I switched from talking about Other Zadie—*her*—to talking about me.

"And it's not Jason's fault," I tell Marcus hurriedly. "I know if I brought up my dad, he would listen. My friends would listen. But part of being Zadie, part of being me, is that I don't just fall in a heap and, like, cry. I get shit done. I ran for student council at the worst point in my life. I take care of my mom and never let her down. I'm *good*, you know?"

"Yeah," Marcus says. He's looking at me, but I refuse to turn and meet his gaze.

"I just wish someone—anyone—had been like, 'It's okay to fall apart.' Even if it was a lie. Even if it was just for a few moments."

I feel utterly stupid, blathering on like this.

And this is why I don't like the memory.

The Zadie in front of me is clearly hurting.

She needs something, but I don't know what.

Still, it tells me about Zadie, about me. It doesn't tell me anything about me and Jason.

"Zadie," Marcus says in a soft voice. "It is okay to do whatever you need to when you lose someone you love."

I sniff. "No, it's not, but it's nice when people say it."

I feel Marcus starting to argue, but luckily that overpowering suctioning feeling is starting. We are being pulled out of this memory, out of this picture of Zadie and Jason and their friends. I feel relieved as pieces of Marcus disappear, as pieces of me vanish, one by one. Relieved and confused.

I'm wondering why we were ever here to begin with.

* * *

I'm somber the next day. That lonely feeling of having to keep everything bottled up inside lingers, but it comes with the weirdly grateful realization that having Marcus there made reexperiencing New Year's bearable.

I continue visiting Jason every morning, and later in the week, I finally get an appointment with my doctor for after school.

Dr. Carruthers is an older woman with a thin build and kind eyes, and when I explain to her that I've been getting migraines for a few weeks, she's concerned but in a calm, motherly way.

"My best guess is that it's the whiplash from the accident causing these headaches," she says. "The good news is that there are a couple of different options we can try here."

Dr. Carruthers ends up prescribing a medication that she says is great to take as soon as a migraine attack begins.

When I get home, I'm so lost in my thoughts that, at first, I hardly notice my mother sitting in the living room, frowning and pointing the remote control at the television we never use. When I do notice, I freeze.

"Mom?" My heart plummets because something is wrong. Something has to be wrong.

But when she glances up, she looks normal. Tired, but normal. It's been ages, years, since I saw her sitting in the living room. It had to be even before Dad left, before any of us knew how much life was going to change.

"Oh hey, honey," she says. "Thank goodness. I'm trying to figure out how to watch an old DVD."

"A DVD," I say, because she might as well be telling me she wants to retrieve a dinosaur from before the Ice Age. It's so unlikely and so weird that I'm genuinely scared. "Mom, what's wrong?"

"Nothing, nothing," she says with a little laugh. "There are just some shake-ups happening with the city council, and so I surprisingly have a bit more time on my hands. Something has been bothering me, though, for weeks, so I wanted to confirm with the DVD."

I look at her, then at the TV again. Is this somehow connected to the dream and the TV we didn't watch at Jason's on New Year's?

No, it can't be.

I take the remote from her and switch to the right channel for DVDs.

"The disc is already in there," she says, so I press play, and I feel the world fall out beneath me as I see what DVD it is. My dad is wearing a burgundy suit.

Dad is laughing and mouthing something to someone we can't see until the camera turns and pans to her. Mom is in a strapless white dress with tiny, intricate beading, grinning from ear to ear as she walks toward my father.

"It's your wedding video," I say, hardly able to get the words out over the lump in my throat.

"I don't think I've ever seen it," Mom admits, and I stay quiet instead of telling her how many times I've seen it. How often I used to watch it secretly in the early years, soon after the divorce. Zoom in on Dad's expression when he's watching Mom come up the aisle, freeze it on the moment right before they kiss, the way their eyes twinkle when they turn to face the crowd before they leave the church. Both their arms raised as though they've done something massive, accomplished something, been given some-thing. I used to just stare at the amount of joy in their faces and wonder what it felt like to love somebody that much. Wonder what happens to all that joy and hope when love dies. Wonder what exactly makes one person stop loving the other, and whether it could have been prevented and how. How do you know if the thing you've found is really love, and if it is, how do you not let it die?

"Your dad's sister swears we had this DJ that your dad and I loved there, but I have no memory of that," Mom is explaining as

I hand her the remote again. Instead of skipping to the reception, though, she lets it play from the very start.

I perch on the arm of the chair and watch with her. I'm expecting it to all look different now that I'm older. I'm expecting that knowing how things ended will make it look artificial and fake and temporary, but it doesn't. They look happy. Their joy looks real. The hope is still on their faces.

Mom looks amazing, regal, poised. And Dad. Dad looks like Dad, with a questionable fade (involving an Afro-mohawk situation) that we're still laughing about and pants that are slightly too short. He reads something during the reception that makes Mom cry, in a world before everything about him just made her impatient and sad and disappointed. Somehow, here, they match. They are right for each other and enough for each other.

It hurts to see my dad on-screen again, but I like to believe that he's as happy where he is now as he was on his wedding day. It mattered to him that he was happy, mattered more than what people thought or believed about him.

We sit there for the whole ceremony and then the reception, talking casually about people I recognize and people I don't. I ask questions, Mom reminisces, and for one moment in time, we go back to the past where everything was messy while being good.

I'm feeling content, softer, when I curl up on my bed and open up Instagram a couple of hours later.

And then I see the newest message from the anonymous account: I want my ring back.

Nineteen

The words aren't, technically, a call for my demise and the demise of everyone I love, but they might as well be. They feel like a threat.

The most unnerving part is that literally anybody could be behind the DMs. Which is why I sit down with blank paper and markers and try to recall every odd interaction I've had in the last week. Everyone is a suspect. From the freshman who bumped into me from behind five days ago to Mr. Tan giving me *another* 98, when I can clearly argue for full marks, to Tyler vetoing my graduation speaker ideas to Penny wearing a similar jacket to the one I wore two weeks ago.

I end up with arrows going everywhere, infinite possible candidates for the person targeting me on Instagram.

Truthfully, it's a little ridiculous. And hard to read.

"Okay, new plan," I tell myself as I get up and light a lavender candle. It says on the box it came in that it's supposed to encourage sleep. Or at least, peace and relaxation. Which is probably necessary for dreams.

The dreams have been like a magnifying glass, zooming in on things I never noticed and answering questions I never thought to ask. This last dream was different because there was no one moment or incident that was drawn out, so I have to believe that I was supposed to get something bigger from it. Something less specific, but I have no idea what it was.

Which all comes back to me needing as many dreams as I can get—to clarify things, to answer my original questions, to home in on things I've been ignorant of. I wonder if more dreams don't just have to show me what happened with Jason. Maybe they can show me other things too. Maybe they can lead me to who I should be suspicious of, help me narrow down who might be out for my blood.

I try a bunch of dream-stimulating techniques I find online, including visualization and journaling and yoga. I suddenly can't even nap, as though that's ever been a problem for me.

Finally, after an entire afternoon of trying and failing to force a dream, there's really only one place I can think to go.

Marcus's dad's car shop, The Fix, is on the upper north side of town. It's attached to a single house, three cars lining the front of the shop, three others parked in a line beside the curb.

As I leave my car, dark streaks of grease are like a trail leading me up the long driveway. The air smells of engine oil and cigarette smoke, and rock music is playing in the background. There are leaves almost all colors of the rainbow littered on the ground. I'm wearing a puffer vest because it's been raining the last couple of days. The weather has fully committed to chilly, stopped hopscotching between summer and fall.

I hear tinkering beneath a car deep in the garage; I imagine all of them are in varying states of disrepair. I'm not sure where to go, but then, as if summoned from the belly of a demonic whale, a body slides out from the bottom of the car where all the noise was coming from.

It's Marcus. His hair is tied in a ponytail, and he's wearing a ratty gray T-shirt covered in oil. I expect him to look like a kid playing with toys that are too big for him, but he doesn't. He looks different and serious, older or something.

"Hey," he says, sliding all the way out. He looks just as surprised to see me as I feel to be here.

Before I can answer, the door of a small office with glass windows opens, and out comes Tommy Riddick, Marcus's father. I saw him at the hospital the night of Jason's accident and at the lunch for Jason, but this is the first moment I realize how much older than Jason's dad he looks, despite being the younger of the Brothers Riddick. He must have heard me come in—they must both have heard me come in—because he calls out a "Hello?" as he shuffles out of the office.

"Hi, Mr. Riddick," I say.

Marcus gets up. "Dad, it's okay, I got it."

"Good man," Marcus's dad says, turning around.

Marcus is wiping his hands on a rag, and there's something perplexing about this idea of Marcus as a good son, a hard worker, someone who has been helping to carry the weight of keeping his father's garage open. But also, he seems like more than sleepy Marcus Riddick here. Capable and solid and relaxed. He feels like a hot stranger, and I suddenly wish I'd thought to wear something cuter.

"So, hi," I say turning back to him. "I'm here about the dreams."

"Really? I thought you might be here about *Little Women*," Marcus says with a smirk.

"Oh. I mean, if you wanted to talk about some of the links I sent you . . ."

"I really don't," Marcus says, and he's giving me a strange look.

"Listen," I say finally, because this is more than a little awkward.

"This whole dream thing is obviously a . . . very weird thing that happens."

I have no idea what I'm actually trying to say, and it shows. "I don't know why it happens the way it does, with it always being my memories and . . ."

"Was there a point to this?" Marcus whispers, stepping forward till the tips of our shoes are almost touching. For some reason that I'll never understand, my stomach dips.

You're beautiful as fuck.

"I've never been able to make one happen. Even when I sleep, I have other dreams. Normal dreams, but not like *our* dreams."

"You know, when you phrase it a certain way, Zadie Cartwright, it kind of sounds like you've been dreaming about me," Marcus says, back to being his annoying self.

I roll my eyes. "And let me guess, you . . ." My voice fades as I catch sight of something behind Marcus. "Holy shit, is this one?"

I'm moving past Marcus to look at the palm-sized bird made out of light brown wood. I can tell that it's not totally done, with just the basic bird shape and the head recognizable. There are no wings yet, and I can see the start of a tail but not much else. And already it looks incredible.

Marcus seems embarrassed as he comes to where I'm standing. "I just started this one," he says. He pulls out paper drawings of a bird from a workbench. "This is the template." He puts one of the drawings over the wood so I can see how it's starting to take shape from a two-dimensional drawing to a three-dimensional bird.

"This is so cool," I say, and I'm not sure why I'm whispering. "Can you . . . do a little bit?"

"It's really not impressive. Just something to pass the time," he mumbles. "I just like working with my hands."

But he picks up one of the knives on the bench. He shaves pieces of wood off the body of the bird, carving until it's more rounded. His hands work quickly and easily, and then he holds out the knife to me. "Your turn."

I guffaw. "Yeah, right. I like my fingers, thank you very much."

"It's easy," he says, explaining what a whittling knife is and then showing me more slowly how to carve with it. When he gives me the knife, the handle is warm from his hand. I carefully follow his instructions and am immediately alarmed by how sharp it is.

"Nope," I say, handing it back. "I don't want to ruin your masterpiece."

Marcus grins. "First, not a masterpiece. Second, I have too many of them already. This one can be yours."

"Do you sell them?"

He nods. "The birds are more for me these days. But I do turtles, fish, mice, mini furniture and sell those. It's all just a hobby for now, but we'll see."

I find myself feeling weirdly sad. Wishing I had something I was indisputably great at. Something that could give me even the slightest hint on what to do with my life.

"That is really, really cool, Marcus," I say.

Just like when he first told me about carving, his cheeks are pink, and after a bit, I realize we are just standing there smiling at each other.

"So, the dreams," he says.

"The dreams," I say, remembering what I came for. "I still don't know what happened with Jason *and* I don't know who the Instagram bully is, but I think the dreams could show me both. Which is why I think we should make one happen. A specific one."

Now, he looks at me like I'm crazy. "Damn, Cartwright. I didn't realize that, in addition to making a mean yearbook, you knew how to control REM sleep."

"Somebody has been doing their research."

Marcus smirks.

I sigh. "There has to be a way, right? I mean, there's a science behind everything, and we know it involves me and you and a place and a memory."

Marcus seems to consider this for a moment. Then he looks at me. "Are you thinking what I'm thinking?"

"Maybe," I say. Feeling a tickle of excitement, I add, "Let's say it on the count of three. One. Two. Three . . ."

"Mind melding," I say at the same time Marcus says, "Pot brownies."

"Are you kidding me?" I don't bother to hide my disappointment.

But he maintains his arrogance. "*Mind* melding. That's your brilliant plan?"

"Our minds would be overlapping, sharing thoughts—only this time instead of it happening on its own, we'd *make* it happen," I explain. "I thought we could try to go to this one memory; it's the closest thing to a fight that me and Jason ever got into. You guys had an away game, and I hadn't been able to reach Jason all night. But then there he was on TikTok, doing shots with his boys and these cheerleaders from another school."

Marcus narrows his eyes. "And that's the memory you want to see *because*?"

"Well, it is Jason and me at our most imperfect. Even if we did end up resolving it very maturely," I can't help but add. "There could be something in the memory that shows when things started to fall apart. Plus, if someone does have it out for me, they'd probably be thrilled about me and Jason fighting. Maybe this dream can show me who my haters are. All we need is to get into that specific memory."

"Just get into it," he says, solemn. "Like a cabinet or a bank. An enemy compound. We'll scale the walls. Break in."

"You don't sound like you have a ton of faith in me, Riddick," I say, hands on hips, pretending to be annoyed.

"Oh, I have faith, Cartwight," Marcus deadpans.

I hide my smile. "You should. I have methods. Do you have time now?"

Marcus sighs and makes a big show of checking the clock in the garage, but fifteen minutes later, we are sitting crisscross applesauce on a blanket Marcus pulled out of the back of one of the cars. It covers the dusty, oil-stained floor of The Fix, since Marcus claims to be too filthy to go inside. With our outstretched hands connected and eyes closed tight, we try to think the same thought.

I find myself hyperaware of absolutely everything, from how sweaty my palms are to how taut my skin is against my knuckles to how long his fingers are.

"Zadie," Marcus whispers. "You're stroking my hands."

"Oh my God!" I jump. "Sorry, I was just trying to . . . It's part of the mind-melding process."

"No, I know," Marcus says, with faux seriousness even as my face heats up. "It's one of your methods. You want the digits to really connect, right?" He is trying not to laugh and also clearly doesn't buy my "mind-melding process."

"Just close your eyes," I order as Marcus chuckles and we rejoin hands. I breathe in deep because it's taking all my concentration not to trace the lines across his hands again. It feels comfortable, easy. I can't even begin to understand why.

After more than five minutes of silence and attempting to *meld*, something tells me to peek with my right eye. I'm horrified to see Marcus staring straight at me. "Marcus! Do you not understand the concept of closing your eyes?"

"I was," he insists. "I just needed to scratch my eye."

I shut my own eyes again, trying to set a good precedent, but I can hear the smile in his breath. I feel my cheeks warming at the realization that he's just been staring at me. How *long* has he been staring at me, and what was he thinking? A month ago, it wouldn't have mattered one bit to me. Or, at least, I would have denied that it mattered even an iota. But now, in this upside-down world where he has seen into some of the most special and sacred memories of the past year, it turns out I do care what he thinks.

I wonder if *he* cares what I think.

We are quiet a grand total of about a minute before Marcus speaks again. "Things I did not have on today's bingo card: holding hands with *the* Zadie Cartwright and trying to teleport."

"Shhh."

I swear I hear it again, the smile in his breaths, as I try very, very hard to force us into a dream. But nothing happens. My hope was that, given the synchronicity of our brain waves or whatever, all we had to do was really concentrate and focus on transporting ourselves to the correct time and space.

But alas, we remain in Tommy Riddick's garage.

*　*　*

Fifteen minutes and a Marcus bathroom break (and a Marcus snack break) later, we are inside Marcus's house, the one attached to the garage. It is smaller than I expect, smaller than it looks from the outside, but cozy. With many pictures of Marcus and his sister in various stages of growth and toothlessness, the walls are a warm light blue color. Mom would not say their house looked like a museum. In fact, she'd probably say they had achieved peak attainability. I plop down on the couch of the well-lit living room as Marcus eats a bowl of cereal and checks soccer scores on his phone. He offered me my own bowl and I turned him down.

A few minutes later, while he's upstairs cleaning up, I catch up on socials. Check again if the Instagram bully/Ring Bandit has done or said anything new. They haven't.

"Ready to try again?" I say when Marcus comes back.

I offer my hands out to him, and he takes them, both of us facing each other on the couch.

At exactly that moment, a girlish voice that definitely does not belong to Marcus gasps from across the room.

"What the frig!"

My eyes snap open and land on a girl dressed in pink from head to toe. She has her blond hair pulled up in a perky ponytail and is wearing high-tops. She looks a prime total of nine.

Marcus groans. "Kangaroo. I thought you were at a playdate this afternoon."

"Three things. Stella . . ." she says, each word slow and deliberate, "hasn't picked me up yet." She counts off on her fingers. "I answer only to Joey. And I don't have playdates. I'm ten. We're going to *afternoon tea*."

Ten it is, then.

As the girl's staring continues, I realize I'm still holding hands with Marcus and quickly take my hands back. I give her a little wave, but she just continues to look wide-eyed in my direction.

"Marcus," she says. "What is she *doing* here?"

Joey's expression is a cross between scandalized and awed, which seems a little strange.

I'm not sure she recognizes me, so I say, "I'm Zadie. Marcus and I go to school together."

"And kiss?" Joey asks, completely shameless.

"Sorry?" I almost choke on my saliva.

"Do you go to school together and kiss? Because you kind of look like you'd be kissing if I wasn't here."

I think I'm overheating, but Marcus gets up, goes to put his sister in a headlock. "No, we don't kiss, you rascal."

She grins as he tugs on her ponytail, then remembers herself and bats his hand away.

"I . . ." *have a boyfriend*, I start to say but catch myself. I don't know what I have. "I, um, like your shoes."

In a normal type of family, I would probably know Joey better since she is also Jason's cousin and our town is that small. But it's almost like the Brothers Riddick only remembered they were related when Jason's accident happened.

Joey beams. "Thrifted," she says. "It's the only way to do it."

"The only way to do *what*?" Marcus looks incredulous. "Joe, I think I hear Stella's mom's car. Maybe you should go check?"

But she is already moving toward me, sitting on the arm of the couch. "You know, I kind of already know who you are. You're, like, famous at my school."

I grimace. "I am?"

"Oh yeah," she says. "You were the Grand Supreme spelling champion three times in a row! Plus, you're really pretty, so every time I see you, like that time in Jason's hospital room, I remember. I like your braids. Are you popular in high school?"

I'm not sure how any of those things are related, and I shoot Marcus a look for help. "Thanks, and I guess?"

"Oh, she's popular," Marcus says with a twinkle in his eyes.

"Sweet," she says. "I really need someone to . . ." She trails off as she squints at her phone. Then she tucks it into her pink purse and resumes the conversation. "Sorry, I don't mean to be rude. I'm so glad you're here and you're normal because Marcus is not."

"Here or normal?" I ask, teasing.

"I wish I wasn't here," he says with a half-embarrassed groan.

"I wish he was normal." Marcus's sister sighs deeply. "I've been worried because obviously I'm starting high school, like, tomorrow . . ."

"You are?" I say, trying to do the math. If she's ten . . .

"Okay, not tomorrow, but I have to start planning, you know?" she says solemnly. "I know what happens to kids who aren't popular. They get stuffed in lockers and their head gets flushed down a toilet."

"How many times have I told you that movies are not real life?" Marcus says, but she ignores him.

"I obviously need to be preparing, so I asked Marcus but he said he doesn't know what's cool for girls to wear. If I turned up at school dressed like him, I think I would *die*."

I laugh. She just might be the spunkiest ten-year-old I've ever met.

"Oh, absolutely." I lean forward, enjoying playing along. "The other day he wore a beanie to school."

"No!" she gasps. "I'd die."

We hear the sound of a car pulling up in front of the house.

"You should give me your number so we can touch base," Joey says.

"Touch base?" I say, trying not to laugh. I'm concerned about her cultural references.

"No," Marcus says before either of us can move. "Nope. No exchanging numbers."

"Why?" She sulks. "If this is about my phone bill from last month, I told Dad I was sorry, and he's already punishing me by making me eat a banana every morning."

"No, it's about your incessant need to talk innocent people's ears off."

Joey looks chastened as she heads to the front door.

"Don't worry. We'll keep in touch," I promise her before she leaves.

"Text when you get there safe," Marcus calls out.

"It's five minutes away!" she protests.

"Great. So I'll expect a text in five minutes." Joey glares at her brother. "Four minutes and fifty seconds."

"Aaargh," she says, then squeals as her friend runs at her. Their high-pitched excited voices drift toward us before Joey yells one last "Bye, Marcus!" and then the front door slams shut.

"Wow," I say.

"Obviously, you don't really have to keep in touch," Marcus

says before I have the chance to say anything else. "Thanks for seeming so into everything she was saying."

"I *was* into everything she was saying. She's feisty."

Marcus gives me a wary look, and then he seems to relax. "She has a hard time at school because, as you can tell, she's a little intense, and ten-year-olds are brutal."

Marcus tells me how last year Joey would talk about nothing but horses even though she is allergic to them. How her best friend, Stella, is a self-professed "fashion guru" and how together they're on a mission to spread pink far and wide. Everything about Joey sounds delightful, but especially the way Marcus's face lights up when he talks about her. It reminds me of the Marcus I met last July.

"Dad and I are, like, ogres. Who knows if we're doing or saying any of the right things to her?"

I laugh, but the obvious amount of love Marcus has for his sister makes my heart melt.

"I know I just met her," I say, even though I'm not sure it's my place, "but she honestly seems like she's going to be just fine to me. Which tells me that you and your dad are doing an amazing job with her."

Marcus ducks his head. "Thanks," he says a little shyly. "Should we go back to mind melding?"

"I actually just remembered—there's this one bookstore I forgot to put on your list. My dad was friends with the owner."

Marcus wanders over as I pull up the website on my phone, then draft an email to the owner. His face is inches away from mine, his breath warm. If I leaned just the slightest bit to the left, we would be touching. A slightly different angle, and we would be kissing. The idea is . . . not repulsive, and I immediately feel guilty.

But then the same thought I had when Joey was here hits me: I'm not anyone's girlfriend.

But Marcus, *Zadie?*

He's the worst . . . or so I thought.

"You smell good," he says, voice husky, a second before I can break the spell by saying something stupid.

He's Jason's cousin.

My heart pirouettes in my chest.

"Thanks," I say. "Let's get back to business."

Twenty

"Are you really not going to college?" I ask Marcus from where I'm now sitting on the bench in his garage, watching him work. It's high enough that I can swing my legs off it like a little kid, and it's strangely delightful.

Marcus looks up from where he's leaning over the innards of a car and gives me a wary smile. "Having fun there?"

"You don't even know," I say.

We were in his living room trying to mind meld again after Joey left when Marcus started getting antsy about all the things he wasn't doing. I'd never have put Marcus down as a secret workaholic. I *should* have taken the hint and gone home, but I was actually having fun hanging out with him, so here I am.

"Probably not," he says, in answer to my question about college, and swipes the back of his wrist over a spot on his face.

"But what about soccer?" I ask.

"I know I'm important, Cartwright," he says, "but the sport *will* continue on without me. Unlikely as it seems."

I roll my eyes. "I bet you could get scholarships."

"I'm still figuring it out," Marcus says, with no sense of urgency. "I like making things, working with my hands. Helping my dad out. College-level soccer would probably also be great. And contrary to popular belief, my grades don't suck that badly. I have a lot of options."

As I'm trying to wrap my mind around this, he says, "It's not mandatory, you know. College. Princeton."

I feel a strange tightness in my chest at his words. Most likely because this kind of talk is forbidden in my daily life, in my mind. It takes me back to the night we met, the only time I've ever allowed myself to admit the truth about how and why I chose my future out loud. That it was based on criteria that had nothing to do with me.

It still mortifies me to think I told him that, but I would have answered anything Marcus asked that night. I *did* answer everything Marcus asked.

"Do you know what I liked about you last year?" I ask him, voice soft.

"Like, a body part?"

I sigh. "Can you be serious for one second?"

"I've been told I have a trustworthy face," Marcus says with a grin.

"Yeah, no, that wasn't it," I say. "I liked that you were a stranger."

When I say this, he frowns. "So you would have talked to anyone?"

"Maybe at first," I admit. "But then it seemed like you really wanted to know me."

Sometimes people will ask you about yourself and all they really want to know is who you are on the surface. In high school, it's so often where you fit in the big picture: jock, nerd, valedictorian, president, teacher's pet. But with Marcus, I got the sense that he knew that stuff didn't matter; he didn't just care about the surface-level stuff. He wanted the deep, the significant, the random, the weird. The things that mean you really know a person. That's why he asked so many questions. That's why This or That never went away.

And even though it's been so long since then, everything I told him the July before last never got out. Neither has the Jason thing or the Princeton thing. Marcus is trustworthy.

He's getting the inside look at all my memories, so he better be.

"Of course I wanted to know you," he says softly.

"Can I ask you a question?" I ask. "Why didn't you want me to come to the game?"

"Next question. What else do you have?"

"No, seriously," I say.

He sighs. "Because there was no way we were going to win. And people are used to Jason winning. It wasn't just you I told to stay away."

I don't know if that feels better or worse, hearing that I was among a group of people he didn't want there.

"You were worried about losing?"

"I wasn't worried about losing," he says. "It was about how we were going to lose. Badly. Brutally."

"But you won."

"The universe is a strange place."

"Or," I say, "or you're kind of good at soccer."

"Thanks, but let's not get ahead of ourselves. Jason owns that team, and they carried us to the win."

"What if you had lost?" I ask now.

"Well, that would have been on me."

I frown. "So it's the team if you win and you if you lose."

Marcus shrugs.

"Wow, that is some egomaniac type of stuff," I say.

A dull thumping has just started in my head. I ignore it and keep speaking.

"Seriously though," I continue, "it wouldn't have mattered to me if you guys had lost. I mean, it would have been sad but I'm not going to, like, think less of you if you lose a soccer match."

"That's what you say, but think about if it's really true." I try to do just that—and I don't think it does matter, but maybe there were times I let it seem like the Silvers winning, Jason winning, was the most important thing in the world. Especially when to him it was. "My whole identity in people's eyes is about how inferior my soccer skills are compared to Jason's."

"Because you're Plan B."

I'm only repeating what people call him, but it seems to be the absolute wrong thing to say.

Marcus's body stiffens, his eyes instantly losing their light, and for the first time today I feel like I'm talking to a stranger. But there's a false joviality in his voice. "Or Backup Marcus. Pick your poison."

"You don't have to laugh about it, if you don't think it's funny."

"Oh, I think it's funny. I think it's hilarious."

Something about his belief that he *has* to take the comments makes me feel sad for him. I want to ask more questions, but he says, "Do you know what I liked about you that night? Jason didn't come up once. I can count the number of conversations I've had in this town where Jason didn't come up."

He's right. I didn't even know he was related to Jason when we met.

"When he found out we were moving here, Jay told me in no uncertain terms that he ran this town. He owned it, and there wouldn't be any room for me. I tried to convince my dad to let us stay in California, but he wanted to come back because of his health.

"Meeting you felt like this . . . sign that it would be okay. That I could find a way to belong here."

I'm surprised about the picture he has of Jason in his mind. The Jason I know is tough, sometimes cocky, but would he tell his cousin that there's no space for him in Sterlingwood? I don't think so.

"It must suck to constantly be compared when you both have your own strengths," I say, treading carefully. And it's true. There are things I'm sure I can go to Marcus for that I can't go to Jason for. Conversations I've *had* with Marcus that I would never have with Jason, and it's not because one is better than the other. They're just different.

Marcus looks horrified. "I hope you're not feeling bad for me."

"I'm feeling bad for me. I think the mind melding is starting to work," I say as I massage my temples.

"Why would you say that?" Marcus asks, frowning when I tell him about the headache.

"They seem connected somehow. I'm not totally sure how, but it does seem like every time I get a bad headache, I dream. *We* dream. I went to the doctor a few days ago and got some pills, but I'm waiting till I figure out the Jason thing before I start taking them."

Marcus frowns. "Please tell me you're joking, Zadie."

"It's not like I'm *giving* myself migraines. I just know that . . ."

"And you're getting one now?" he interrupts. "I'm taking you to urgent care."

187 * * *

"Oh, relax," I say. "It's completely fine. I occasionally get migraines. They just might happen more since the accident but . . ."

Marcus walks over and bends so he's looking me right in the eye.

"Zadie, I don't care if you never dream again," Marcus says, no hint of levity in his voice or expression, "but I'm not going to stand by and watch while you mess with your brain."

I give an incredulous laugh, because this is all a little too much now. "Marcus, I'm fine. Worry about your own brain."

I don't know what I'm expecting, but it does not involve Marcus rubbing the back of his neck and saying, "The night Jay broke up with you, I felt so . . . powerless. Like there was nothing I could do to make things better. To make sure . . . everyone was going to be okay."

I frown. "Because of the accident?"

"Uh, yeah," he says. "Because of that. It happened again the day you were sick. And I know you don't want *my* help. I get it. Jason is your person."

The words jolt my chest awake.

I haven't thought about Jason the last five minutes, and I've thought about Jason every hour every day since we started dating.

Does that mean he's not my person anymore?

No. No, I'm not having this conversation with myself. I banish the thought before it takes root. I'm supposed to be fixing the breakup, not asking questions, creating doubts.

Marcus is still talking. ". . . and so if there's a way I can think of to help, I want to."

It's like these two versions of him keep shape-shifting into one another, contradicting one another.

Nobody hides their true self better than Marcus Riddick, and I just don't get why. Why be this half-hearted, careless guy who laughs everything off, when he could be thoughtful, sincere Marcus?

I open my mouth to ask just that, to reprimand him and bring up everything I've been thinking the last year, but he's already speaking.

"Do you need me to beg? Because I'll do it," he says.

"Oh my God, fine," I say, like this is the biggest sacrifice of all time on my part. "I'll go home and take a pill. I should get going, anyway."

"Are you sure you're okay to drive? Let me give you a ride home at least," Marcus says, but I shake my head.

"Nope. It's just a tiny headache. I also think you know too much about my life. Too much ammunition."

Marcus grins, earnest and warm.

"I know too much? How come all I want is to know more?" He says the last part quietly, and I bet if I look hard enough, I'll find something sweet in that comment. Instead, I stick my tongue out at him.

The pain in my head is growing, but I hop off the bench and start out of the garage.

I walk past Marcus's truck, parked on the side of the street. I had to leave my car almost down the block because of all the cars in front of The Fix. I see my white Ford when I reach the end of the driveway, so I turn and wave to Marcus.

He gives me a smile that I feel all the way to my toes.

But when I look up again, my car is gone.

Twenty-One

I'm in a meadow.

A meadow with blue poppies and yellow daffodils and dande-lions.

"Here they are again," I say. I reach for one of the blue flowers. It's soft, slightly wet with the air of spring.

I look around until I find Marcus lying on the grass, hands be-hind his head, feet crossed at the ankles.

"We have got to stop meeting like this," he says, the definition of casual. Serious Worker Marcus is gone and Dopey Marcus is here, but I'm starting to understand that they are just different sides of the same coin. "How's the head?"

"Fine. What's that *noise*?"

I tip my head to the side at the sound of ice-cream-truck music.

"Let's find out," Marcus says, standing and following the sound.

As we get farther and farther down the hill, a full-on fair comes into view. There are merry-go-rounds and clowns on stilts, chil-dren holding bags of cotton candy, all behind a massive gate in a tall chain-link fence.

"Where is this?" Marcus asks.

I stare at the lively mayhem behind the gate, trying to figure out why this suddenly feels very, very familiar, but it's not until we're close enough to read the orange banner with the words WINFIELD CARNIVAL on it that I remember exactly what day this is.

And things just got exponentially better.

"Marcus! I love this place. This is where Jason and I snuck off to one weekend last year." I try to explain it to Marcus as we approach the tail end of a line stretching out from the parking lot.

"Oh my God. We had the best time. Like, one of the best days of our lives."

We'd been together for months then, and Jason had been pretty proud of himself when he'd planned the date. He wouldn't give me any details about where we were going or why, but his Cheshire grin told me he thought it was one of his best ideas.

"I'm practically an expert on date organization," he bragged when I met him at my front door. "Some think it's a hobby, that maybe he's born with it, but, friends, it's a skill. A skill he works very, very hard for."

I laughed as he spoke. "Oh, yeah. And where did you get all this skill from? All the people you dated?"

"See, it might seem that way," Jason had said, eyes twinkling as he led me into his car, "but all of those girls, all of those dates, were just practice for you."

"Aw, I like that you're a giant cheeseball," I teased Jason as he started his car.

"What else do you like about me?" He looked over at me like he was genuinely curious. Like he didn't know. He was clearly fishing for compliments, but I indulged him.

"You're great at soccer. Everyone likes you—like seriously not one person has a bad thing to say about you. It's very annoying."

Jason was biting his lower lip, focusing hard on the road. "What else?"

"What, that's not enough for you?" I joked. I didn't think he

191 * * *

was *actually* insecure, so I didn't pick out my words carefully like I might have otherwise. "I like that you're really going places. Most high school boys are obsessed with the here and now, but you know what really matters. We both do. Oh! And you're a great captain. Leadership skills unmatched."

"A great captain," he repeated. "I guess there's a consensus then. Everyone likes me for the same reason."

"It's called universal appeal," I told him.

I'm practically bouncing on my toes now with anticipation as I try to share the memory with Marcus, but I notice that he isn't even listening. He has stuck his head between the people in front of us, his face uncomfortably close to both of theirs as he tries to read their tickets.

"Marcus!" I hiss. I tug on the back of his shirt. "Do you know what's creepy? People who stand too close in line."

"Relax," he says, all ease. "I was checking what tickets they need to get in. God, I love being invisible."

"It feels wrong to go in without paying," I say. "Or at least waiting in line."

But Marcus is already weaving his way to the front.

"Spare me the lecture, Cartwright. There's no rules in dreams."

I huff. "And you would know because?"

But of course, he's right. The ticketer doesn't blink as we push through the line into the carnival. The security guard does nothing as we walk past him.

It feels like with this many people all clumped together, there should be more bumping elbows and stepping on toes and unreciprocated *excuse mes*, but as always, nobody feels a thing as we walk through them. There are no jolts, no particles clashing. Just me and Marcus, breaking the laws of matter.

It suddenly feels exhilarating, what Marcus said—being totally invisible, immaterial, unseen. I bulldoze right through scores of people, running and skipping and jumping. Euphoric for some reason.

Marcus is grinning when he catches up to me. "Having fun?"

"Have you ever felt like you could do absolutely anything you want and not have a single person judge you? Felt like you don't have to answer to anyone even if you make a mistake or say or do something stupid?"

"I have," Marcus says, because he *doesn't* care what people think.

"I haven't," I admit. "I'm always worried. Worried about doing or saying the wrong thing, seeming stupid, rude, unfriendly, ungrateful. There is always, *always* something to think about."

"It doesn't have to be that way, you know."

I give him a skeptical look.

"Okay, listen, I'm not going to pretend that you can do whatever you want and not have to pay the consequences. That's just unrealistic. And people are going to judge you—that's a fact of life. But you can control how much energy you give their judgment. You can let it affect you, or you can let it roll off you."

"You didn't," I point out. "The day you played the Buffalos."

Marcus sighs. "That's different. A lot of people were counting on me."

My face tells him I'm not buying it.

"Okay, fine. I did care. I didn't want to embarrass myself in front of . . . everyone," Marcus says, cheeks turning pink. *Everyone* sounds suspiciously like *you*. But why does my opinion of him matter at all?

"Oh, look at *this*," Marcus says, breaking our silence and helping himself to some random guy's fries, dipping a couple in a plate of ketchup.

I make a face. "You're going to eat a stranger's food?"

"Pretty much," he says with zero shame. "That okay with you?"

"I might be judging," I tease.

Marcus gives a small smile. "Judge away, Zadie Cartwright."

We walk another few steps and then Marcus is distracted again. "Fuck, why is the food so good in your memories?

"Do you want some fish sticks?" Marcus shouts toward me, closing in on somebody else's food. "These are some good-looking fish sticks."

"No, thank you." I don't hide my repulsion.

He chews with aggression. "It kind of boggles the mind, doesn't it?"

"How you can eat so much of other people's food and not get sick?" I ask.

"I was going to say, I don't get why some things we can, like, manipulate. Like say, food. Game machines. We can touch each other," he says, taking that time to touch my cheek. I freeze at his nearness. He never takes his eyes off me. "And other things," he says quietly, "we just pass through, completely inconsequential."

"I know," I whisper.

"How's your head?" he asks again.

"It's always fine *in* the dreams."

Marcus is frowning. "I really think we should find a way to stop doing this," he says in a soft voice.

I've only just realized how close we're standing, but I don't take a step back. "Doing what?"

"These dreams," he says, gesturing around us. "I don't want you to get hurt."

"I need to find out what happened between Jason and me," I say.

I regret saying his name as soon as I do. It's like turning on the lights in the middle of a dark theater, a blender in a library; it disrupts everything about the moment.

"Yeah," Marcus says. "I guess you do."

We start walking again until I stop at a tent on our right, trying to read the descriptive panel in front of it.

"So what was so great about the last time you were here?" Marcus asks, and there's a new distance in his voice. A cautiousness.

I can't hide the smile in my voice. "Well, over spring break, Jay picked me up in the morning and refused to tell me where we were going. He stopped at a gas station, and we loaded up on junk food, and then we rode in his car for like three hours, listening to country music.

"Finally, we pulled up in this parking lot. It's way in the back outside," I tell him. "I never told Jay, but I was a little bit disappointed that the whole thing had been about getting to a carnival. I mean, carnivals are fun, but they're not, you know, *romantic*.

"But Jason *made* it romantic. We walked in those gates we just came through, and the first thing we did was buy corn dogs." I point out the corn dog stand not far from us.

"I could really use a corn dog right around now," Marcus says. "I should've taken that guy's corn dog."

I ignore him. "Then, we got our faces painted over there. Jason was . . . The lady painted this little sunflower on his face." I look around. "I thought we might have seen them . . . us by now, but maybe we're not coming."

"You and Jay?" Marcus asks, and I nod.

"Want some onion rings?" He raises his voice as I start to walk away from him.

"Gross. Race you to the bumper cars?" I say, then burst into a run as I get deeper into the carnival.

"You sure you're up for that?" Marcus asks, but he's already running straight for me. I look over my shoulder at him, pump my arms and legs even faster, but he's closing in on me. I take a wild right turn and keep sprinting.

I can see the bumper cars up ahead, just a few feet away, when I feel Marcus grab my waist. As I try to wriggle out of his hold, I stumble over my own feet, and we fall in a heap on top of each other.

I'm laughing too hard to breathe and then he's laughing too, and we are a rowdy messy pile on the ground in the middle of a carnival and our faces are dangerously close, our smiles wavering. Marcus moves in even closer, and I start to shut my eyes.

But right before I do, I see them.

"Oh!"

Marcus sits up, gaze following mine all the way to us.

Me and Jason.

Past Me and Past Jason, walking hand in hand into the carnival. We are the quintessential couple. So happy and so in love that we're even swinging our hands between us.

"What we've been waiting for," Marcus says, his voice a whisper.

"Yeah," I say, but my voice is dry, and I have to clench my hands into fists to stop myself from grabbing the front of Marcus's shirt, making him stay exactly where he is. Pressing my lips to his.

The absence of Marcus's body weight feels like an insurmountable loss.

His voice is hoarse as he stands then offers me his hand. "What are we doing, then?"

I take his hand so he can pull me up, and we silently hurry after them.

Twenty-Two

"Yeah, right!" Past Jason is saying. "You were turning green by the end of that ride."

Past Zadie laughs. "*No*, that was you, Mr. I'm Not Scared of Anything Riddick," she says. "You were squeezing my hand so tight, I think a couple of my bones are broken."

Now, they're both laughing.

We're so close we're almost right on top of them, but it still feels like they are an entire world away from us.

"In less than a year, I've discovered three different types of your kryptonite," Other Zadie says smugly.

"Three?" Jason is incredulous. "I can't even think of one!"

Zadie untangles her fingers from his to count them off. "Arcade games slash dancing."

"Okay, true," Jason concedes. "That wasn't my best performance."

"Heights," I whisper dully at the same time as Other Zadie says it to Jason.

"*Heights?*" Jason sounds flummoxed, and for a second it's like he's answering me. Talking back to me, as if we can hear each other. It is a jarring feeling, like speaking to a dead person. "I'm scared of the Big Dipper, not heights. I'm completely fine with heights."

"Sure, Jason," Zadie says.

Beside me, Marcus is dead quiet.

"Okay, what's the third? You said three?" Jason asks.

Zadie stops walking, and so the three of us do too.

"And me," Zadie says with more certainty than she feels. "I'm your kryptonite."

Jason leans down with a smile that takes up his whole face, kisses her on the nose.

"That one," he whispers, "I won't deny."

They make out right there in the middle of the carnival, and for one or two seconds, everyone has to go around them. The kiss is passionate for how public it is, and I feel my heart very literally split in two. How can anyone deny that we were anything but unstoppable together? On the other hand, I feel like Marcus and I shouldn't be here. That we should be somewhere else.

Until someone with the type of booming voice that only a sports coach possesses yells, "Mr. Jason Riddick!"

I groan and cover my eyes. "Oh God, here we go. I can't even watch this."

Before Marcus can suggest that we *shouldn't*, I shush him.

Zadie's the first to jump back, and Jason's eyes have gone wide, a timid expression on his face. "Coach Feathers," he says.

"Who's Coach Feathers?" Marcus asks, frowning.

"You'll see," I say.

Coach Feathers has a full beard sprinkled with white and a head that is almost bald, but not quite. "I thought that was you, dipping into the chocolate milk, but it was hard to tell," he says with a smirk. The words make me flinch even though it's obviously not the first time I'm hearing them.

"What the fuck did he just say?" Marcus says, disbelieving. He's as shocked as Jason and Zadie feel, if their stunned eyes are anything to go by.

It's always like this, a moment when you are least expecting it, when someone says something that pulls the rug out from under you.

"Did he just imply what I think he implied?" Marcus asks me. I nod, trying for no expression, but I'm clenching my fists so hard my nails dig into my palms. For days after this encounter, I would question whether Feathers actually said what I thought he did, whether he meant it the way I thought he did, whether I should have told him how much of an asshole I thought he was, or whether I did the right thing staying quiet.

"How's Sterlingwood?" Coach Feathers asks, patting Jason once on the shoulder, the man's authoritative voice making me feel small, even now that I'm invisible. Even now that he technically has no power over me; he's just a memory.

"Um, good, sir," Jason says.

"And how's that heading technique we talked about?"

"Wait," Marcus says, "why isn't Jay beating his ass? What am I looking at?"

"He can't," I explain, even though I feel warm all over. "It's UMaine's soccer coach."

"Right." Marcus looks furious, and not just at Feathers now but at his cousin, who is saying, "Much better. I'm looking forward to showing you how much it's improved this coming year."

"That's what I like to hear," Feathers says.

"Jason can't say anything," I point out, my voice small. "It would ruin his prospects with—"

"Zadie," Marcus says with the utmost seriousness, "fuck his prospects." He's looking at me like he can't believe what he's witnessing. Feathers pats Jay on the back again, then walks off. As soon as he's gone, Past Jason gives Past Me a guilty look.

"Zad, I'm sorry," he says softly. "I forgot how much of a tool he is."

"That's convenient." Marcus is fuming.

Something tiny in me feels vindicated, seen somehow by Marcus's reaction, even though I'm sure it's easier to be mad in a dream than in real life. It's easier to call someone out for doing the wrong thing than to do the right thing yourself. For all I know, if I'd been at this fair with Marcus and Coach Feathers had made a ridiculous comment, Marcus might have just given me his own apologetic smile.

Somehow, though, I'm not completely sure of that.

Other Zadie waves the whole thing off. "He's not the first or last ignorant person," she says, feigning a smile. She takes Jason's hand again, and we—they—keep walking. In real life, I feel slightly ill as I watch them. Even though it's only been five months since this moment, I am not sure I would react the same way now. Not sure that I would take Jay's hand and pretend everything is okay.

My dad would have made a scene.

Always easygoing and cheerful and fun, unless somebody hurt me or Mom, he would have told Feathers where to shove it, and he would definitely be looking twice at Jason. Not that it's Jason's job to save me, but he could have handled this way better.

Still, it's Mom's voice Other Zadie is hearing when she plays it off—Mom's voice I typically hear in moments like these. *Keep smiling. Don't give them something to talk about.*

Softer eyes and kinder smiles and fewer whispers.

For Other Zadie and Jason, there is a notable damper on everything, like looking at the world under an overcast sky compared with a bright sunny sky. But they try to make the best of it.

They go back the way we came, to the bumper cars. After playing on them for a while, they attempt a video game. They take photos with a clown on stilts, and Jason even convinces one of them to let him try on their stilts. To disastrous effect. Other Zadie takes pictures of all of it, and eventually they're laughing hard, holding the stitches in their sides. I smile too as I watch, tell myself with every second that passes: you and Jason. This is what makes sense.

When they get back down to the ground from their last ride, it's sunset, everything a reddish orange as it burns up the sky.

"I'll be right back," Zadie tells Jason before she goes to the bathroom.

"Hold on," he says, kissing her softly first. "*Now* you can go."

She heads off, eyes twinkling, smile big.

"Who do we follow? Him or her?" I ask Marcus, mood still dampened as Zadie gets farther and farther from us.

"Listen, Cartwright," Marcus says, and I can tell he's trying to put the joviality back into our day. "I know you don't want to miss a thing, but there are laws against following someone to the bathroom."

I give a strained laugh, focusing on Jason, who is reading a message on his phone. I get close, then even closer, and all I can make out is Monique's name. Why were Jay and Mo texting? Before I can read what the actual text says, though, Jason turns off his screen and slips his phone into his pocket.

Just then, I remember that this memory takes place in April, and Past Jay is going to decorate Past Zadie's locker with flowers in a couple of weeks with Mo's help.

"Hey," Jay says, stopping at the stall just a few feet away. There are bears of all shapes and sizes in the stall and a plastic bow and arrow to shoot the one you want. "How much is the big one?"

The stall worker looks a couple of years younger than Jason, so he's probably a freshman or so. "The big one?" the boy asks in a bored, nasal voice.

"The biggest one," Jason amends.

"They're not for sale. You *play* for them."

"Okay, how's fifty bucks?"

"You want fifty turns at shooting?" the boy asks, sliding Jason a set of about ten arrows. "Have at it."

"No, man," Jason says. "I think you're misunderstanding me. I don't want to play. I want the really big one for my girlfriend."

"This is sweet, right?" I say, getting a little more into this.

"It is," Marcus says.

"I believe I said it's not for sale," the boy says.

Jason looks around the corner to make sure Zadie isn't back yet and turns again to Stall Boy. "Listen, man, one hundred bucks." He puts down a fresh bill. "We'll just say I won it."

Stall Boy takes the hundred bucks, holding it up to the light as if testing its validity. "All right," he finally agrees. "Congratulations, *man*, that was a great shot." He hands Jason a bear that is almost as big as him over the counter. But it's not Zadie who comes up to Jason—it's a curvy brunette girl with makeup and skin that is, literally, without flaws.

"Aw," she says, taking the bear's paw. "Is this for me?" She bats long eyelashes at Jason.

"And who are you?" he asks, immediately falling into Hot, Confident Soccer Captain mode.

She stands much closer than she has to. "Alana Duncan."

"What the hell?" I whisper. This is also new for me.

"Uh, wow," Marcus says, seemingly waking up for the first time in minutes. I try not to let it irk me, the fact that Marcus is clearly attracted to this very attractive girl, who if I didn't know better, I would say is trying to hit on my boyfriend.

"Who are *you*?" she asks, all bouncy and casually gorgeous.

"Jason Riddick."

She cocks her head to the side. "Your name sounds familiar. Do I know you?" Jason doesn't hide the fact that he's pleased about this. He's not hiding the fact that he's pleased by any of it. And I'm speechless watching the interaction. I've seen Jason with dozens of girls in my presence. But right now, he is not reacting with the level of indifference that has always made me feel safe, made me feel like I didn't have to compete with every girl on the planet.

"Maybe you do," he says, with those dimples that very rarely come out. "Though I'd remember you if we'd met."

"No, seriously, why does your name sound so familiar?" she asks. If I had to bet, I'd say she's never heard of him in her life.

"Maybe we should go," Marcus says, and I almost consider agreeing. I don't want to watch my boyfriend flirting with some girl while I'm mere yards away. But my feet are rooted in place, a dozen branches starting to stem out from them. I can't just go now, after all these weeks of wanting answers.

"I play soccer," Jason says matter-of-factly. "That's probably it."

The girl twirls one of her curls with her hand, a signature move from all the movie versions of Hot Girl Flirting. "I like soccer players," she says. "My ex-boyfriend played soccer."

Jason grins. "Your ex, huh?" He leans toward her, drops his voice a little lower. "Is that your subtle way of telling me you're single?"

I'm stunned by how good Jason is at this. He is effortlessly charming. Having experienced it myself, I know flirting comes easily to Jason. Last September, even in the worst season of my life, I noticed him. Or rather, he noticed me. He was warm and comforting and funny when those were exactly the things I needed.

The girl beams. "So what if it is?"

"Listen," Marcus starts to say, touching my shoulder. "We both know Jay is a flirt. I really don't think—"

"Marcus, just leave it." I don't snap when I say it, but it still feels harsh in the air.

Marcus clears his throat. "Yep. Sure."

"Noted," Jay says now, "but I have a girlfriend."

The resignation he says it with is slight, but it still hurts. It feels like a slap in the face.

"I don't see her anywhere," the girl says, taking a step even closer to Jason.

He laughs and glances back toward where I've gone, probably realizing I'll be back any second. "You're kind of a troublemaker, aren't you?"

She smiles and finally, finally takes a step back. "If you're sure about that girlfriend, at least give me something to remember you by."

For a second, I'm terrified it's going to be a kiss, and my heart starts beating impossibly fast. But the girl says, "I want the bear, but I'll settle for your number."

Jason chuckles, shakes his head. "It's like that, huh?"

He glances over his shoulder once more before reciting the number I know by heart. The girl puts it in her phone, and then Jason's phone vibrates loudly. He pulls it out and reads the screen.

"Nice to meet you too, Alana Duncan."

She gives him one more flirtatious smile, then she turns around and is gone.

Just in time for Other Zadie to wander back. The radiance she always has in these dreams is dulled. It is my worst nightmare: I look somehow . . . insufficient. Not bubbly or cute or anything enough.

"Oh no, what did I miss? The lines were endless," Zadie says, and I can see her eye makeup is less smudged, a new layer of lipstick applied. It feels like she's been gone an eternity, but it probably hasn't been up to five minutes.

"Not much," Jason says modestly as he hands the bear over to her. "I just won this." It's taller than Zadie. She *aww*s and leans forward to kiss him, and I feel like the dumbest person on the planet. Not only did Jason just lie to me, but he had a full-on reciprocal flirting match with a really pretty stranger. He acted like what Coach Feathers said was completely fine. And here is Past Zadie feeling bright and confident, lucky to be with him.

"I can't keep watching," I murmur, ready to turn my back on the two of them and wander away. Something stops me, though.

A song is playing. It's "Everyday People" by Sly and the Family

Stone, and it instantly sends me back to that memory of running through the supermarket with Dad. I hadn't even known there was a song attached to that memory, but the connection is so clear in my head that I'm winded. A memory is so much more than a picture in our minds.

Past Zadie freezes for a second at the song, but then she dismisses it. Doesn't make the link in her mind.

But I do. I know this song.

It is suddenly so overwhelming. Coach Feathers, the ways Jason has let me down today, the grief.

I feel a hand on my shoulder.

"My dad," I whisper, and Marcus finds my hand and squeezes.

I'm feeling so many things at once.

I want to go back to that afternoon. To the fun and lightness that I would only ever experience before Dad was gone. I want to choose not to leave him in the canned food aisle, but I still feel the judgment of other eyes.

I feel the utter shame of Jason lying to me, giving some girl his number as he organizes date after date with me.

"Maybe it's her," I whisper to Marcus, and even without context, even without explaining what I'm talking about, I know he understands. We have been through so many memories and dreams together. "Or me, I guess. It's me."

Somehow, no matter how hard I've tried to be good and attractive and smart and funny, to keep it tidy, I have failed. I am not enough.

Marcus curses. "It's not you," he says. "This is all him. It's all Jason."

I feel desperately sad, and then Marcus reaches out and pulls me to himself. He smells clean and cottony. I feel safe in Marcus's arms, and I'd like to stay there for hours, just standing with him, having him hold me.

But as usual, the dream gods have their own plans, and even right there in each other's arms, Marcus and I start losing each other. His face blurs, his torso becomes air. Over my shoulder, Jason and the other Zadie are walking, leaving through the gate they came in from, while Marcus and I are disappearing, fighting an unseeable force, being sucked into the tornado of the real world.

Twenty-Three

The text.

It takes on a whole new meaning now.

That's my ring, Zadie.

On the night he broke up with me, Jason swore that there was nobody else. But what if he lied and he really gave the ring I've been wearing to someone else?

I'm so uninterested in getting up the next morning. In fact, I probably *wouldn't* get up at all if there wasn't someone on top of me. Actually, physically on top of me.

"What the hell?" My words come out muffled as I push the log of weight off me and sit up.

Mo bursts out laughing as she and Ambs end up in a heap on the ground.

"Aw, I told you it was too mean," Amber says, standing up and throwing her arms around me.

"Your mom let us up," Mo explains. "We were going to let you sleep, but then we thought *nah*."

"You did look super serene, though," Amber says.

"Really? Because I was having the worst fucking night," I say, wiping the sleep from my eyes. Both my friends stare wide-eyed at my language.

"Well, it *was*," I insist.

"Was it a bad dream?" Amber sits on the edge of my bed and

takes my hand in hers as Mo goes over to my closet and rifles through it.

"Something like that."

Ambs squeezes my hand. "Do you want to talk about it?"

"Not really," I say.

"Well, we're going to Tanner's to drown our sorrows in pancakes and Canadian maple syrup," Mo announces. "Do you want to, like, wash your face? Or is dry drool your new look?"

I sigh, pull myself up, and quietly start putting an outfit together. There doesn't seem to be a need for an open secret today. My misery is written all over my face, and I can't hide it no matter what I wear.

Behind me, Amber clears her throat, and I turn to face her. "So, um, I have news," she says.

Mo's look says, "Please don't let it be Talon-related."

"I applied to UMaine," Amber says.

Mo and I stare at her, dumbfounded.

"But you're going to New York," I point out.

"Well, maybe not," she says, tucking a strand of hair behind her ear. "I always thought I would be dying to leave, but I don't know . . . now I think I might want to stay."

"Please tell me this isn't about Talon," Mo says, voicing my exact thoughts.

Amber blushes, but she says, "Talon's not going to UMaine. I just don't want to leave my people."

"Ambs, that's great," I say, reaching over to hug her, even as tears prick the back of my eyes. Days ago, Mo was the odd one out, the one getting left behind, and now I'm the only one who's leaving. If I was looking forward to going, actually excited about Princeton or wherever, then it would be fine. But I'm not.

* * * 210

"Sorry," Ambs says, looking guilty.

"Don't be silly. Wherever you go, you're going to kill it. And they'll be lucky to have you," I say.

Mo and Ambs hug, and I head to the bathroom. Alone, I stare at my own face in the mirror and try not to cry. The first term of senior year was not supposed to be this awful. I've even kind of slacked off on documenting it for the yearbook.

Jason is in a coma.

I haven't been able to bring myself to continue my Princeton application.

And now, worst of all, Jason was most likely cheating on me.

My phone vibrates with a text as I'm getting dressed.

My heart does a weird stutter when I see that it's from Marcus. Marcus, who saw my humiliation in our dream. Who has seen *all* my humiliation, including the fawning over Jason, the clueless faith, the undue optimism.

Marcus has drawn a sketch of two Smurfs. A Smurf and Smurfette, really. At Winfield Carnival.

At first, I think it's me and Jason, but on closer look—I see my braids instead of Past Zadie's bun. I see Marcus's long hair.

It's us, him and me.

And the "him" Smurf has a thought bubble that says *Wow, we're kind of hot for Smurfs.*

I smile and text back.

Me: Stop objectifying Smurfs.

He texts back, How are you?

Me: I feel like death.

Marcus: . . .

Marcus: . . .

Finally, he says, Next time I see you, can I give you a hug?

I can't help another little smile.

Me: In dreamland?

Marcus: Or in real life . . .

I bite my lower lip.

Me: Okay.

And suddenly I'm looking forward to the next time I see Marcus. But only because when he hugged me last dream, it felt so good. He's a good hugger. That's all there is to it.

I tuck my phone into the pocket of my leggings and brush my teeth.

It's not long before her name comes back into my mind again, hovering like the melody of a catchy pop song.

Alana Duncan.

It sticks in my head for the whole morning, and by the time we're halfway through brunch, everything I've convinced myself about being evolved and mature enough to not stalk a stranger has dissolved.

"I think Jason was cheating on me," I blurt out to my friends. I touch my chest as I say it, because it hurts like hell to admit it.

Mo has been telling us about the bug she's fixing on her Zebra app, but she immediately pivots.

"I'm going to kill him," she says, and it's like she doesn't even need the details. I see a version of the past year where she's been waiting for him to fuck up, and now he has.

"Are you sure?" Amber asks.

"I don't trust him," I say, and it feels like a giant release after all this time. To simply tell the truth.

I know this is as good a chance as any to tell them about the dumping, the dreams, but at this point things have gotten so far that I don't think I can. Besides, Jason cheating on me would be mostly a Jay-is-a-douche kind of problem, mostly his fault, rather than a situation where I've lied to them for more than a month. I'm sure I'll tell them the whole truth at some point. Just not *now*.

"With who?" Amber asks.

"Yeah, how did you find out? Piece of shit." Mo mutters the last part under her breath.

"It's complicated," I say, "but basically there's a girl named Alana Duncan who looks like a brunette Sabrina Carpenter, and I found her number in his phone."

"Could it be a mistake? Maybe he has the girl's number for another reason?" Amber says, forever cautious to take up arms against someone she likes.

"They're into each other. Just trust me on this," I say.

"I believe you," Amber says, and I want to kiss her for choosing my side, always. "What do you want to do? I mean, have you looked up her socials?"

"Not yet," I admit.

"Okay, but how aggressively stupid can one guy be?" Mo asks, stealing a bit of bacon from my plate. "I told you it was weird how he was suddenly into you, didn't I? As if he didn't know you all his life . . ."

Amber shuts it right down. "Mo, seriously. More support. Less . . . whatever it is you're doing."

They glare at each other. Mo relents. "Fine. What's her name again?"

I repeat her name, and all three of us search for her.

"I have her Instagram," I say, and both of them lean in to look at my phone.

"She's hot," Amber says, stating the obvious.

"Oh my God, her dog," Mo coos. "Can the two cheaters eff off to an island and give us the cute dog?"

Amber smacks her, and Mo giggles.

"She has so many friends," I say, looking at the vast array of faces on her grid.

Alana hasn't updated her Instagram in over a year, but there are a few pertinent things we learn about her. She's great at golf. She's great at playing the bass. She's older than us—in her first year of college. And she has three older brothers.

"God, it's like a page of testimonials," I say, looking at her tagged photos.

> **@northernAlana** You are the funniest, sweetest, most loyal friend I have ever had. You have been there for me ALL our lives, through thin and thicc (iykyk, hahaha). Even tho we don't share blood, you are my SISTER for life and the kindest soul I have been priviliged to know and I miss you now that we're on separate coasts.

"Separate coasts?" Mo says. "Oh, it looks like she moved out west for school."

After some back and forth, we decide I should DM Alana and send this message: Hey Alana, I wanted to ask a couple of questions about someone you know. Do you have time to chat?

She doesn't respond throughout our brunch, and by the end of the day, there's still no reply.

The next several days are late October gloomy, cold and rainy.

There's nothing from Alana, and it begins to occur to me that she might never respond. And even if she does, who knows if she'll tell the truth? Who knows if she's the only girl out there? Jason didn't exactly look new to the whole flirting-while-having-a-girlfriend deal. Until he wakes up, I might never be able to answer the question of whether Jason really has been cheating on me. Plus, all my original questions still remain: whether Jason loves me, why he broke up with me, what I'm supposed to do until he wakes up.

I haven't been to see Jason since Friday morning, and I don't know if I can go back.

In the quiet of my room and with no one here to notice, I let myself cry over everything that has happened the past few days. Things weren't supposed to be like this. They weren't supposed to be this uncertain or this painful.

Crying has made a brand-new headache start to blossom, a kind of faraway ringing in my head. I reach for my nightstand and take one of the pills the doctor prescribed, but it doesn't make the ache disappear. It just makes me feel different, like there's electricity in my head. The door to my room is gone, a distinct rectangular hole in the world, but it doesn't last. It's like a dream is threatening to start, but something is stopping it from happening.

Maybe it's the medication.

Finally, the dream gods win out, and it happens the way I'm used to: My walls collapse, and the world restarts.

Twenty-Four

In tonight's dream, we're indoors. The space is familiar—a dimly lit house with tall ceilings and widely spaced walls, shiny marble floors, all of it with its own great big pulse. Everything is out of balance for a second or two, and I'm unsteady, nervous, until I locate Marcus just a few feet away from me. I grab for his hand, and he lets me, as a synth-pop song plays loud enough to fill an arena. Kids our age are grinding and drinking, talking and making out to its soundtrack.

Marcus leads me through the party now, our fingers intertwined. When I was a kid, my dad read me a book about being "snug as a bug in a rug," and that's how my hand feels now. Snug, warm, enclosed by Marcus's much bigger hand. It's a weird thought to have about Marcus, but not as weird as the agreement we made that we'd hug tonight.

Marcus is mouthing along to the music as he checks something on his phone.

"Where are we?" I shout to be heard over the music. I could swear I've been here before. Something about the cabinets—the color of the wood, the host of those same purple-blue poppies on the dining table, and even the giant painting of a safari on the far side of the room.

Marcus leans in closer. "What?" he yells.

"Where *are* we?" I say, each word accompanied by its own feeble gesture.

Marcus is too busy bopping his head to be of any help. He shrugs.

"Let's try and figure it out!" I shout.

"Maybe?" he yells back, clearly not on the same wavelength. This is officially the most distracted I've ever seen Marcus. Probably because this party with its chaotic energy, girls in skintight clothes, and sweaty packed bodies is exactly the scene I picture him thriving in. Grateful for our entangled hands, I take the lead now, dragging him toward the entrance of the room.

And then it hits me.

"Penny!" I shout.

Marcus just looks at me.

"Penelope Miller's house! That's where we are!" I'm ecstatic to have figured it out. And right on cue, as if to verify my theory, Penny comes stumbling out of the kitchen in a leather miniskirt, crop top, and tall boots. She's laughing with a guy I don't know.

This is the party Penny threw in the summer last year. The party I met Marcus at. But the dreams had been becoming more recent, and this is going way back to the start. Plus, there's something odd about the house. The light of the room or the proportions or something is off. It doesn't look right.

We keep walking around, pointing out kids from the soccer team and yearbook and student council and dance. The people don't look quite right either, as if we're peering through glasses with the wrong prescription. My head is beginning to pound in direct opposition to the music, a thunderclap of discomfort, as I tug Marcus toward a long hallway.

Boom-BOOM. Boom-BOOM. BOOM, BOOM, BOOM.

I push into the first room on the right, seeking relief. I never get headaches in the dreams.

"Oh my God!"

Two people are standing in a corner, making out. Like *aggressively* making out. The girl I recognize as Jazz King. The guy's back is to me, but I don't think anything of it. I'm about to go out and shut the door when something stops me. A low throaty laugh I recognize.

Boom-BOOM. Boom-BOOM. BOOM, BOOM, BOOM.

I'm trying to place the voice when an identical one cuts into my thoughts, only slightly less sleepy and breathy. "I really think we should—" Marcus whispers, trying to lead us out of the room. I snap to attention.

"It's you! This is *your* dream!" I say, smacking his chest hard. The shaggy-haired guy making out with Jazz is Marcus.

"Oh. No way," he says with zero conviction. He gives a half-hearted chuckle. "That explains a lot."

"You're such a liar," I say, because he clearly knew from the minute we got here where in space and time we were. "Ugh, of *course*, this is your dream. Typical."

"Now, Cartwright, did I judge any of those dreams where you were slobbering all over my cousin?" he says, rubbing the spot on his chest where I hit him. It occurs to me that if this is Penny's party on the night I met Marcus, then it's early on that night—which is why there is no sign of me or my friends. We aren't here yet.

"You are such a good kisser?" Jazz King says, or rather, *asks* Marcus.

He laughs. "I'm a man of many talents."

"I'm double-jointed?" Jazz says. "Wanna see?"

"Nope, nope, not in this lifetime," I say, exiting as fast as I can.

We reverse through a hallway and try to find another room to go into, but everywhere is too full and too loud.

Boom-BOOM. Boom-BOOM. BOOM, BOOM, BOOM.

Before I can head for the front door, though, I spot someone wearing a familiar cropped knitted vest, leaving one of the rooms.

"It's Mo!" I point out to Marcus. Even though she can't see or hear me, I'm glad to see her. A friendly face among my wasted classmates. As usual, Mo seems completely sober. But she's acting strange, adjusting her top and pulling the door tightly shut behind her like she doesn't want whatever is in there to get out.

It hits me in that moment. Our suspicions have been correct. Mo's Zebra app is, at least, part human. As in, there's someone she's been hiding.

"Ohhh."

"Who's she with?" Marcus asks, at the same time I freeze.

"Hold on," I say. "She told me she wasn't allowed to come to this party."

Marcus looks at me, so I continue. "Ambs and I are going to show up later, but Mo never comes out tonight because her grandparents didn't let her. So how is . . . she . . ."

I'm already looking at the door she shut before it even starts to swing open. I'm anticipating the person coming out of the room, the person who has been in there with Mo.

Jason.

Jason has been in there with Mo.

He comes out of the room and immediately slams into Josh Faraday.

"Yo, dude! Where you been?" Josh asks as Jason distractedly

slaps his back. "What have you been doing, or should I say *who* have you . . ."

Jason smacks the back of Josh's head, but they're both laughing. "Go to hell."

I bend to the ground because the world does not feel steady.

"Zadie," Marcus says, dropping down beside me, but I can't look at him. Can't talk. Can't breathe.

I spring up from the ground, race through the hallway and through the kitchen and out the front door.

Relief from the noise and the putrid air and the general *too much*ness of everything floods me as I slump onto the concrete and gasp desperately for oxygen. More oxygen. *More.*

I face away from the streetlights as I collapse in a heap on the steps and knead my temples with my thumbs. This is the first time a migraine has really followed me into the dream like this.

"What do you need me to do?" Marcus asks, voice a whisper. "Do you need water? Do you need . . . What do you need?"

"Mo and Jason" is all I can say. "That's what all this leads to."

A hundred pieces fall together in my mind. Mo never quite trusting Jason. Her fury when we thought he was cheating with Alana. Mo having a mystery guy. Maybe Mo is the girl Jason really bought this ring for.

Marcus helps me up then, pulls me into a ferocious hug. "Come here," he whispers into my hair. I am solid at first, resistant, and then I melt into it.

"She's my best friend. This doesn't make any sense."

My head is resting on his chest. I can hear his heartbeat. It's fast and choppy and loud. It's not like Jason's. Jason's heart is rhythmic and steady, but Marcus's arms feel safe.

I nuzzle even closer to him, enjoying the feel of him, the roughness of his unshaven face on my cheek, the warmth radiating off him.

It has always been Jason for me. From the very beginning, even during these dreams where I've seen thing after thing that makes me question him. I haven't wavered. But now I realize it doesn't have to be this way. It never had to be this way. I am so tired of it being this way.

"Marcus."

He looks down at me at the exact moment I stand on my tiptoes and kiss him.

He's completely not expecting it. "Fuck," he says, stumbling backward, but a second later, he kisses me back, gruff and hungry and impatient.

Marcus kisses like he has everything to lose. As with so much else, he is not disciplined or strategic, and his hand trembles as it cradles my jaw.

"Zadie."

The kiss is messy and full of wanting and confusion. It is the most honest kiss I've ever gotten or given.

"Not like this," Marcus whispers even as he keeps kissing me, our mouths roaming and incautious.

"Mmm," I respond.

I wrap my arms around him more fully, slipping my hands under his coat.

"Zadie." He takes a step back. *Fuck.*

He pushes a hand through his hair. "Not like this."

I blink as I come back to reality, like I'm squinting against sunlight. "Like what?"

221 ⋆ ⋆ ⋆

"Not when Mo and Jason and . . ."

"It doesn't matter," I say, reaching for the collar of his shirt again. "I don't care."

"You *do* care," Marcus says, and all of a sudden he is angry. "Who am I to you?"

I frown. "What?"

"Me. Who am I to you?"

"Marcus Riddick?" I say. "Don't be weird."

"And who is that? Who is Marcus Riddick?"

I search for words, unable to understand why we stopped kissing for this. "Soccer player. You read books and carve birds. And, I don't know, you're Jason's cousin . . ."

"That's right. I'm Jason's cousin. You're kissing *me*, but how do I know it's not because you can't have him? Tell me I'm not a stand-in, a backup plan."

I stare at him and open my mouth to speak, but no sound comes out.

The disappointment in Marcus's face is devastating, and I start to argue. "No, this isn't just about Jason. I like you. I liked you first."

But Marcus looks at me like he can't hear me.

And then after a second, I realize it's because he can't.

There's a blurry haze surrounding him, keeping him separate from me. Because soon we're dissolving, both of us breaking into less and less until there's nothing left of either of us.

But instead of waking up in my room, in my bed, I'm in a large room with fluorescent lights and lockers everywhere. In another memory. And Marcus is still by my side.

Two dreams in a row—this has never happened before.

Is this another side effect of the medication?

I don't know and I don't find out, because by this point, *I'm* angry. "Why does everything have to be a pissing contest between you and Jason? Seriously. Maybe I just like you. Has it occurred to you that that's a possibility? That I just like you?"

"If you liked me, why are you dating my cousin?"

"Because your cousin asked me out?" I say. "Because he didn't just never talk to me again as soon as he moved to my school. He didn't avoid me in the halls and act weird around me until I started hearing that he didn't like me. So, *yeah*, I fell in love with Jason. Sue me."

Marcus shakes his head. "Come on."

"Come on, *what*?" I ask, fired up.

"You didn't fall in love with Jason. You chose him because he was safe. You chose him for the same reason you choose everything else: because it's good, it's what you're *supposed* to like."

I am furious. Livid.

So furious and so livid that I shove Marcus hard in the chest.

To my annoyance, he doesn't budge. And right then, the smell of dirty socks and mildew becomes impossible to ignore.

"Oh, Jesus." I pull my shirt over my nose.

I realize we are in the boys' locker room at school. In this memory, Marcus and Jason are talking, surrounded by other boys in various states of undress.

"Are you really going to tell me . . ." Marcus blinks. Seems to realize where we are now too.

"Oh, come on!" he shouts up at the sky. Except because we're indoors, he's shouting at the ceiling. "Hilarious. Really hilarious."

"What?" I ask.

"Nothing, but we don't need to watch this," he says, taking me by the shoulders and trying to guide me out of the locker room. I shrug him off.

"I want to see."

"Of course you want to see. There's nothing to see."

Except, clearly, there is. Because Past Jason and Past Marcus are sitting down on opposite sides of a bench. Jason and Marcus are both a year younger. I can tell because Marcus's hair is slightly shorter, like it was when I first met him. Jason, meanwhile, hadn't yet gotten on the protein kick that would make him even bigger than he is in this dream.

As we watch, Jason whacks some kid walking by with a towel.

"Ouch!" the kid says at the same time I, in this future moment, flinch too. In front of us, Past Marcus is starting to get dressed. "Hey, do any of you know Zadie Cartwright? She's kinda cute."

My eyebrows shoot up. "You thought I was cute?"

"No, I thought you were incredible," Marcus says, still annoyed. "And funny. And smart. And a lot of other things."

Against all odds, my anger begins to fade. The girl Marcus said he's been trying to get over all year . . . could it be . . . am I her? "But you never asked me out," I say quietly. "And you were such a jerk when school started."

Marcus sighs. "Just watch," he says.

"Oh no, no, no," Jason says, standing too now. He hooks an arm around his cousin's neck. "Stay far away from that one. Trust me, we've been in the same classes forever, and she wants a Ken doll."

I open my mouth in disbelief. I've never heard Jason talk about me like this before.

Young Marcus laughs uncertainly. "A Ken doll?"

Jason nods. "Four-point-oh GPA, no personality, no sense of humor, and no balls."

Several of the guys who are overhearing laugh.

I am shocked.

Real-life Marcus opens his mouth like he wants to say something, but then doesn't.

"So, you?" Young Marcus says, making a belated joke.

Jason punches him in the ribs, but it's good-naturedly. I think.

"You're not her type. Let it go."

"Wow," I say, more stunned even than hurt. Where the hell is this Jason coming from? I feel like there's so much I never knew about the boy I dated, the boy I loved. "So you listened? He told you I sucked and you just took him at his word?"

"Well, *no*, I was trying to figure out what was what, and next thing I know, the prick is dating you."

"So then you start insulting me."

Marcus sighs. "I never insulted you. But I was angry. I was angry with him, hence why I said you were out of his league, and angry with myself for listening to him for those two weeks. Giving him time to make his move."

Already, we are melting out of that dream. Body parts disappearing, the magnetic pulling feeling of being yanked out of a force field. It is disorienting and happening too quickly to stop. But instead of waking up, we find ourselves in another memory.

We are going through Marcus's dreams lightning-fast, and I can't figure out why.

In this memory, Marcus and I are outside now, on the track field behind our school.

Before either of us can speak a word, three people appear. Past Marcus, Past Jason, and Past Jason's dad. It's early morning in the dream, only just sunrise. There are patches of grass with morning dew that feels like an exhale and flowers, purple-blue poppies, the color of daydreams.

"Oh shit," Marcus mumbles, clearly realizing what memory we're in.

"What?" I ask. My voice is hoarse from the argument, and I look between the Marcus beside me and the Marcus on the field. Both Past Jay and Past Marcus are in sweaty gym clothes, working out as Jay's dad coaches them through reps of push-ups and sit-ups and running up and down the bleachers.

"Come on, Marc!" Jay's dad yells. "You've got to pick up that pace. Is that the best you got? That's it? That's how much you want first string? Jay is blowing you out the water. Leaving you behind."

"Jay is welcome to go," Past Marcus grumbles under his breath.

"What's happening here?" I ask Marcus. The air is end-of-summer crisp, and I wrap my arms around myself.

The real Marcus mumbles something indecipherable.

"I asked you something!" I say, unable to believe I was just kissing the crap out of him two memories ago.

Marcus says nothing.

"Wow, really mature," I say, then turn back to watch the scene in front of us. They are warming up their arms, making circles in the air, when suddenly Past Marcus jumps into Past Jason's face.

"Try saying that again," he hisses, his teeth bared. I've never seen Marcus that angry or that serious.

"And what happens if I do?" Past Jason taunts his cousin, moving in on him too. Now they are in each other's face, and neither of them is moving. And then Jason breaks it and laughs. Immediately, Marcus punches him in the jaw.

"Oh my God!" I exclaim in shock. Jason ducks, then goes for his own punch, misses, ducks another blow from Marcus, and jumps on him. And now the two of them are full-on tussling.

"What's going on? What are you so mad about?" I ask the Marcus next to me, instinctively heading toward them before I remember that I can't do anything to stop them. I can't separate them or talk sense into them. "Is this where you find out me and Jason are together?"

"No, this was more recent. But I should have beat his ass then too."

"So what is this?"

"Nothing," he says, but his jaw is clenched and he's watching Jason like he wants to jump him all over again.

"Ow. Back *off*!" Jason says as they fall to the ground. Marcus knees Jason in the stomach, and my heart beats fast in my chest as I watch the whole thing.

"Marcus, what *is* this? What's going on?" I ask, then wince as Jason tugs Marcus's head by yanking on his hair.

"What the hell is this?" Mr. R says, returning from his phone call just before they kill each other. "I leave for five seconds and you two are acting like three-year-olds."

He pulls Marcus off Jason.

"He started it," Jason tells his dad, and as he stands, I notice he has a busted lip. The busted lip he told me happened during a soccer game a week before the accident. Just last month. It came from *Marcus*.

"Is this usual?" I ask Marcus. "Is this a thing that happens with you two?"

227 * * *

I'm realizing more and more that there were many things Jason didn't tell me about, things he let me believe even though they weren't true.

"Only once," Marcus says, barely looking at me.

I turn to Marcus, gesturing at the scene in front of us. "Hurry up and explain this to me."

Marcus makes no move to do so.

"You're being so ridiculous! I told you what was happening in all my memories," I point out. "Even when it was uncomfortable."

"I didn't ask you to," he says in a voice that I can only describe as dull, dead, indifferent. "I didn't need to hear every twist and turn in you and Jason's feelings for each other."

I'm stunned. "Then you should have asked me to shut up! Instead of laughing along and hugging me but secretly resenting me."

He turns to me, surprised, a look in his eyes that might be hurt. Then he laughs. "Wow. So all this time and that's what you think I've been doing? That's what you think of me?"

"You have no idea what I think of you," I say, and he just laughs again.

"You know what? Fine," I say. "I think you're a fraud. I think you're someone who has two faces, and for a while I thought your real face was the face you wore that night when we met, but now I think I was wrong."

I look him up and down. "This," I say, "is your real face. You *don't* give a fuck. You *didn't* care at all that night. You *haven't* cared about me all this time."

Marcus reaches out to touch my shoulder. "Zadie . . ."

But I shrug him off. "Don't touch me. You don't like being compared to Jason? No wonder. Because he's so much better than you will ever be."

I blink hard after what I've said. Because it surprises me too.

"I didn't mean . . ." I start to rephrase, but it's too late. Marcus has a hard look in his eyes.

"You're right," he says, and starts to walk away from me, hands in his pockets.

Every time he catapults back to my side, he just keeps walking again. Like he can't stand to be next to me.

And finally, the gods put us out of our misery.

We're sucked out of that memory, hurtling through space and time again.

The electric feeling in my brain finally stops.

I wake up in my own bed, in my own room, with even more questions now than answers, and a heart that is unexpectedly broken.

Twenty-Five

I wake up to someone shrieking at full blast. No, not someone. *Something*. Our security alarm is shrill and banshee-like, and given that it's an hour before my typical wake-up time on a weekday, I jump out of bed, terrified.

I grab a baseball bat from the linen closet, where I've always had one stashed just in case, and rush into Mom's room. But her bed is empty.

"Mom?" I whisper in case the burglar is close by. "Mom!"

Did Mom never come home last night? Or has someone already gotten to her?

My heart is beating so hard I feel like it might explode out of my chest.

"Ahh!" When I hear a squeal from downstairs, all thought for myself flees, and I storm down the steps ready to go to bat (literally) for my mom. But when I burst into the kitchen, the air is smoky and Mom is already in there, fanning below the alarm with an oven mitten. It's the smoke alarm, *not* the security alarm.

Most disconcerting is that she's still in her pajamas and there's a glass of red wine in her hand.

I stand there, simply unable to comprehend the sight in front of me. "Mom," I say, "what are you doing?"

"I don't know!" she says, harried. "It won't shut up!"

And then she takes another sip from her wineglass.

"You need to open a window," I say.

"Really?" she says, abandoning the fanning. I rush for the window myself.

Fresh air moves into the smoke-filled room, gradually making it more breathable and less cloudy. Then, finally, the alarm stops.

"Mom," I say, looking at her. She is still holding the wineglass. "What is going *on*?"

"I'm so sorry. Did that wake you?" she asks, as though it is remotely possible a single human being could have slept through that ruckus. "I was just trying to make breakfast, which I know I haven't done in some time, but I don't remember it being *this* hard."

And then she does the most unthinkable thing: She giggles.

"I need to sit down," I say, grabbing the nearest counter stool.

"Aw, I feel so bad. Will you get back to sleep?"

"I usually don't," I tell her. Once I'm awake, I'm up for the day. It's the kind of minor detail a mother should know, but the thing about us is that while Mom focuses on the big picture—the overall problem—the tiny details are up to me. I've done my own hair since I was a kid. I picked out my own outfits. Made my own breakfast and snacks, especially after Dad left. "Why aren't you getting ready for work?"

Why aren't you at *work?* is a better question.

Mom sighs. Then walks over and takes the stool next to mine.

"I wanted to make breakfast and talk to you about life over food the way we did with big things when you were younger. Remember?" I frown because she never used to do that. *Dad* used to do that. He did it when my grandpa died. He did it when he told me he and Mom were having problems. But I get the feeling she needs to believe this, so I let her.

"Yeah?" I say.

"There's been . . ." She sighs again. Puts down her glass of wine. "I made a mistake."

At first, I'm sure I've misheard her.

"You did what?"

"I screwed up," she says. "Made a mess of everything. I'm turning my resignation in to the city this afternoon, effective immediately."

My heart rolls into my stomach, or maybe it's just my stomach that rolls. Either way, my organs shift out of place because this is the single most insane thing I've ever heard in my life.

"Are you *drunk*?"

"Honestly, maybe a little," she says, the most sober she's sounded all this morning. "But that's the story. I wanted you to hear it from me first."

I can't stop shaking my head, and now a cold panic is starting to set in. My mom has lost her mind. She's having a breakdown.

Who do I call if my mom has a breakdown? I no longer have a father, another parent.

I almost start bawling on the spot, but instead I manage to speak over the lump in my throat. *Stay strong, Zadie. Just fix it.* "This isn't making any sense."

"The thing . . . I guess . . ." Mom is stalling like she doesn't want to have to say the words. Normally I would fill them in, help her where she needs it. But not this morning. I have to understand what's happening. "I had a workplace . . . relationship. It went south some months ago. I didn't expect Brian to threaten to go to the media—Brian, of all people . . ."

"Who is Brian?"

Mom laughs. Actually laughs, like there's anything funny or remotely normal about any of this. "A junior staffer. We had . . . a connection."

I cover my face with my hands. This can't be happening. It really can't.

"If you resign, everyone is going to know."

Mom stares at me for a second and then touches my cheek. "Oh, honey," she says, all tenderness. "I'm so sorry."

"Everyone at school. All the teachers, the parents, your friends. My friends. Your constituents. Your *constituents*, Mom."

I emphasize that word in the hopes it will reach her. That is a word my mother knows. Even in a breakdown, she will correct her posture, put on her lipstick, and *deliver* if there is even one constituent involved.

She nods. "By next week, yes," she says. "Or even as early as this afternoon, if it leaks."

"How is this happening?" I ask, looking around at the room instead of her. I am positively and completely mystified.

"How could this have happened? You've blown up our lives!" The explosion comes out of me without my permission, and I want to apologize, take it back, make amends. But if I do, she won't know how serious this is. I don't think she gets how serious this is.

How can my mother, Wendy Cartwright, not understand the gravity of a situation like this?

And then to my shock and absolute horror, she loses it.

"I'm *such* an idiot," she says, bursting into tears. "Such a fool. I don't know what I was thinking."

She covers her face with her hands and just starts to weep, quiet shuddering breaths and heaving shoulders.

I can't move at first.

And then I reach for her.

"Mom," I say, panicked. "Mom, it's okay."

"It's really not," she says, still crying. "My whole career is over. You're going to have to deal with the fallout—we both will. I was just so fucking *stupid*."

I've never heard her curse before. Never heard her break down like this.

Heart beating wildly, I pry her hands from her face.

"It's okay, it's okay," I promise, even though I know it's not. She's right that her career is over. She's right that we're both going to have to deal with the fallout. And it's going to be painful. Especially in this town, with these people, who have always viewed us as other.

I run for a box of tissues, a glass of water.

Mom blows her nose, and finally, finally, she can speak again. "I just don't know what to do from here. What do I *do*?"

For one second, I'm afraid she's really asking me.

Asking who and what she is now without the career she has worked so hard for, because the truth is that I don't really know.

I am afraid, in my heart of hearts, that she is ruined.

But I don't want to tell her that.

I can't.

She wipes at her eyes, sips her water again. We're silent for the next two minutes, and then I say, "I have to get ready for school."

"Of course," Mom says.

"I love you, and we'll be okay," I tell her, because it feels like the right thing to say. She squeezes my hand, then lets go.

I mean it when I say those words, but by the time I get upstairs, shock and weariness have given way to anger. No, not anger. *Fury.*

I'm furious that she screwed us over like this, that she's going to make us the talk of the town for the next however many months. She's blown up everything she's worked for, everything *we've* worked for. What was the point of it all, if she threw it away just for one short relationship? Some random guy I don't even know.

I scrub hard at my skin in the shower, get dressed, come back down. She's still sitting in the same spot. The water I got her is gone, but her wineglass is fuller than when I saw it last.

"Zadie," Mom says, looking a little more like herself. "Why don't you stay home today? Maybe we can come up with a game plan."

She looks so small, so hopeful, and that, too, makes me angry.

She's screwed us over, and I can't even be furious and yell at her. I have to comfort *her.*

"I can't do that. People are going to notice if I'm not there."

"Maybe they'll think that you are ill?" Mom offers. "I can call the school. I can tell them you woke up with a sore throat."

In eighteen years, Mom has never offered to let me play hooky. Unless I was actually sick, she's never deemed one of my personal crises important enough for me to stay home and watch TV all day. Dad let me once, when my second-grade friends turned on me for a couple of days, and my mother flipped out. Went on a rant about how we had to deal with things, not just run away from them. Now, because it's something that affects her, it's worth staying home for.

"It's fine," I say, turning around to leave.

Then I stop.

"And, Mom? I think I want to take a gap year."

I shut the door before I can see or hear her reaction.

I hadn't planned to announce this. The thought hadn't really even consciously crossed my mind, but as soon as I say it, I know it's the right decision. The fact is that I don't know what I want to do next. Knowing what other people think I should do next, even knowing the objective *best* thing to do next, is not enough. I have to make the decision based on who I am, what I want, and as Dad would say, what I love.

I wish having clarity on this one issue would solve everything, but it doesn't.

The drive to school feels nonexistent. One second I'm getting into my car; the next I'm getting out of it.

I genuinely can't tell how I got to school, but I pull down my mirror before I get out of my car. Since the autumn rain stopped a few days ago, the sun is bright again, good for light but not quite heat. I wipe the last few tears off my face, double-check my makeup, and paste the most natural-looking smile I can manage on my face. I'm wearing a vintage choker today, because it feels impossible to breathe.

All the way into the school building, every glance my way is a potential threat. Do they know about Mom?

I don't think anyone knows.

At least for today, nobody knows.

When I get to my locker, my heart drops. Marcus is leaning against it, waiting. He gives me something that isn't quite a smile or a frown. It's a searching look, an appraising look.

I don't meet his eyes.

"Do you need something?" I say as I wait for him to move so I can grab my books.

"We should probably talk about what happened . . ." he begins.

"It shouldn't have happened," I say.

Marcus looks closer at me, takes a step forward. "Hey, are you okay?" He is so gentle. And he's paying attention to what I'm not saying as well as what I am.

"Please don't ask me that," I say, my voice a warble. "I can't here."

"Then where?" he asks. "Do you want to take off for a . . ." He puts his hand on my shoulder.

"I'm serious, Marcus." I lower my voice. "No."

No to talking. No to taking off for a bit. No to us. No to everyone talking, gossiping, judging. No to more dreams. No to kissing, hugs, fairs. Just no.

He backs off. He lets me go.

Mo isn't here today, so as soon as school finishes, I text her.

SOS

I don't even wait for her response before I start driving.

Twenty-Six

Mo's sister Krissie is fourteen, four years younger than Monique, but she claims she's been searching for an aesthetic that matches her soul for years.

When she opens the door dressed in black from head to toe, lips and fingernails included, I don't quite think she's found it. But I can see why she thinks she might have. It reminds me of the wailing widow I wanted to be when Jason first went into a coma.

"Krissie, hey!" I say, giving her a hug.

"Hey, Zadie!"

"Is Mo home? She wasn't at school today."

"She has a cold, but I'm sorry to tell you that she is in the basement, watching the new TV Granddad mounted. Jack and Archie were playing whatever they play and they cracked the screen, and because everyone in my family is a slave to the capitalist agenda of consumerism, they went and immediately purchased another. I don't even believe in screens."

"I *am* sorry to hear that. Good for you for standing strong," I say, right as Mo appears from the basement.

"Oh, hey, Zad! Are you here for dinner?" Mo asks, then blows her nose noisily into a tissue. Just seeing her face, I want to start crying. I don't want it to be true. "Bad night for it. It's the twins' turn, and we'll be lucky if we get peanut-butter-and-jelly sandwiches."

"No," I manage to get out. "Just wanted to talk."

She must hear something in my voice, because she looks up. "Oh," she says. "Let's go outside."

Outside, we sit on the porch chairs her grandparents love. "What's up?"

"I think I was right about Jason. He was cheating on me," I say. The stiffening of Mo's posture is subtle, but I'm watching for it.

"Geez, really?" She sniffs. "What did you find out?"

I close my eyes because suddenly I am just so, so tired. Of lying, of hiding, of trying to get things right. "I know it's your ring."

Mo frowns, opens and shuts her mouth. "Sorry, what now?"

"The ring," I say. "I know it's yours, and I know that you're the one who's been messaging me on Instagram."

Mo stares at me a moment, then laughs. "I'm sorry, Zadie. I have no idea what you're talking about." Her eyes widen and she sniffs again. "Wait, did Alana answer? Or did a different girl contact you on Instagram?"

"Yes," I say. "You!"

Mo is looking at me with genuine concern now. "Zadie, is everything okay?"

"Just tell me the truth. I'll respect you more if you just look me in the eye and be honest with me," I say. "Maybe we can still find a way to be friends."

"What do you want me to say?"

"The *truth*," I say, getting more and more frustrated. "I know about you and Jason."

Monique blinks, sniffs. "You think *I'm* cheating with Jason?"

"Aren't you?"

"No!" she practically bellows. "What the fuck! Why would you even think something like that?"

239 * * *

The strength of her reaction is making me doubt myself, but then I remember that people can be damn good actors. It had never even crossed my mind before he broke up with me that Jason might be cheating on me. Now, there are so many possibilities for ways he could have betrayed me. From falling out of love with me to being with my best friend.

"I know you were with him at Penny's party and God knows when else."

"Penny's party?" Mo looks confused. "I didn't even go."

"Oh my God, I *saw* you!" I tell her, not caring if she tries to make me explain. "You were leaving a room with him."

She frowns like she's trying to recall this. Finally, she says, "Oh, you mean *before* Penny's party?"

I sigh. If she's going to try to skirt this with a bunch of technicalities, I don't have time for it. *It wasn't at Penny's party; it was before Penny's party. I didn't hook up with Jason; he hooked up with me!*

"I saw you, Mo," I say again. "I know for a fact you hooked up with him."

A light repetitive thud is starting in my brain.

Mo looks disgusted. "I absolutely did not!" she cries.

"Then why were you alone in a room with him?" I ask, finally losing all semblance of control.

"Because he's investing in my app!" Mo spits. "Or we were talking about it, anyway. I would *never* hook up with Jason."

I blink at her. "Then why were you adjusting your top when you left the room?"

"Because that top is itchy?"

"And why did Josh imply Jason had been hooking up with someone?"

"Because Josh is an imbecile and likes to start drama? I don't know! Ask him."

In addition to the thumping in my head, that electric sound is back again. It's a loud buzzing noise, and I have no idea what to think or believe. "But you've been absent a lot."

I'm expecting her to use the excuse of her app again, but she surprises me. "Because I've been visiting Jason," she snaps. "I found out what he'd done to you—that he'd been with another girl—a couple of days before the accident. So I cornered him and told him exactly what I hoped became of him. I might have called him a couple of names, cursed him and his children, and then he goes and gets in a stupid coma. I feel terrible, okay? So, yeah, sometimes I visit him."

I remember the time her sister "hurt her leg," but that's not what makes my voice small. "So he did cheat?"

Mo is quiet a minute, then says, "Not with me."

"Why didn't you tell me? Any of it—the cheating, the visits."

She shrugs. Wipes her nose. "He promised he'd tell you himself," Mo says. "And why did I have to tell you about the visits? I didn't think you'd care or fucking think I was hooking up with him!"

She seems really genuinely hurt. "I would never, ever hook up with a boy you were dating. Which, by the way, was never even a possibility if you or *anyone* bothered to ask questions or bothered to *see* me."

"What the heck are you talking about?"

"I don't like Jason!"

"Okay?"

"I don't like guys," she tells me, quieter this time.

I blink. "Oh . . . oh, Mo, I didn't . . ."

She swats the hand I'm reaching out to her. "I don't like girls either."

"Wait, so you're like . . ."

"I don't know *what* I am, okay? I'm figuring it out, but I've been pretty much screaming that for four years, and you and Ambs are so obsessed with *your* own love lives that you've never taken the time to ask about mine. Instead, it's just like this assumption. 'Why don't you ask this guy to prom?' or 'Would you ever hook up with him?' or whatever else."

"Oh, God, Mo." I feel like the absolute worst, most selfish person on the planet. "I'm so, so sorry. I didn't know . . ."

"You don't have to know, but people who don't know? Ask. They don't *assume*." She gets up now, is pacing back and forth. "You actually collected yourself to come all the way to my house to accuse me of sleeping with *your* piece of shit boyfriend after I've been your best friend for four years."

She takes a big breath. "I'm trying to figure out what it means. Is it that four years is not enough time, because you've known Amber for twelve or whatever?"

"No, of course not."

"Well, it's something because this is . . . this is so . . ." She shakes her head and holds up a hand. "I'm done with this."

"Mo, please," I say, getting up too.

"I'm serious. You don't trust me? Then don't act like you're my friend. Don't call me. Don't text me. Just leave me alone."

And then she goes inside her house and slams the door.

I go to her front door and call her name. "Mo? Mo, come on! I'm sorry! Mo?"

The curtains are pulled shut.

I knock. "Mo, please. I'm so sorry."

My phone starts ringing, and I want to hurl it across Mo's front lawn.

"Give me a break," I groan, because it's probably my mother for the twentieth time today. But when I check my screen, it says Mrs. R. Jason's mom.

My heart drops.

I know it's big news immediately. Life-changing news.

I call her back. "Hi, Mrs. R! Is he awake?"

"Zadie, you need to get here as soon as you can," she says. She is not laughing through her tears, not rejoicing, not squealing.

I stop breathing. "Is . . . is everything okay? Is Jason . . ."

"Please," she says, and then she hangs up.

I look over at Mo's door, and then I run for my car.

I rush all the way to the hospital.

Park in a spot I'm pretty sure is reserved for physicians. I run all the way to Unit 4C.

There's a commotion outside Jason's room when I arrive. His parents are looking in through the glass as several nurses and a doctor work on him. They're using a defibrillator.

Mr. R is staring at his son in horror, his face red. Mrs. R's hands are clasped over her mouth, and she's crying.

"What's going on?" Nobody answers as I head for Jason's door, but another nurse stops me and then I'm standing next to Mrs. R, my palm on the glass separating us from Jason. I watch as his lifeless body jumps at each shock, and I'm crying too.

I haven't been to see Jason at all this week.

Please don't go, I beg.

Please, please, please don't go.

243 * * *

1, 2, 3, shock.

1, 2, 3, shock.

The quiet pulse in my head that started in Marcus's dreams, that continued outside Mo's house, starts to get faster and more insistent.

"Has anyone . . . Is Marcus coming?" I ask, speaking over the noise in my brain.

"We can't reach Marcus."

"Should I . . . I could try . . ." I start to suggest, but Mrs. R's sudden shriek makes me turn back to Jason.

She's weeping like a mother who is losing everything.

I cry even harder.

I'm terrified that we're watching him take his final breaths.

That he's dying.

That he's dead.

The wailing gets even louder. Unbearable. The pain in my head is too much.

Please let this be a dream, I plead with everything.

Please.

And suddenly, just like that, the walls start to peel. The ceiling dissolves.

"Is anyone . . ." I say, pointing to the melting doorframe. "Can you see that?"

1, 2, 3, shock.

The wailing is getting louder and louder.

"Mrs. R," I say, reaching for her, but like everything around us, she is vanishing.

I look around and I am the only thing that's real.

Twenty-Seven

I wake up by the ocean.

I know it's a dream because it's summer and there are clusters of families and friends and children milling around, building sandcastles that I step on without trampling. Sand pies that I stumble over without smashing.

I accidentally step on limbs as I run from person to person, searching each face for that smile. The one that says unknowable things.

Marcus.

I'm looking for Marcus.

This is the first dream I've ever been in without him, and I feel it acutely, like hearing the echo of my voice in a tunnel. The sound is full but filled with an aching aloneness.

There is a magic to being unseen. To running to the water, scooping it up and letting it slip between my fingers. Allowing grains of sand to sift then burrow between my toes.

But the other magic—the magic of being alone together—is gone.

Marcus is gone.

I'm just alone.

Twenty-Eight

"Oh my God! She's awake!" Amber exclaims as I open my eyes. She tackles me where I'm lying, where I'm blinking my eyes to adjust to the sunlight.

"It's been so long," Mo says, taking my hand. "We've missed you. Let me go grab your mom."

I start to protest. I don't want to see my mother. And I don't want Mo to leave. If she does, I'm terrified she won't ever come back.

Leave me alone, she said.

"Mo!" I call out, my voice sounding weak to my own ears.

"She's coming back," Amber assures me. "God, we missed you so much. I'm so glad you're okay."

Before I can respond, Mom bursts into the room and she's crying again. Silent tears stream down her face.

"Oh, honey" is all she says. "You're back."

I don't know what to say to her. Don't know what people know or if the news has broken yet.

"How's Jason?" I ask as she hugs me.

"Jason is fine. He's on his way," Mom says.

And right on time, Jason sprints into the room and to my side. "Babe. I'm so glad you're okay," he says, teary-eyed.

I blink at him, at my hand in his. *Is he pretending?*

How is he standing, walking, when he was taking his last breaths the last time I saw him?

"When . . . How long have you been awake?" I ask, not sure where to put my hand on his neck or head or hair. I pat him uncertainly.

Jason moves back to see my face. "You mean this morning? Well, we had practice, so maybe five o'clock?"

"You went to practice?" I'm incredulous. I sit up straighter to see his leg. The cast is entirely gone, and I didn't notice a limp when he ran in.

"Of course," he says. "I had to. Who would play my position? A sub?"

He chuckles at the absurdity.

I shake my head, frustrated at his inability to understand me. "No, I mean, when did you wake up? From the coma?"

Jason gives an uncomfortable laugh. Mo and Amber exchange glances, and Mom steps forward again. "Maybe you should just rest. Mona, can you grab Nurse Patrick?"

"Sure," Mo says, hurrying out of the room.

"I am pretty tired," I concede now. My head hurts and my body aches like it's been through a battle.

I'm falling asleep when a chatty male nurse comes in. He tinkers with my IV line, checks my blood pressure, medications.

When I wake up next, it's with the pressing urge to pee. I know from when I got my appendix out how to maneuver my IV stand, so I'm able to get out of bed and drag it with me. I'm halfway to the bathroom when my legs give way.

The nurse comes running as I hit the ground. "Hey, Zadie! Out of bed so soon? We were going to give those legs a chance to get stronger."

I look at him in confusion. "I run track," I say. I don't appreciate being told my legs look weak. And yes, it's the offseason, but I've kept running consistently.

The nurse chuckles, then helps me the rest of the way to the bathroom. He gives me privacy and talks from outside the door as I pee, stand, and very slowly, very carefully make it to the sink.

As soon as the water starts running, he's on my case again. He opens the door to "help" me. But I'm focused on the reflection in the mirror. I look haggard. A massive bandage on my head. Fading bruises on my face.

"What happened to my head?" I ask.

"You were in a little accident," Nurse Patrick says.

He helps me get back in bed.

Later that afternoon, during visiting hours, I ask Jason the most important question. "What happened? How are you fine?"

What happened to *me*?

"What do you remember?" Jason asks, and I know him well enough to know he's being careful. There's something he doesn't want me to say out loud. The breakup? It's a good thing we're on the same page about that, but what I want to know about is when he nearly died in the hospital. I need to understand how he's okay, how he's here.

"You couldn't walk. You were about to die, and they were shocking you and your mom was here and your dad was there, and everyone was crying . . ."

Jason looks at my mom. "I don't know what you're talking about, Zadie. Did you have a dream or something?"

I nearly laugh.

A dream. Hilarious.

"It wasn't a dream," I say.

Three bewildered faces are staring at me.

I switch tacks, turn to Mo. "Are you still mad at me?"

Mo is wide-eyed. "Me? Why would I be mad at you?"

"For . . ." I'm suddenly not sure how comfortable she is with me talking about what we discussed in front of everyone, so I just say, "Yesterday. At your house?"

Mom touches my face, more tenderly than she ever has. "Honey, you were in a coma yesterday," she says. "And the day before. And the day before that."

"You've been in a coma for weeks," Amber says. "We were so scared."

Now I'm seriously confused. "Is this a joke? I'm fine. *Jason* was the one in a coma." I search their faces for any signs of laughter, but not one of them even comes close to breaking. "He's been in a coma for . . ." I count the weeks. "Four weeks."

Jason's laugh must be one of confusion. "I don't think so, Zad. I've been right here. Waiting for you to wake up."

I sit up straighter, because this is getting seriously ridiculous. "Do you guys think this is funny or something? Jason had a head injury. Jason nearly *died*."

"No," Mo says, "*you* nearly died."

I open my mouth to argue, but one more look at their faces and I know. They think they're right.

"I don't have a head inj—" I start to argue, but then I realize . . . I do. Or did.

But that was a temporary thing, something that triggered the migraines and dreams. I'm fine now. I haven't had a real head-ache in . . . How long has it been? How long have I been in this hospital?

"I haven't had a headache since Mrs. R asked me to come and see Jason," I say. "That was the last one I had."

"Mrs. R?" Mom repeats.

Jason frowns. "My parents have been on a cruise for the last two weeks."

"They went on a cruise?" I can't even fathom the heartlessness of parents doing that while their kid is in hospital, unconscious. And here I thought they adored him beyond anything. "God, I'm sorry, Jay."

"Zadie," Jason says carefully. "Do you remember the accident?"

"Of course I do." Even answering the question feels pointless to me, but I do it anyway. "We were coming back from the dinner where . . ." I swallow. Jason shifts where he's standing. He doesn't want me to say it any more than I want to say it. Funny how I can suddenly read him. Now, after he's screwed me over and there's nothing left of us. "We were coming back from our anniversary dinner, and Jason, you suddenly braked, I think? And that caused a four-car pileup."

Mom and Amber are nodding, so I go on confidently. "Which put Jason in a coma for a month, and gave me a slight head injury. I remember everything."

They are all wearing the same look, a mixture of pity, fear, and concern. I start to pull out more facts that everybody knows. "We were working on college apps. I decided to take a gap year. Amber, you decided to apply to UMaine as well. Mom, you resigned, and Marcus played Jason's position. And . . ."

I freeze.

Marcus.

My heart pinches.

I so desperately want to see him, to touch him.

"Where's Marcus?" I ask.

"He came out of it before you did, thank God," Jason says.

I'm back to being confused again. "Came out of what?"

"Marcus was also in a coma," Amber says. "The three of you were in the crash—you and Jason, and then Marcus was in his truck, two cars behind."

"Jason got a little roughed up," Mom says, "but he's been okay. We've been waiting for both you and Marcus to wake up."

"Let me get this straight: You want me to believe I've been in a coma while all of you have been awake? And Jason has been awake all this time, but Marcus has been asleep?"

"Unconscious," Mo says, trying to use precise terminology.

"Do you understand how ridiculous—how unbelievable—that sounds?"

"You have to know that it sounds even less believable for us," Mom says, "that you feel you've been awake. I mean, on what planet would you take a gap year?"

Mom calls in my neurologist.

"Explain to her why she's confused," she orders.

The doctor, a bald man in his forties, starts to ramble, something about how coma patients can often hear and interact with the world mentally even when they're unconscious. "REM intrusion theory proposes that the brain can live in this hybrid state of being awake and sleeping, so it could be something like that going on," he says. "We don't know nearly enough about comas or sleep, if I'm being honest. But as for what you remember, you probably overheard a lot of conversations and mixed in fantasy with reality."

Partway through, I look at Mom and Jason, and they're eating

251 * * *

the whole thing up. Mo will buy anything someone in a white coat sells her, but Amber? Her usually unmovably supportive face is slack, worried.

And that's the point where I stop fighting.

They won't believe me no matter what I say.

It's their word against mine, the four of them a united front. But I do have one more ally, the person who has witnessed my life, witnessed with me the start and end of Jason's and my relationship, the only proof I have that it happened: Marcus.

"Can I talk to him?" I ask after the neurologist leaves. "Can I talk to Marcus?"

Jason looks hesitant. "You want to talk to my cousin? Sure, but . . . I don't know that it will help anything. You know how he can be."

"Yeah, I do," I say, trying to keep my voice in check. "I know exactly how he can be."

"I'll tell him you want to see him," Jason says.

I try to text Marcus, but I can't find our message thread. Our conversations are gone. It's like we've never spoken in our lives be-fore. Could everyone be right that the last month just *didn't* happen?

"That's impossible," I whisper to myself. Clearly, my phone glitched out at some point. The timing is suspect, but the only other option is that someone purposely deleted some conversa-tions off my phone. I don't *think* anyone would do that.

* * *

Mo and Amber show up with home-baked goods for me the next day.

"We've missed you like crazy," Ambs says. "I hope you get that you're crucial to us."

"You know you said almost the exact same thing to me in the . . . after Jason's accident." Amber blinks in confusion, and Mo frowns. "I mean *our* accident."

The conversation is stilted and awkward, like they are afraid to hear my version of reality.

"How's your app?" I ask Mo.

She beams. "It's coming along really well."

"I like the name," I say. "Zebra."

It's a tiny flex. How would I know the name of her app if I wasn't there when she came up with it? If I've been unconscious all this time?

"It's called Stripes," Mo says, "but Zebra's cool too. I'll write that down."

Disappointment feels like something heavy pulling me to the bottom of a well.

I try again with Amber. "You changed your mind about going to CIA in New York." Before she can answer, my voice turns pleading. "See? I knew that because I've been here. I've been awake."

Amber can't hide the fact that she feels bad for me. "Actually, I talked to you about it while you were sleeping. Saying it out loud helped me make the decision."

Oh.

I frown as I stare down at the starchy hospital bedsheets.

Ambs squeezes my arm. "It's okay," she says. "Nobody thinks you're lying."

"But you think I'm crazy," I say.

"You heard what Dr. Chukwu said. All the stuff people were

saying to you while you were unconscious somehow worked its way into your mind," Mo says. "Of course you remember things."

It's the most depressing explanation she could have given me, because it means that they still don't believe I lived it. They don't believe the last four weeks have been real.

I can't convince them, but if I can just talk to Marcus, I know everything will start to make sense.

Twenty-Nine

By the time Mom pulls into our garage the day I'm discharged, I'm rabid with impatience. I've even tried calling Marcus on the phone, but it just goes to voicemail.

"I'm going for a drive," I announce right after Mom has helped me up the stairs to my room.

"You absolutely are not," Mom says. "You know the doctor said no driving before your next follow-up. You're walking like a toddler, and you want to drive?"

"Driving is just sitting."

"The answer is no," Mom says firmly. She has been acting like mothering is her full-time job ever since I woke up. "Where are you even trying to go?"

"To see Marcus."

"Marcus Riddick?"

I try to hide my impatience. Is it so unbelievable to people that we might have something to say to each other?

Mom sighs. "Get settled in for the night, and if you still want to go, I'll take you tomorrow."

As much as I'd like to go right this second, I realize this is my best option.

When I wake up the next morning, it's to Mom telling me that I have a guest.

I hurry down the stairs as fast as I can.

Marcus is standing in the living room, his back to me. He's looking at the picture of me and Dad. Our bodies buried in sand, with only our faces showing.

"I'm six in that one," I say.

When he turns, my heart rockets into my throat. Marcus looks like sunshine in my living room, like light and hope and warmth.

I hurry across the room and throw my arms around him.

"Hey, hey," he says, gently wrapping his arms around me, then cradling the back of my head with one hand. I sob into his chest. "It's okay."

"It's not," I say, refusing to let go. "It's really not."

We stay like that for another minute, and I think, despite the circumstances, *this* is our best hug yet.

"I got something," he says, and I step back, watch as he digs around in his backpack. I'm expecting one of his birds. Maybe he brought the one I saw him making in his car shop. But what he pulls out is the paperback of *Moon Over Hanover*, Dad's book.

I stare in stunned silence because I haven't seen a copy that wasn't Dad's for years. But here it is, in Marcus's hand, looking frayed and used.

"I was in a used bookstore, and I found it. I'm only halfway, but it's really good," Marcus says.

I take it from him, open it, reverent and quiet. There are high-lighted passages, underlined words, and I don't think they all belong to Marcus. Some, but not all.

I thought there would never be another person who went out looking for Dad's words, but Marcus did. And somebody before him.

I throw my arms around him again, hug him tight, fighting even more tears.

"I want it back," Marcus jokes. "I paid three whole dollars for it."

I disentangle from Marcus, but it's so I can lean up, wrap my arms around his neck, and kiss him. Marcus's lips are soft and familiar, but he doesn't kiss me back. He takes several steps away from me.

"What are you doing?" he asks.

Then I remember: Jason. Everyone still thinks I'm dating him, in this reality. Marcus probably wants to do things the right way.

"Sorry," I say, feeling defeated. "I have to sit down." I'm so tired from the effort of all the standing that I immediately sink into a couch. I pat the cushion next to me.

Marcus sits but leaves a respectable space between us. All his movements are surprisingly tentative. "You, er, wanted to see me?" he asks.

I nod, tucking my feet under my body. "Did they tell you the same story?" I ask, and I can't help the derisive tone in my voice. "We were both in comas and *Jason* was the one who was awake."

Marcus frowns. "You *don't* think we were in comas?"

"Do you?" I ask. Before he can answer, I say, "And for a month? There's no way."

He rubs the back of his neck, speaks to the ground. "There's pictures, you know. Medical records."

"It's bullshit," I say, dismissive, right as I see that what Marcus is actually looking at is his left foot. It is in a cast, but not the same type as Jason's. "What happened?"

"I might not play again," Marcus says, his voice quiet. "They've done two surgeries."

"Oh my God," I say. "Marcus, that's . . ."

He's not laughing and downplaying it at all.

"How are you?" I ask.

"Devastated," he says. "It's stupid, but it has taken me a long time to realize how much I love it."

Marcus looks at me. "I'm going to try to get better. Try to keep playing."

I'm so happy he's not giving up. "I bet with physical therapy and the right doctors . . ." Then something occurs to me. "Why were you even there that night? Why were you in the accident?"

Marcus rubs his neck. "To see you."

I'm confused, but I wait for him to go on.

"I know about the breakup," he tells me, which, of course he does.

"You overheard me in the hospital bathroom the night of the accident."

"No," Marcus says slowly, "Jason told me. And we got into it . . . physically." He seems embarrassed about this fact.

That's what the fight was about? That Marcus knew Jason wanted to dump me? "*That's* how you knew he dumped me? You didn't hear it in the bathroom?"

Marcus frowns. "What bathroom?" I'm silent as I try to understand everything that is happening. "No, he told me straight out that he was going to break up with you. So I hit him."

"But why?" I ask now.

"Because he was being so . . . so fucking careless with your heart," Marcus says, and his voice is angry and quiet. "And then

that night, I was at Harrison Smith's party, and there was this
rumor that Jason was planning some epic surprise for you for your
one-year anniversary."

He swallows. "Obviously I knew there was no surprise," he says.
"Not a good one, anyway. And I knew you'd . . . I knew he was
going to break your heart, and I just wanted . . . I don't even know
what I thought I'd do. At the very least I'd give you a hug or a ride
home or . . . something. I knew he wouldn't have thought anything
of doing it in public or someplace where it would be less awful for
you. I know it matters to you that things are . . . perfect."

At this point, there's just so much Marcus is saying that I'm
struggling to comprehend.

He sighs. "Jay can be such a tool."

"So you drove to Apollo's to . . . what, save me?" I don't know
why the thought fills me with both embarrassment and anger.

Marcus curses. "No, not save you. I mean, I . . . I wasn't
thinking."

He pushes his hand through his hair. "I got there too late, of
course. Jason's car was driving out as I was driving into the parking
lot. I turned around and immediately started to head back to Sterlingwood too, a car behind him. Next thing I know, someone had
rammed into me from behind. A truck. And then I woke up in
hospital two days before you did."

"Two days," I repeat numbly. He really thinks our friends and
family are right. Meaning our recollection is entirely wrong.

"My foot was broken. Doctor's telling me they did a couple of
surgeries and need to do another, that I had a head injury too."

I reach out for him, reach for his hands in his lap.

"Zadie, I don't want you to feel sorry for me," Marcus says, not reacting to the fact that we are holding hands. "But they don't have any reason to lie."

I'm stunned into silence.

"So what, we just imagined the whole thing? All that time? All the dreams?"

"What dreams?" Marcus says blankly.

"Our dreams," I say. When he looks at me like that, I stop breathing. "The co-dreams. The memories we went into," I say, still trying to be calm at this point.

Marcus says nothing, and now my pitch has started to escalate with increasing desperation. "Our dreams, Marcus. All the memories of the past year. Most of them were my and Jason's memories, but we saw some of yours too. And we talked, and nobody could see us . . ."

He just looks at me. "I don't . . . I'm sorry, I don't know what you're talking about."

"I'm talking about the carnival, the arcade, sitting outside that party just like we did last year . . ."

I wait for the look of recognition—a light—to enter Marcus's eyes, but it never does.

"You don't remember?" My voice is tiny.

"Obviously I remember Penny's party from last year, but I don't remember any dreams. I'm sorry," he says, pushing his hand through his hair again, and he looks like he means it. "I wish I could say I did, but I . . . I don't."

"You don't remember *anything*? Even the boat or . . ." I sit up straighter. "What about when we ran through the fair?"

I know the answer before he says it: He has no idea.

I stare at the ground, trying to comprehend this. How to explain this, how to change this, what to do next, what to say. But absolutely nothing comes to me.

He doesn't remember.

"That's impossible," I whisper, mentally working through a dozen possibilities. I try to explain it all to Marcus again. We connected, we kissed, we told each other the truth.

He looks so, so sorry.

Because, at the end of the day, everything I felt and thought and saw—everything I became. Everything I wanted—was all in my head.

And me and Marcus, us being an *us*. Us being anything was the biggest lie of all.

Thirty

Marcus texts me after he leaves.

Marcus: I'm really sorry Zadie

Marcus: I'll keep thinking about it, see if anything comes up

Marcus: . . .

Marcus: Please call me if you need me

I shouldn't respond.

What's left to say?

I've gone crazy. No, not crazy, but my memories are all false. I imagined them. I was unconscious the whole time.

Everything was not real.

But for some reason, I text back. I feel like I'm in a bad dream

Marcus: Yeah, it sounds like a nightmare honestly

Marcus: 😉

Me: We made a lot of dream puns

Marcus: . . .

Marcus: What else did we do?

I tell him.

I text him things I remember, random moments from the dreams.

I keep them friendly, though. Keep out all talk of the kissing, the hugs. We were friends in the dreams.

We're just friends now, as we text back and forth throughout the days.

After all, I'm still with Jason. I couldn't break up with him right

after the coma. Everyone would call me out for being erratic, accuse me of going crazy after all. I can't deal with a whiff of drama
right now, so I haven't even confronted him.

*   *   *

"I thought," Jason says, pulling out containers of Chinese from a
brown paper bag as we sit at a picnic table at the lake on this ab-
normally warm fall day, "that we could just have a chill date."

I started back at school this week and am still trying to get into
the swing of things. People have been gracious and patient.

Jason has been gracious and patient.

I say nothing as he pulls out forks. He hands me a can of soda
then attempts to clink his with mine. "Bon appétit."

"Bon app . . ." I don't think Jason notices that I don't finish the
sentence. Which is for the best. How else would I explain that I
just keep reliving all the days and nights, all the half days that were
spent with Marcus?

"So, uh, what did you and Marc discuss?" he asks, chewing, and
it's like he's read my mind. We both look over at a couple playing
with their toddler in the grass. "Did you like compare notes on
your comas?" Jason chuckles at his own joke.

"Something like that," I say half-heartedly.

Finally, Jason sighs and sets down his food. "Zadie," he says
gently, "I get it. You're upset about the breakup."

"The breakup," I say. "Who broke up?"

Jason's brows basically vanish into his hairline. "Us," he says.
"You and me."

"The breakup happened?" I ask dully.

I really had thought we were just going to pretend none of it ever happened.

"Of course it did," he says. He stands and comes over to sit on the same side of the table as me. "I was so upset from it that I pretty much caused the accident."

I frown, because that's not how I remember it at all.

"But anyway, I broke up with you and it was a pretty crappy thing to do and you're hurt," he says. He takes my hands and looks right in my eye. "Let me explain why."

"Why?" I ask.

This is it. The moment I've waited for. The moment I've searched countless dreams and memories for. He's finally going to tell me when and how he fell out of love with me. Maybe he'll tell me who the other girl is, the one he cheated with.

"I love you," he says.

I stare at him. Then I guffaw. "You love me? That's why you broke up with me?"

Jason nods. "It's true . . . Why are you laughing?"

"Because that's the biggest pile of horseshit I've ever heard," I say, giggling despite being so far outside of this moment that I might as well be across the lake. Lately, around Jason, I feel like I'm not myself but rather an actor playing myself.

He frowns as a light wind picks up around us. "Zadie, stop laughing. That's so disrespectful."

"No, what's disrespectful is dumping me, in public, on our anniversary when you *knew* I thought you were going to do something else," I say, untangling my hands from his. "What's disrespectful is you acting like nothing happened when I woke up and expecting me to go along with it."

I have gone along with it, but now I am angry and confused.

"What's disrespectful is you cheating on me with some girl and then having the audacity to say you . . ."

Jason's eyes are as big as footballs. Then he groans. "Zadie," he says, "please don't tell me you think I cheated on you."

I blink. "You did."

"And where did you get that from, this 'dream' you had that lasted a month? Where you thought *I* was in a coma and you were fine?" he asks, then takes my hands again.

"Y-yes," I say, but it sounds more like a question.

"Babe, please. Listen to yourself."

"Hand me your phone," I demand.

"Are you serious?"

"Yes," I say. With a heavy sigh, Jason pulls his phone out of his pocket and hands it to me. I search for Alana Duncan, but she's not in his phone. I find Jason's thread with Mo. They barely have a thread.

I shut my eyes. "You're saying I . . ."

"Made it up?" Jason says, taking his phone back. "I don't want to make you doubt everything you think, but yeah. You kind of did. You *definitely* did."

I stare at him, trying to see if he's telling the truth, if there are any signs of deceit. And I see absolutely nothing.

I have apparently never been able to tell whether Jason has a secret or not.

"You think I . . . I dreamt it?"

"Yeah," he says, a look of apology on his face. "And it kind of sucks that you'd go by some dream rather than completely trust me. That you'd let go of everything we were just because you imagined something."

"I didn't *imagine* . . ."

But I did.

"I didn't think . . ." I knead my thumbs into my temples. This is officially the first headache I've had since I woke up, and part of me is waiting for the world to shake then dissolve away, waiting for Marcus to show up.

Shit.

Shit shit shit, I think as my eyes fill up.

In what version of reality could that ever have been true? That doesn't happen.

Worlds don't just dissolve, give way to memories.

Why did I start to believe, start to accept, that they did?

Because I was unconscious.

Because I had something wrong with my head, a traumatic brain injury as Mo calls it. Mo, who is definitely still speaking to me and remembers nothing about some random fight on the porch of her house. Because that was also a dream.

I swipe at my tears. "But you did still break up with me," I say, defensive. "That really happened."

Jason nods, somber. "It did," he says, then looks ashamed. "I did it because I was afraid. Zadie, I'm in love with you. More than I should be at eighteen. More than *anyone* should be at eighteen. And I was terrified."

I'm speechless but finally manage to ask, "Why?"

"Because then we're it. We're forever. From now until the end," he says, taking my hands again. Forever *is* scary, I want to say. It's so many more memories and versions of me and him. I can't even comprehend forever, but he touches his lips to my hands. "And I started off so afraid of that, but nearly losing you . . . it showed me what a stupid fear it is to love someone *too* much.

"The fact is," he says, "we are a perfect match. We make sense. Everybody knows it."

I've waited so, so long to hear him say these words.

"I was wrong. Stupid," he says. "And I'm sorry."

Jason stands, then seems to feel for something in his jacket. When he starts to pull out a box, I panic.

"No, Jason," I say. "Stop. Don't."

But he ignores me. He drops to one knee. "Zadie Cartwright."

Oh my God.

The couple are looking over.

A few walkers on the path have stopped to watch us. Someone pulls out their phone.

"Jason, get *up*."

"I can't," Jason says. "Because I've fallen deeply, mercilessly, irrevocably in love with you. And I'm not afraid of forever, just as long as you're in it."

He opens the small green box in his hand.

"Ugh, Jason," I say, unable to meet his eyes. This is horrible.

"Don't worry," he says, "it's not an engagement ring. But it is a commitment, and I think we're ready for it."

In the corner of my eye, I can see a small crowd gathering. I can't say no in front of all these people. Embarrass Jason. Embarrass *myself*.

Besides, before the accident, I was so sure.

Surely that certainty is still alive. Somewhere deep inside me.

"Jason, please get up," I whisper, but somehow he hears me.

"All right," he says, and then to my horror, he hops up on the bench and then on top of the table. He asks it again, standing, ring held out grandly to me, "Zadie, love of my life, will you swear to wear this promise ring?"

Jason is very rarely this exuberant, and I feel my horror giving way. I feel both mortified and unable to help laughing.

"Yes, fine, sure," I say. "Just get down from there."

"She said *yes*, folks!" he yells, then hops down from the table and kisses me. It's a familiar kiss. Not too long or too short. Controlled, audience-appropriate, no tongue.

The ring is emerald-green, different from the one in the dream.

"We're the best together," Jason tells me, repeating the words I've thought a dozen times. I nod, because I'm trying to believe it's true. It used to be true, anyway, and maybe can be again.

"I know," I say.

Thirty-One

Word about the promise ring spreads like an infectious disease. People are texting me and tagging me on socials before I get home.

Amber and Mo send several texts, demanding details.

By the time I'm home, I'm exhausted even though I haven't really seen anyone but Jason.

Marcus and I are texting about used bookstores.

Mom calls me into her room as soon as I get upstairs.

"Do I go purple pantsuit or chiffon dress?" she asks, holding up each outfit even though she is in her pajamas. The city is honoring the end of Mom's first and only term as mayor tomorrow.

"They're very different," I say. "A power suit is good for a last impression."

Mom smiles. "A girl after my own heart," she says, setting down the dress. My mother has been saying things like this ever since I woke up from the coma. She's been warm and funny and tender, available, things I never thought my mother could even be.

It's making me doubt if I imagined the last eighteen years of my life, if the loving but distant mom I had only existed in my mind.

"Mom," I say, sitting on the edge of her bed as she tries to select a matching handbag and shoes to pair with the suit. "I feel like . . ."

I genuinely have no clue how I'm supposed to make sense of the different versions of my mother. The last time I saw her—the coma her, at least—she was about to lose everything. Now she's getting some incredible honor by the very city council that wanted her out.

"Is something going on? Is the city *really* honoring you for a successful first term?"

Mom looks at me, sighs, then puts down the suit. "I should have known you wouldn't be fooled."

"Fooled by what?" I ask.

Mom sits on the other side of the bed. "No," she says. "Honey, I'm actually being forced out by the city council. Because of some . . . bad choices on my part."

"Was it an affair?"

Mom's eyes widen. "How did you . . ."

The only person who knew, who could have told me this in my sleep, was my mother. And she clearly did not.

But I just frown, ignoring her question. "Right, and nothing says forced out like a giant party?"

Mom plays with a loose string on her comforter. "It was a deal I struck. If I agreed to resign, give up my reelection bid, and concede on some of our political gains and wins over the past three years, they'd let me resign and leave with my head held high."

"I'm so sorry, Mom," I say.

"It hurt like hell," Mom says, "but I think it's for the best. A stronger person might have refused to bend and chosen to bear the consequences of what they'd done, but I just . . . I worked so hard for their respect, you know? And for the sake of every other Black politician that enters local politics after me, I didn't want to leave such an ugly stain."

I feel a sudden hot rage rise in my chest. "Maybe you shouldn't have done it, then."

Mom's look of surprise takes up her whole face. "Excuse me?"

I should back down. I *know* I should, but I am just as furious as before. Furious that she made such a big, careless mistake that could have cost us everything. Furious that she wanted me believing she really was being honored by the city. Furious that in the coma version of reality, *I* had to comfort *her*, despite the fact that she had screwed up. But most of all, I'm furious that something happened in the coma that *was* real and she wasn't going to tell me. I'd have gone on thinking everything from the coma was wrong, when it turns out some things were spot-on.

"You're a hypocrite and a liar," I say, ignoring the alarm bells going off in my head, warning me that I'm going too far. "For years, you've pretended to be perfect. Judged everyone who wasn't. Accepted only the highest standards.

"If I brought home a report card with an A minus, you'd fixate on the minus. When I came second in track, your whole thing was how I could come first. Be the first Black girl to be district champion. If I talked too loud during one of your events, you said it reflected on all of us."

"Of course, I always want you to be your best," she says, defensive.

"If you wanted me to be my best, why were you only ever concerned about what other people thought? If I tripped, you'd probably ask who saw me."

I'm surprised by how spiteful I sound.

"Nothing Dad did was *ever* good enough for you. From how

clean his closet was to his friends to how he took care of me, there was always, *always* something wrong."

Mom blinks. "I was just trying . . . I wanted the best for all of us."

"That's what you say, but you mean you wanted everyone else to be the best and you just wanted to look good, *look* like the best."

My mother flinches like she's been slapped. "That is not true. Where is all this coming from?"

"Did you even *think* when you were sleeping with stupid Brian of how it would affect us? How it would affect me?" I ask. Something has turned Mom's expression from hurt to shock, but I don't stop to find out what. "Or does that only count where other people are concerned?"

"Zadie, I have no idea what has gotten into you, but I'm not going to listen to any more of this."

"Well, then I'm not coming to your party tomorrow."

That catches her attention. Mom hates to miss an opportunity to show me off, me with my great grades and my Jason and my *everything*. Her voice is quiet. "Why are you doing this?"

"Because it's unfair!" I yell. "Because Dad is gone, and all he ever felt the whole time he was here was that he wasn't good enough."

Mom shakes her head. "That's not true."

"Yes, it is! You hated everything about him. He was too messy, too impractical."

"I *knew* your father was a mess when I married him," Mom insists. "I loved him in spite of it."

Bullshit, I think.

"And yes, I may have demanded the highest standards for you

* * * 272

and him, but I demand that of myself too. Absolutely," she says.

"I just thought you'd care that you had come so close to destroying everything we built."

"And what would that look like if I cared? Self-flagellating? Cursing myself? What exactly would be good enough to you?" she asks. "I made a mistake. Sometimes people make mistakes."

"Dad's mistakes were never okay."

"I don't understand what you're talking about."

"He died alone!" I shout. "He died alone because of you. Because he didn't fit into this image you had of who he should be."

Mom blinks like she's stunned. "What do you think caused my and your father's divorce?"

"You weren't happy," I say with a shrug.

She is quiet a moment and then she says, "Your father ended it. He thought we just didn't fit together anymore like we once did, and at first, I didn't agree. But over time, I saw it."

My turn to look shell-shocked. "*He* ended it?" I repeat. "But he . . . he couldn't write and that frustrated you."

"Because it frustrated *him*."

"He was disorganized."

"Oh, Zadie," Mom says. "He was the most disorganized man I've ever met, but if I didn't leave him when he made us miss the flight to our honeymoon, then no amount of disorganization would have done it."

"So he . . . *wanted* to be alone?"

"I don't know if he wanted to be alone, but he liked the life he had. He was happy. Happier than he'd been with us," Mom says. "And don't take that to mean he loved you any less than he did, but being free was important to him. And he was free."

A giant lump sits directly in the base of my throat, making it impossible to speak.

"About the . . . other things you've said, I know I haven't always been the best mother, that sometimes I've let you down, but you have to know that your opinion of me has always mattered the most to me. Not some stranger or acquaintance, *yours*. And if you don't know that, I must have failed you in a big way, because it's always been true."

Her eyes get fierce. "Everything in me wants to fight back against the council, to point out that, despite my mistake, I've served this town well and don't deserve to be shunned. But I don't want to make things worse than they have to be for you. That's another reason why I took the deal."

Mom leans over to me and extends her arms. "I love you, Zadie."

I swat a tear from under my bottom eyelashes and close the distance between us. "I love you too."

I'm still hugging her when I speak into her shoulder. "Mom? I really am taking a gap year."

I hear Mom take a big breath before she gently lets me out of her hold. "Okay," she says cautiously.

It is not an agreement; she is simply open to the discussion. So, we discuss. We talk about Princeton and majors and the future, and I tell her about wanting to have things I love. Choosing things because I love them and not because I should.

"I hear you," Mom says, "but a job doesn't always feel like falling in love, Zadie. It's hard work. Your father loved to write but it was hard for him. Things you love can still be difficult."

"I know," I say.

A few minutes later, right before I leave her room, Mom says,

"By the way, how did you know that it was Brian, at work, who I . . .?"

"Just a hunch," I say.

She gives me a weird look.

The fact that some things in the coma world were real changes everything. I'm not crazy.

For the first time in days, there is a glimmer of hope.

Thirty-Two

Mom's end-of-term party, and with it her retreat from public life and politics, is an all-star event. The previous mayor is there, members of the city council. So many of my classmates and teachers and friends, all tucked into city hall, which is decorated in balloons and streamers, like a child's birthday party.

I'm wearing a navy-blue suit dress, fresh braids in my hair, Jason on my arm. I'm also wearing a brand-new red lip, closer to burgundy this time. Today's open secret is that I am confident but still sad.

Mom manages to look a mixture of touched, surprised, and humbled by the lengths people have gone to to celebrate her. I don't know how she does it.

"I shouldn't be crying," Amber tells me, where we are hidden beside one of the refreshment tables. I've caught her sobbing twice already today. "*I'm* the one who broke up with *him*, you know?"

"I get it, though. It still hurts," I say, hugging her. "And Talon's a nice guy."

It's hard to admit it, but he is.

"A really nice guy," Mo says, "the kind of person you'd *think* you'd want to end up with." My head injury must have made me slow because I can't figure out for the life of me how Mo's words are supportive. She's basically telling Amber she was stupid to let go of Talon.

Amber says nothing, just swipes under her eyes with a Kleenex.

"Do any of these foods have banana?" a girl's voice says. I whirl around to find Joey Riddick, with Marcus arriving a little behind her.

"Hey," he says.

My eyes immediately fix onto his quiet, easy smile, but I fight to bring my attention back to Joey. Behind me, my friends try to make themselves less conspicuous.

"Hey, Joey, are you allergic to bananas?" I ask.

Marcus's sister is frowning at me. "How do you know my name?"

"I, um . . . we . . ."

"We're friends," Marcus says. "Zadie and I."

I mouth a silent thank-you to him. He knows it's probably something from the dreams. "Plus, um, you're Jason's cousin. I feel like we're old friends."

Joey doesn't look totally convinced, but she turns her attention back to the food. "I'm deathly allergic to bananas. Just looking at one makes me feel itchy."

My eyes widen.

"Please ignore the little kangaroo. Honesty is not her strong suit."

Joey looks mortified. "Marcus! You're not allowed to call me that."

I hear her telling him off some more under her breath, but Marcus just grins.

"Hey, Joey," I say. "Will you be in high school soon? You seem like an almost high schooler."

"You think?" she asks, helping herself to a sandwich.

"Oh definitely. Maybe sometime we should talk about what's cool to wear, so you're prepared," I suggest.

"What the frig! That would be so cool!"

"Then it's a plan," I say, right as I spy my mom heading upstage with a microphone. I tell them bye, then hurry to stand near the front, clapping and looking appropriately proud of her. As soon as Mom is done thanking everyone for the honor of serving as their mayor, etc., I slip through the crowd and head for the bathroom.

Right before I can leave my stall, someone bursts into the outer room.

"God, Mo, I don't know what you want me to say!" Amber sounds so upset, I'm immediately alarmed.

"I want him back," Ambs continues. "I love him."

My eyes widen. I keep being surprised by how serious things between Amber and Talon seem to have been.

"You love him so you can just have him, is that it?"

"He loves me too; he just feels trapped. He feels he *has* to keep dating her."

"Ugh, do you *hear* yourself?" Mo asks. What even is her problem? I swear I'm about to push the door open and snap at her for being so consistently awful to Amber, but I think of the ways I misjudged Mo already, and something stops me. "You love him, so it's okay to treat other people like trash? Talon? Your best friend?"

My heart starts to beat faster.

Amber is silent a minute then starts to wash her hands. "I don't *want* to hurt Zadie. Neither of us does. We just want to be happy."

What does any of this have to do with me?

"She is going to be hurt. She's going to be devastated," Mo says.

"We didn't ask for any of it to happen," Amber insists, "and it's honestly been really difficult for us too."

"Oh my God," Mo says with a groan. "Please spare me the details of how inconvenient your friend's coma has been for you and her boyfriend. You and Jason are not star-crossed lovers. You don't want me to tell you what I think you are."

Amber sighs as they both move toward the door. "You don't have to be such a bitch." They're still talking as they leave.

I sink down onto the cover of the toilet, unable to move for at least five minutes.

Amber and Jason.

Amber. And Jason.

That's who Amber has been in love with all this time. That's who she's going to the University of Maine for instead of New York.

Her *soulmate.* Everything inside me wants to fall apart.

I do the opposite.

I fix my makeup, go back out into the large hall, and run right into my mom and a group of women. "Zadie! Let me introduce you to the ladies who are behind this . . ."

I barely hear a word she says, but I know I'm smiling and shaking hands and nodding. "Mom, I'm going to leave," I whisper.

She looks caught off guard. "Are you okay? Do you need something?"

"I'm fine," I say, give her a reassuring smile, and start a hasty exit across the hall. Only to see the three of them—Jason, Amber, and Mo—standing in a little group right in my path.

I freeze, don't know whether to turn around and go back into the bathroom. Or march past and ignore them.

"Zadie!" Amber says, waving me over with a huge smile.

It's too late. I take tentative steps toward them. Mo notices my artificial smile, the glazed look in my eyes, but she mistakes it for illness.

"Zad, you don't look so good. Do you want us to drive you home?"

"No, I can drive myself," I say. "Thanks, though."

I start to walk away from them.

"You look like you're a second from passing out," Jason says, catching up with me.

"And you just got out of a coma," Amber says.

She's looking at me with pity, but I'm hearing her tell Mo in the bathroom just now how hard things have been for her and Jason.

"I'm okay," I assure them.

A voice in my head is telling me to stop acting. For the first time in your life, stop acting, Zadie.

But I don't listen to it.

We're in public.

Mom is actually going to get away with the mess she made.

She actually found a way to clean it up.

Keep a low profile and go.

It's when Amber catches my elbow and says, "Zad, are you sure you're okay?" That's when I lose it.

No, I don't lose it.

I decide I'm done.

Done working so, so hard to be perfect when everyone else is allowed to be a mess.

Done being so good that I'm never allowed to actually feel anything.

Done watching my three best friends lie through their teeth to my face and still caring the most about what everybody else will think.

Softer eyes and kinder smiles and fewer whispers.

I turn around, reach for the nearest thing around me (an abandoned glass of orange juice), and toss it in Amber's face.

Amber squeals and jumps backward.

Mo gasps.

Jason freezes. "Why would you . . . Ambs, are you . . ." He goes between us like some sort of pendulum. Freak out on girlfriend or check on fellow cheater.

"No, go ahead," I tell Jason. "Find out if she's okay."

He actually follows my direction, turns to Amber. "Are you hurt?"

Hurt.

I threw orange juice at her, not arsenic.

Amber shakes her head bravely then gives me another stunned look.

Jason, meanwhile, has grown some balls. He steps forward. "Why would you do that?" he asks.

"It's a thank-you," I say, "for sleeping with my boyfriend."

Amber's mouth opens and shuts. What she says shocks me. "It wasn't just a hookup. I love him."

I laugh, even as a small crowd gathers around us. "You love him," I repeat. "So you were, what, stringing Talon along?"

"I told him we were just having fun," Amber says, defensive. "It's not my fault if he didn't take me seriously."

I shake my head, tummy turning. "I can't even look at you." I look at Jason. "Or you."

"Hold on," Jason says, grabbing my arm. I shrug him off and reach for the nearest thing—a pitcher of water.

Jason takes a step back. "Whoa, whoa, whoa."

I've lost it. I know I have, but I can't even help it. "You lied to

281 * * *

me. You broke up with me because you *loved* me too much? How stupid do you think I am?"

He has the decency to look ashamed. "I do love you." Then he remembers Amber. "And . . . you. I love both of you."

"That's not what you told me," Mo says, stepping forward. "You told me it was Amber for you. That she was the love of your life."

It is the single most humiliating moment of my life.

It's like being set on fire and also finding yourself naked on the roof. It is like being set on fire while naked on the roof.

Everyone knows I'm the one he didn't love, the one he won't choose, the one that wasn't enough.

Amber looks touched. "R-really?" This must give her some type of strength because she juts her chin forward and meets my gaze. "I'm not going to apologize for loving him. It's how I feel."

I remember the conversation we had weeks ago, in the coma. Amber's question: *You don't think anything goes if love is involved?*

"And do you know how *I* feel?" I say, surprised to realize I'm yelling. "I feel stupid. I feel used, and ashamed, and angry and alone and betrayed. By all of you."

I look at Mo. "Even you."

"I wanted to tell you, but they promised . . . I gave them the chance to tell you themselves."

"And you didn't even have enough of a conscience to do that," I spit at the two of them. "You just kept lying."

"Love is complicated," Amber says.

"Oh my God, enough about love!" I snap. "You're not the first person who's ever felt it. You're not even the first person who has felt it for someone they shouldn't."

I steal Dad's words. "Every story is about love," I say. But then I add my own piece of truth to it. "But love should make you better, not worse. You two aren't special for being in love. What you are is a coward and a traitor."

With that, I turn and race out of the building. But I haven't gotten very far before Jason is catching up with me.

"Zadie, please," he says, slowing me down. "At least let me explain. You owe me that much."

I nearly guffaw. "I don't owe you anything."

"Fine, you don't. Just please let me explain," he says more softly. He opens his mouth to speak, but no words come out.

"Well?"

"Marcus and I—"

"What does Marcus have to do with this?" I ask, confused.

Jason ducks his head. "We've been competing all of our lives," he says. "And you've met him, right? Everybody loves him. It's so *easy* for him. Whereas I have to bust my ass, morning and night, to get anything."

"What are you talking about? You're the team captain. Everyone loves *you*," I point out.

"Because I work nonstop for people to like me," Jason says, and something about his words feels so familiar. Feels so understandable to me.

"I don't see what that has to do with me."

"I'm getting there," Jason says. "I've worked hard to make a name for myself in this town, and I didn't want anyone to take that away from me. Especially not Marcus."

"I'm not a town, Jason," I say, losing patience.

"He liked you, okay?" Jason says. "As soon as he came to

Sterlingwood, he liked you. So I thought I'd flirt with you a little to ruffle his feathers. Even take you out on a date or two."

The words sting like acid. They are truly humiliating. "But then as we started talking, I actually started to like you. So yeah, I asked you out." He shrugs. "It wasn't even about him anymore, at that point, but it didn't hurt that it pissed him off."

I shake my head, eyes starting to burn from unshed tears. And to think I ever thought anything between us was real. "And let me guess, this love you had for me was so real that you were sleeping with Amber a few months in."

"No, of course not," he says. "Ambs was . . . unexpected. We just connected in a way I haven't connected with anyone. She doesn't like me for my name or my stats or anything but who I am, and that feels nice."

"I didn't like you for your freaking stats either," I spit.

"Okay, but is that true? Be honest with yourself—why were you with me?"

"What?" I have no idea where he's going with this.

"Why were you dating me? Look me in the eye and tell me part of the appeal wasn't dating *Jason Riddick*."

I shake my head. "What are you even talking about?"

"Jason Riddick. Not me, but him."

I hear it the way he means it. I'm not *me*; on the best days, I'm Zadie Cartwright. I'm good and smart, who everyone wants to be. "So?" I say.

"So," Jason says quietly, "Ambs is with me for me. Not who I'm supposed to be, but who I am. With everyone else, there's some kind of . . . I don't know, persona. But with me and her, we're people."

I blink hard as I hear the words. Part of me wants to mock them:

We're people. It's so completely stupid and pretentious. Everybody is people.

But the unfortunate thing, the unfortunate truth, is that I get it. I hate that I get it.

"If you and Amber are so meant to be, why the hell did you give me a promise ring days ago? Shouldn't you have given it to her?"

Jason has the decency to look ashamed. "I was going to. I mean, that was the plan—after you and I broke up, I was going to give it to Amber. She and I had talked about it."

He shuts his eyes briefly. "But then I broke up with you and the accident happened. I didn't know if you were going to be okay, and I started to think maybe it was a sign that I *shouldn't* have broken up with you. Maybe the universe was saying something, you know?" He takes a step closer, looks at me with earnest eyes. "I thought about us again and, on paper, it works, Zad. Maybe . . . maybe even after all of this, you and I are still what makes the most sense."

He looks almost hopeful as he waits for me to speak.

I stare at Jason because I can't quite believe this is happening. "Wow," I say, at last. "I can't believe even now you're willing to screw Amber over to do what 'makes sense.' I would rather absolutely nothing in my life *make sense* than to waste another minute trying to make myself worthy of you."

Amber and Mo have crept up behind us while we were speaking. Thankfully the party seems to have continued after our dramatic exit.

"And with that said, I hope you and Amber are very happy together," I say, twisting the ring off my finger. It takes everything in me not to toss it into the bushes and let him have to find it. I drop it in Jason's palm. "I'm done with both of you."

285 * * *

I look specifically at Amber, and I realize that when I thought I lost Jason originally, it broke my heart. Losing Amber is like losing a part of myself.

I can feel one tear starting to fall, and I know that if they start, they won't stop.

"Love *is* magic, but it isn't just romantic, Amber. I wish you had loved me back," I say, then turn away from them.

I hurry into the parking lot, get into my car, and drive away even as I spot Marcus at the door, trying to come after me.

I drive to where the park overlooks the lake, one of my favorite places to go with my dad.

I sit in the grass and pull my knees up to my chest and cry.

I cry until I can't breathe.

My heart is so broken I barely know where it fits inside me.

Mo texts me: Z, I'm so so sorry.

Mo: Tell me where you are and I'll come with you

Mo: If you want me to

Mo: Just please tell me you're all right

I have a text from Marcus.

Marcus: I'll be at The Fix if you need me

Marcus: Call me anytime

I don't respond to either of them.

Instead, I talk to my father. "I miss you," I whisper. "So, so much.

"I just want to talk and argue over books one more time. I wish you were here for one more story—I swear it's the most important one."

My story.

I wish my father was alive to see it and read it and be part of it.

But he's not.

My father is gone, and with him, all the words that he will ever say to me.

Through my blurry eyes, I notice a small blue poppy sticking out of the grass a few feet from me. The flowers have followed me from dream to dream to dream. I pull out my phone and search for their meaning. *Remembrance.*

I pluck the flower from the ground now and realize it's the only one of its kind here. I remember that one of those times when my father held his arms out wide and asked me what I loved, I held mine out wide too and declared, "Everything!" because then he'd have to get me the whole store. Dad laughed and hugged me and said, "You can't have everything, Zadiebug, but you have enough."

I used to think it was tragic that he never finished more books, because it meant he didn't leave more of himself behind. But the truth is that he is in books we read together. He is in a Sly and the Family Stone song. He is in the Yellow Mart where we will be restacking cans of baked beans for the rest of our lives. He is in my smile that looks so much like his. I don't have everything, but I have enough of him for the rest of my story.

Thirty-Three

The next day, I don't leave my room.

When Mo comes to visit after school, she hovers at my bedroom door like she's not sure whether she's allowed in.

"Explain it to me," I say from where I'm sitting at my desk. I have finally made it to the twenty-fifth book. Soon, I will be on twenty-six. More and more books without Dad. I've been working on the yearbook too. I made so many decisions about it in the coma, decisions that haven't been made in this world yet. But at least I know what will work. "You knew all along that Jason and Amber were together?"

"No, just a couple of weeks before the accident. I saw something shady on Amber's phone."

"God, Mo. I'm so mad at you." I'm starting to cry again. At this point, I've cried so many tears I'm probably dehydrated.

Mo wraps her arms around me. "I'm really sorry. I'm sorry."

"They just used people," I say, but Jason's words about me using him don't leave me either. I am guilty, in my own way, of the same thing.

Social media is ablaze with talk about the fight, especially the part where I ran Amber over with a truck. Or some other ridiculous rumor that is a clear escalation from *I poured orange juice on her.*

"Why were you so against Talon?" I ask Mo. "He wasn't even the problem."

"He is a nice guy," she says. "Honestly, I hated him at first, but then I realized she didn't deserve him."

Mo sits on my bed.

"Don't ever lie to me again," I say, but as I do, I realize that I'm a big freaking hypocrite. I'm still keeping so many secrets.

So I tell Mo. Every single one.

In the coma world, I had Marcus to confide in, to share the most important things with. In the real world, it's Mo for me. And, hopefully, me for her.

Mo stays for a couple of hours, and we talk nonstop until she leaves.

I spend the hours after doing research on the best ways to spend a gap year. Traveling, volunteering, working, eating tours, band-chasing tours, bookstore-hopping, film festivals. I feel overwhelmed with the possibilities.

That night, when I sleep, I find myself in a world I recognize.

It's Corner Books, except it's brighter than the real store. Wall-papered with bluish flowers. As I'm looking through the shelves, the door opens and in walks Marcus Riddick. My heart trills at the sight of him.

Him, him, him.

"You're here," I say.

"*You're* here," he says. "I've been waiting for you."

"Really?" I say.

"You seem sad," Marcus says, linking his fingers with mine.

My breath grows shallow at his touch.

I'm silent a moment and then I say, "You forgot me. In the real world, you've forgotten *this*."

He sighs. "I'm sorry, Zadie Cartwright. I don't know what happened."

I look down at the ground, then try to sound optimistic. "Well, at least we'll always have this. I'll always see you in my dreams."

"And you in mine," he says, but as I stand there, he starts to fade, getting more see-through. The walls of the bookstore begin to disappear.

I give a heavy sigh.

"I'll see you soon," he says, kissing me even as the world around us keeps melting away.

And then I'm waking up to the sound of someone's voice coming from outside.

"Zadie!"

I panic at first, because I don't know anyone who would stand under my window and yell for me. At least, I don't *think* I do.

"Cartwright!" the voice shouts again. I think I hear a negligible attempt to whisper-yell, but it's not very successful. Finally, I open my window, and Marcus is standing on the grass.

"Come down," he says, and he's speaking too loudly, too excitedly.

"Shhh!" I hurry out of my room then let him in. "Are you *drunk?*"

"I remember. Everything we did and said," Marcus blurts out, as soon as I open the door. "Zadie, I remember *us.*"

I shake my head, clear my eyes, because it's too good to be true.

I keep talking like he didn't just drop something huge on me. "You're lucky my mom is catching up on, like, four years of sleep. She'd kill you if she wasn't passed out in her room," I tell him as quietly as I can. "Come upstairs."

When we get into my room, he repeats it. "I remember us."

"Don't say that if it's not true."

"It *is*," he insists, "and I remember the last dream. We were arguing about whether I care or not, about why you started dating Jason."

He stands closer, takes my face in his hands. "Of course I care," he says.

I struggle to inhale. "Be honest. Am I the girl?"

A frown crosses Marcus's face. "What girl?"

"The one from before, the one you've been trying to get over." I pull his hands down, keeping mine in them. "Because if not, it's okay if you want to try with her and . . ."

Marcus laughs. "Cartwright, please can I just kiss you?" he asks. "Yes, you're the girl. I fell for you that very first night that we met. And a whole year later, you're just starting to give me the time of day."

I feel so happy, I could float away. "I didn't want to make it too easy for you," I tease.

He snorts. "Trust me. I know."

I stand on my tiptoes and close in on his lips, but instead of kissing me, he leans away slightly and picks up the poppy on my dresser.

"Hey, it's Hanover's seal."

I'm pretty sure Marcus is speaking gibberish. "Sorry?"

"From your dad's book," Marcus says. "The character's signature is a blue poppy. He signs every letter with it."

I take a step back. "My dad's book?" I repeat. I run to my shelf for a copy of *Moon Over Hanover* and leaf through it until I come upon the first mention of the blue poppy. I flip a few more pages. Another mention and another.

The one and only time I read Dad's book, I was eleven, so I have absolutely no recollection of blue flowers.

"The dreams," I say all of a sudden. And then I'm crying. "Blue flowers. I think they were from my dad. That's what he left me."

I explain it to Marcus, who still has no memory of seeing any poppies. Still, I know like I know my own voice that the dreams were a gift from my dad. Every dream in which I found Marcus, every dream in which we found ourselves.

It is a reminder that I still have him, through all the things I will ever love.

Marcus wipes my tears with his thumb, and then he leans down and kisses me.

I . . . did not know Marcus could kiss like this. Slow and gentle, careful like a secret. I wrap my arms around his neck and draw him in closer, wishing I could do this forever. When we pull apart, it's so we can both catch our breaths.

"What do we do on Monday?" Marcus asks hoarsely.

"Monday?" I ask.

"I'm surprised you haven't thought this through already. Amber's going to be there with Jason, and you and me are . . . unless you don't want a . . ." His voice fades, and I can see him rethinking everything, wondering if he got too far ahead of himself. "Shit, maybe you . . ."

"I *do* want a you and me." I take a deep breath. "And people might stare and talk. In fact, they will."

She traded one cousin for the other. Talk about a downgrade. She's such a slut.

I hear everything they could possibly say, and more.

"But I don't care," I say. "This is what I want."

Marcus grins, eyes twinkling. "You sure, Zadie Cartwright?"

"I'm positive."

"Okay, then," he says. "You and me."

"You and me," I repeat, grinning.

"You know something we haven't done?" Marcus asks.

As he appears to be looking at my bed, my cheeks are immediately on fire.

He looks up, smirks. "Get your mind out of the gutter, Cartwright. I was just thinking, we never tried summoning a co-dream in the most obvious way, by falling asleep together."

He yawns. "And quite frankly, I'm exhausted. May I?"

He's already taking off his shoes, stretching out on top of my comforter.

"Sure, Marcus. Make yourself at home." I feign an eye roll.

I climb onto the bed so we're both on our sides, facing each other. Now I have to yawn too.

"That's how I remembered, you know," Marcus says now. "I dreamt about you."

My smile is too big to be contained. Is this real life, or am I dreaming yet again? "Maybe I dreamt about *you*."

"I don't think it matters," Marcus says. "You know how dreams work, right?"

I pretend to sigh. "No, but you're going to tell me, aren't you?"

"If two people share the same dream, then it's meant to be."

"*It's* meant to be?"

"*They're* meant to be," Marcus says, planting a kiss on the tip of my nose.

I can always tell when I'm falling into a dream. Everything starts to blur, and some things start to move at double speed. But sometimes, real life can feel that way too. A dizzy, blurry mess. The only way to know for sure is—well, there *is* no way to know for sure. You just have to live it, and sometimes you get to the end and you wake up, and it's all a dream.

I weave my fingers through his as I shift closer to him.

"Doesn't sound like a thing."

"Well, wait till I tell you a story," Marcus says.

Sometimes, though, you wake up, and it's all real.

Acknowledgments

I always used to feel suspicious of people who said they wrote a book entirely for themselves, but I think I get it now. *The Romance Rewind* started as a love letter to one of my favorite holiday rom-coms, conceived simply because I was bored between projects. The first chapters were the most fun I've had writing in years, but for a bunch of different reasons, I never thought I'd finish it. And then! Thanks to the encouragement of some very early readers and with the support and insight of my amazing agent, Suzie Townsend, it started to feel like something that could actually live on shelves someday. Simone Roberts-Payne and Rūta Rimas had an incredible vision for what this story could be and expertly guided me through the editorial process, so that by the end of the book it felt like a homecoming rather than a novel that was never meant to be a novel. Thank you to the entire team at Putnam for taking such good care of Zadie and co. Especially Christine Doran and Marinda Valenti, Abigail Powers, Natalie Melius, Rye White, Madison Penico, Rebecca Aidlin, and Theresa Evangelista. Leni Kaufman couldn't have done a better job designing my cover and bringing these characters to life. Thank you to everyone at Team New Leaf for being consistently wonderful. Olivia Coleman, you're the best! Sarah Gerton and Keifer Ludwig, thank you for everything.

Thank you to my family, who are unwaveringly supportive and kind and would totally let me leave the family business if I showed any discernible talent for building furniture. And thank you to my friends for cheering me on even when (especially when?) I disappear for weeks on end.

To everyone who picked up this book and/or has somehow found their way to my work, thank you for coming on this journey with me!

Finally, there are certain things that make the holidays feel like the holidays. Christmas trees, leaning, Joe Jr., families that choose you, Sandra Bullock, and Peter Gallagher's eyebrows. Thank you, *While You Were Sleeping*.